THE

100

DAY 21

About the author

Kass Morgan received a BA from Brown University and a master's degree from Oxford University. She currently works as an editor and lives in Brooklyn, New York.

THE 100

DAY 21

KASS MORGAN

HODDER

A CIP catalogue record for this title is available from the British Library

Paperback 978 1 444 76690 5
Ebook 978 1 444 76691 2

Produced by Alloy Entertainment
1700 Broadway
New York, NY 10019
www.alloyentertainment.com

Printed and bound in Great Britain by Clays Ltd, Elcograf S.p.A.

Hodder & Stoughton policy is to use papers that are natural, renewable
and recyclable products and made from wood grown in sustainable forests.
The logging and manufacturing processes are expected to conform to the
environmental regulations of the country of origin.

Hodder & Stoughton Ltd
338 Euston Road
London NW1 3BH

www.hodder.co.uk

For my parents and grandparents, who taught me to look at both the world and words with wonder

CHAPTER 1

Wells

No one wanted to stand near the grave. Although four of their own were already buried in the makeshift cemetery, the rest of the hundred were still disturbed by the idea of lowering a body into the ground.

No one wanted to stand with their backs to the trees either. Since the attack, a creaking branch had become enough to make the anxious survivors jump. And so, the nearly one hundred people who'd gathered to say good-bye to Asher stood in a tightly packed semicircle, their eyes darting between the corpse on the ground and the shadows in the forest.

The comforting crackle of the fire was conspicuously absent. They'd run out of firewood last night, and no one had been willing to venture out for more. Wells would've gone himself, but he'd been busy digging the grave. No one had volunteered for that job either, except for a tall, quiet Arcadian boy named Eric.

"Are we sure he's really dead?" Molly whispered, edging back from the deep hole, as if worried it might swallow her up as well. She was only thirteen but looked younger. At least, she'd used to. Wells remembered helping her after the crash, when tears and ash had streaked her round cheeks. Now the girl's face was thin, almost gaunt, and there was a cut on her forehead that didn't look like it'd been properly cleaned.

Wells's eyes flashed involuntarily to Asher's neck, to the ragged wound where the arrow had pierced his throat. It'd been two days since Asher died, two days since the mysterious figures materialized on the ridge, upending everything the Colonists had ever been told, everything they thought they knew.

They had been sent to Earth as living test subjects, the first people to set foot on the planet in three hundred years. But they were mistaken.

Some people had never left.

It had all happened so quickly. Wells hadn't realized anything was wrong until Asher fell to the ground, gagging as he swiped desperately at the arrow lodged in his throat. That's when Wells spun around—and saw them. Silhouetted against the setting sun, the strangers looked more like demons than humans. Wells had blinked, half expecting the figures to vanish. There was no way they were real.

But hallucinations didn't shoot arrows.

After his calls for help went unheeded, Wells had carried Asher to the infirmary tent, where they stored the medical supplies they'd salvaged from the fire. But it was no use. By the time Wells began frantically digging for bandages, Asher was already gone.

How could there be *people* on Earth? It was impossible. *No one* had survived the Cataclysm. That was incontrovertible, as deeply ingrained in Wells's mind as the fact that water froze at 0 degrees Celsius, or that planets revolved around the sun. And yet, he'd seen them with his own eyes. People who certainly hadn't come down on the dropship from the Colony. *Earthborns.*

"He's dead," Wells said to Molly as he rose wearily to his feet before realizing that most of the group was staring at him. A few weeks ago, their expressions would've been full of distrust, if not outright contempt. No one believed that the Chancellor's son had actually been Confined. It'd been all too easy for Graham to convince them that Wells had been sent to spy for his father. But now, they were looking at him expectantly.

In the chaos after the fire, Wells had organized teams to

sort through the remaining supplies and start building permanent structures. His interest in Earth architecture, once a source of annoyance to his pragmatic father, had enabled Wells to design the three wooden cabins that now stood in the center of the clearing.

Wells glanced up at the darkening sky. He'd give anything to have the Chancellor see the cabins eventually. Not to prove a point—after seeing his father shot on the launch deck, Wells's resentment had drained faster than the color from the Chancellor's cheeks. Now he only wished his father would someday get to call Earth home. The rest of the Colony was supposed to join them once conditions on Earth were deemed safe, but twenty-one days had passed without so much as a glimmer from the sky.

As Wells lowered his eyes back to the ground, his thoughts returned to the task at hand: saying farewell to the boy they were about to send to a much darker resting place.

A girl next to him shivered. "Can we move this along?" she said. "I don't want to stand out here all night."

"Watch your tone," another girl named Kendall snapped, her delicate lips drawn into a frown. At first, Wells had assumed she was a fellow Phoenician, but he'd eventually realized that her haughty stare and clipped cadence were just an impression of the girls Wells had grown up with. It was a fairly common practice among young Waldenites and

Arcadians, although he'd never met anyone who did it quite as well as Kendall.

Wells turned his head from side to side, searching for Graham, the only other Phoenician aside from Wells and Clarke. He didn't generally like letting Graham take control of the group, but the other boy had been friends with Asher and was better equipped than Wells to speak at his funeral. However, his was one of the few faces missing from the crowd—aside from Clarke's. She'd set off right after the fire with Bellamy to search for his sister, leaving nothing but the memory of the five toxic words she'd hurled at Wells before she left: *You destroy everything you touch.*

A crack sounded from the woods, unleashing gasps from the crowd. Without thinking, Wells pulled Molly behind him with one arm and grabbed a shovel with the other.

A moment later, Graham stepped into the clearing, flanked by two Arcadians—Azuma and Dmitri—and a Walden girl named Lila. The three boys were carrying armfuls of wood, while Lila had a few branches tucked under her arm.

"So *that's* where the other axes went," a Waldenite named Antonio said, eyeing the tools slung over Azuma's and Dmitri's shoulders. "We could've used those this afternoon, you know."

Graham raised an eyebrow as he surveyed the newest cabin. They were finally getting the hang of it; there were no gaps in the roof this time, which meant it would be much warmer and drier at night. None of the structures had windows, though. They were too time-consuming to cut, and without access to glass or plastic, they would be little more than gaping holes in the walls.

"Trust me, this is more important," Graham said, raising the pile of wood in his arms.

"Firewood?" Molly asked. She flinched as Graham snorted.

"No, *spears*. A few wooden shacks aren't going to keep us safe. We need to defend ourselves. The next time those bastards show up, we'll be ready." His eyes settled on Asher, and an unfamiliar expression flitted across Graham's face. His customary veneer of anger and arrogance had cracked, revealing something like real grief.

"Do you want to join us for a minute?" Wells asked, softening. "I thought we'd say a few words for Asher. You knew him well, so maybe you'd like to—"

"It seems like you have everything under control," Graham cut him off, avoiding Asher's body as he met Wells's eyes. "Carry on, Chancellor."

By the time the sun had fully set, Wells and Eric were placing the final shovelfuls of dirt on the new grave while Priya wrapped flowers around the wooden marker. The rest of the group had drifted away, either to avoid watching the actual burial or to stake out a spot in one of the new cabins. Each could fit about twenty comfortably, thirty if people were too tired—or too cold—to complain about errant legs sprawled across their mound of charred blankets, or the odd elbow to the face.

Wells was disappointed, though not surprised, to discover that Lila had once again claimed one of the cabins for Graham and his friends, leaving the younger kids shivering in the cold as they looked warily around the shadow-filled clearing. Even with volunteer guards keeping watch, no one left outside was in for a restful night.

"Hey," Wells said as Graham strode past carrying one of his partially completed spears. "Since you and Dmitri are taking the second guard shift, why don't you two sleep outside? It'll be easier for me to find you when my shift's over."

Before Graham could respond, Lila sauntered up and hooked her arm through his. "You promised you'd stay with me tonight, remember? I'm too afraid to sleep on my own," she said, affecting a breathy, high-pitched voice that was a far cry from her usually snapping tone.

"Sorry," Graham said to Wells, shrugging. Wells could hear the smug grin in his voice. "I hate going back on my word." Graham tossed his spear to Wells, who caught it in one hand. "I'll take a shift tomorrow night, if we're not all dead by then."

Lila gave an exaggerated shudder. "*Graham*," she chastised. "You shouldn't talk like that!"

"Don't worry, I'll protect you," Graham said, wrapping his arm around her. "Or else I'll make sure your last night on Earth is the best of your life." Lila giggled, and Wells fought the urge to roll his eyes.

"Maybe you should both sleep outside," Eric said as he emerged from the shadows. "That way, the rest of us might have a chance of getting some rest."

Graham scoffed. "Don't pretend like I didn't see Felix sneaking away from your bedroll this morning, Eric. If there's one thing I can't stand, it's a hypocrite."

A hint of a rare smile flickered across Eric's face. "Yes, but you didn't *hear* us."

"Come *on*," Lila said, dragging Graham forward. "Let's go before Tamsin gives our bed away."

"Do you want me to take this shift with you?" Eric offered, looking at Wells.

Wells shook his head. "It's okay. Priya's already out checking the perimeter."

"Do you think they'll be back?" Eric asked, lowering his voice.

Wells glanced over his shoulder, searching for any eavesdroppers in the darkness, then nodded. "It was more than a warning. It was a show of force. Whoever they are, they want us to know that they aren't happy we're here."

"No. Clearly they're not," Eric said, turning to look across the clearing where Asher was buried. With a sigh, he said good night to Wells and headed toward the clump of make-shift cots, which Felix and some of the others had clustered around the empty fire pit out of habit.

Wells hoisted the spear over his shoulder and turned around to find Priya. He'd only taken a few steps when his shoulder bumped into something, and a yelp rang out in the darkness.

"Are you okay?" Wells asked, stretching out a steadying hand.

"I'm fine," a girl said shakily. It was Molly.

"Where are you sleeping tonight? I'll help you find your bed."

"Outside. There was no more room in the cabins." Her voice was small.

Wells was overcome with an urge to grab Graham and Lila and toss them in the stream. "Are you warm enough?" he asked. "I can get you a blanket." He'd steal it off Graham's body if need be.

"I'm okay. It's pretty warm tonight, isn't it?"

Wells surveyed her quizzically. The temperature had dropped considerably since the sun set. He reached out and placed the back of his hand against Molly's forehead. Her skin was warm to the touch. "Are you sure you're feeling all right?"

"Maybe a little dizzy," she admitted. Wells pressed his lips together. They'd lost a lot of their supplies in the fire, which meant that rations had decreased significantly. "Here," he said, reaching into his pocket for the protein packet he hadn't had time to finish. "Eat this."

She shook her head. "It's okay. I'm not hungry," she said weakly.

After making her promise to let him know if she wasn't feeling better tomorrow, Wells set off to find Priya. They'd saved most of the medicine, but what good would it be without the one person who knew how to use it? He wondered how far Clarke and Bellamy had traveled by now, and whether they'd found any sign of Octavia. A bolt of fear cut through his exhaustion as he thought about the dangers facing Clarke in the forest. She and Bellamy had left before the attack. They had no idea that there were *people* out there, Earthborns who communicated through deadly arrows.

He sighed as he tilted his head back toward the sky, sending out a silent prayer for the girl he'd risked countless lives to protect. The girl whose eyes had blazed with hatred when she'd told him she never wanted to see him again.

CHAPTER 2

Clarke

They'd been walking for two days, pausing only for an hour or two at a time to rest. The backs of Clarke's legs burned, but Bellamy showed no signs of stopping. Clarke didn't care—in fact, she welcomed the pain. The more she thought about her hamstrings, the less she thought about the ache in her chest, and the friend she hadn't been able to save.

She took a deep breath. Even if she'd been blindfolded, she'd be able to tell that the sun had set. The air was heavy with the scent of the white blossoms that only unfurled at night, making the trees look like they'd dressed for dinner. Clarke wished she knew what sort of evolutionary advantage the strange flowers provided. Maybe they attracted a type of nocturnal insect? Their distinct perfume bordered on overwhelming in the spots where the trees grew close together, but Clarke preferred them to the orderly rows of apple trees she and Bellamy had seen earlier. Her neck prickled as she recalled the evenly spaced trunks, like straight-backed guards standing in formation.

Bellamy was walking a few meters ahead of her. He had gone quiet, just as he did on his hunting expeditions. But this time, he wasn't tracking a rabbit or stalking a deer. He was looking for his sister.

It had been almost a whole day since they'd seen the last set of footprints, and the unspoken truth thickened the silence until Clarke could feel it pressing against her chest.

They'd lost Octavia's trail.

Bellamy paused at the top of the hill, and Clarke stopped next to him. They were standing on the edge of a ridge. Just a few meters ahead, the ground sloped sharply down to a glimmering body of water. The moon above was huge and bright, while a second moon trembled just below, reflected on the surface.

"It's beautiful," Bellamy said without looking at her, but there was an edge to his voice.

Clarke placed a hand on Bellamy's arm. He flinched but didn't pull away. "I bet Octavia thought so too. Should we go down and see if there's any sign . . ." Clarke trailed off. Octavia hadn't gone for an impromptu stroll through the woods. Neither of them would say it aloud, but Octavia's sudden disappearance, the way her footprints suggested she was dragged—she had been *taken*.

But by whom? Clarke thought of the apple trees again, and shuddered.

Bellamy took a few steps forward. "It looks a little less steep over here," he said, reaching out to grab her hand. "Come on."

They didn't speak as they made their way down the slope. When Clarke slipped on a patch of slick mud, Bellamy tightened his hold and helped her regain her balance. But the moment they reached level ground, he let go and jogged toward the water, examining the bank for footprints.

Clarke hung back, staring at the lake as wonder swept away the exhaustion that had settled in her limbs. The surface was as smooth as glass, and the reflection of the moon looked like one of the gems she'd seen occasionally at the Exchange, locked up in a transparent case.

When Bellamy turned around, his expression was weary, almost defeated. "We should probably rest," he said. "There's no point in wandering through the dark without a trail."

Nodding, Clarke let her pack slide to the ground, then raised her arms into the air and stretched. She was tired and sweaty, and there was a days-old layer of ash on her skin that she was desperate to wash off.

She walked slowly toward the lake, crouching down at the edge and skimming her fingertips across the surface. When they'd first arrived on Earth, she'd been diligent about purifying any water they used to drink or bathe, in case it was contaminated with radioactive bacteria. But she was running out of iodine drops, and after watching a fire kill her best friend while her ex-boyfriend restrained her, a little lake water seemed like the least of her problems.

Clarke exhaled deeply and closed her eyes, letting her tension dissipate with her breath into the night air.

She rose to her feet and turned to look at Bellamy. He stood perfectly still, staring across the lake with an intensity that made Clarke shiver. Her first instinct was to slip away and give him his space. But then another impulse took over, and a mischievous smile slinked across her face.

Without a word, she pulled her sweat-soaked shirt over her head, kicked off her boots, and stepped out of her dirt-and ash-streaked pants. She spun on her heel, wishing she could see the look on Bellamy's face as he watched her step into the lake wearing nothing but her bra and underwear.

The water was colder than she'd realized, and her skin began to prickle, although she wasn't sure if it was from the night air or the sensation of Bellamy's eyes on her.

She waded forward, yelping as the water swirled around her shoulders. Water was far too scarce on the Colony to justify baths, and this was the first time Clarke had ever felt her entire body submerged. She experimented with lifting her feet out of the mud and trying to float, feeling strangely powerful and vulnerable. For a moment, she forgot that a fire had taken her best friend's life. She forgot that she and Bellamy had lost Octavia's trail. She forgot that her improvised swimming outfit was going to be see-through whenever she emerged from the water.

"I think the radiation must've finally scrambled your brain."

Clarke twisted around and saw Bellamy looking at her with a combination of surprise and amusement. His familiar smirk had returned.

She closed her eyes, took a deep breath, and ducked under the surface, popping up a second later with a laugh as water streamed down her face. "It's fine."

Bellamy stepped forward. "So your keen scientific mind knew instinctively that the water was safe?"

Clarke shook her head. "No." She lifted a hand into the air and made a show of examining it. "I could be growing flippers and gills as we speak."

Bellamy nodded with mock solemnity. "Well, if you grow flippers, I promise not to shun you."

"Oh, trust me. I'm not going to be the only mutant."

Bellamy raised an eyebrow. "What do you mean?"

Clarke cupped her hands, filled them with water, and splashed it at Bellamy with a laugh. "Now you'll grow flippers too."

"You really shouldn't have done that." Bellamy's voice was low and menacing, and for a moment, Clarke thought she might've actually upset him. But then he grabbed the hem of his shirt and pulled it over his head in one swift motion.

The moon was so large and bright that there was no mistaking the grin on Bellamy's face as he reached down to undo the button on his pants, tossing them aside like they weren't the only pair he had on the planet. His long, well-muscled legs were pale in his gray shorts. Clarke blushed but didn't look away.

Bellamy plunged into the lake and closed the distance between them with a few powerful strokes. He'd boasted about teaching himself to swim during his treks to the stream, and for once, he hadn't been exaggerating.

He disappeared under the water, just long enough for Clarke to feel a flicker of worry. Then his hand grasped her wrist, and she squealed as he spun her around, expecting him to splash her in retaliation. But Bellamy just stared at her for a moment before raising a hand and running his finger along her neck. "No gills yet," he said softly.

Clarke shivered as she looked up at him. His hair was slicked back away from his face, and water droplets clung to the stubble along his jawline. His dark eyes burned with an intensity that was worlds away from his usual playful grin. It seemed hard to believe he was the same boy she'd carelessly flung her arms around in the woods.

Something shifted in his gaze, and she closed her eyes, sure that he was about to kiss her. But then a crack sounded from the trees, and Bellamy's head whipped around. "What was that?" he asked. Without waiting for Clarke to respond, he took off for the shore, leaving her alone in the water.

Clarke watched Bellamy grab his bow and disappear into the shadows. She sighed, then silently chastised herself for her foolishness. If it'd been her family they were seeking, she wouldn't waste time playing in the water either. She tilted her head back, sending drops of water trickling off her face as she stared up at the sky and thought about the two bodies drifting among those very stars. What would her parents say if they could see her now, here on the planet they had always dreamed of calling home?

"Can we play the atlas game?" Clarke asked, leaning over her father to peer at his tablet. It was covered with complicated-looking equations that Clarke didn't recognize. But she would someday soon; even though she was only eight, she'd recently started algebra. When Cora and Glass heard about it, they'd rolled their eyes and whispered loudly about how math was pointless.

Clarke had tried to explain that without math, there would be no doctors, and no engineers, which meant that they'd all die of preventable diseases . . . if the Colony didn't burst into flames first. But Cora and Glass had only laughed and then spent the rest of the day giggling every time Clarke walked past.

"In a minute," her father said. He frowned slightly as he swiped the screen, rearranging the order of the equations. "I just need to finish this first."

Clarke brought her face closer to the tablet. "Can I help? If you explain it to me, I bet I can figure the hard part out."

He laughed and ruffled her hair. "I'm sure you could. But you're helping me just by sitting here. You remind me why our research is so important." He smiled, closed the program he was working on, and opened the atlas. A holographic globe appeared in the air just above the couch.

Clarke swiped her finger through the air and the globe rotated. "What's this one?" she asked, pointing to the outline of a large country.

Her father squinted. "Let's see . . . that's Saudi Arabia."

Clarke pressed her finger against the shape. It turned blue and the words *New Mecca* appeared.

"Ah, that's right," her father said. "That one changed its name a number of times before the Cataclysm." He rotated the sphere and pointed to a long, narrow country on the other side of the globe. "What about that one?"

"Chile," Clarke said confidently.

"Really? I think it feels pretty warm in here."

Clarke rolled her eyes. "Daddy, are you going to make that joke every time we play?"

"Every. Single. Time." He smiled and pulled Clarke onto his lap. "At least, until we're actually *in* Chile. Then it might get old."

"*David*," Clarke's mom warned from the kitchen, where she was tearing open protein packets and mixing them in with the greenhouse kale. She didn't like it when Clarke's father made jokes about going to Earth. According to her research, it was going to be at least another hundred years until the planet was safe.

"What about the people?" Clarke asked.

Her father cocked his head to the side. "What do you mean?"

"I want to see where all the people lived. Why aren't any apartments on the map?"

Her father smiled. "I'm afraid we don't have anything *that* detailed. But people lived everywhere." He traced his finger along one of the squiggly lines. "They lived by the ocean . . . they lived in the mountains . . . the desert . . . along the rivers."

"How come they didn't do anything when they knew the Cataclysm was coming?"

Her mother walked over to join them on the couch. "It all happened very quickly," she said after she'd sat down. "And there weren't many places on Earth where people could hide from all that radiation. I think the Chinese were building a structure here."

She zoomed out the map and pointed to a spot on the far right side. "And there was talk of something near the seed bank, here." She traced her finger to the top of the map.

"What about Mount Weather?" her father asked.

Clarke's mother fiddled with the globe. "That was in what would've been Virginia, right?"

"What's Mount Weather?" Clarke asked, leaning in for a better look.

"Many years before the Cataclysm, the United States government built a large underground bunker in case of nuclear war. The scenario seemed unlikely, but they had to do something to protect the President—he was like their Chancellor," she explained. "But when the bombs finally fell, no one made it there in time, not even the President. It all happened too suddenly."

An uncomfortable question bumped against the jumble of other thoughts in Clarke's mind. "How many people died? Like, thousands?"

Her father sighed. "More like billions."

"*Billions?*" Clarke rose to her feet and padded over to the small, round, star-filled window. "Do you think they're all up here now?"

Her mother walked over and placed her hand on Clarke's shoulder. "What do you mean?"

"Isn't heaven supposed to be somewhere in space?"

Clarke's mother gave her shoulder a squeeze. "I think heaven is wherever we imagine it to be. I've always thought mine would be on Earth. In a forest somewhere, full of trees."

Clarke slipped her hand into her mother's. "Then that's where mine will be too."

"And I know what song will be playing at the pearly gates," her father said with a laugh.

Her mother spun around. "David, don't you dare play that song again." But it was too late. Music was already streaming out of the speakers in the walls. Clarke grinned as she heard the opening lines of "Heaven Is a Place on Earth."

"Seriously, David?" her mother asked, raising an eyebrow.

Her father only laughed and bounded over to grab their hands, and the three of them spun around the living room, singing along to her father's favorite song.

"Clarke!" Bellamy emerged from the tree line, breathless. It was too dark to see the expression on his face, but she could hear the urgency in his voice. "Come and see this!"

Clarke stumbled awkwardly through the water. She reached the muddy bank and, forgetting that she was barely dressed, broke into a run, ignoring the rocks under her bare feet and the sting of the chilly night air.

He was crouched on the ground, staring at something Clarke couldn't make out.

"Bellamy!" she called. "Are you okay? What was that sound?"

"Nothing. A bird or something. But look at *this*. It's a footprint." He pointed at the ground, his smile shimmering with hope. "It's Octavia's, I'm sure of it. We found the trail."

Relief coursed through Clarke as she knelt down for a better look. There seemed to be another print a few meters away, in a patch of mud. Both looked fairly recent, as if Octavia had walked by only hours earlier. But before she could reply, Bellamy stood up, pulled Clarke to her feet, and kissed her.

He was still wet from the lake, and as he wrapped his arms around her waist, her damp skin clung to his. For a moment, the world around them faded away. All that existed was Bellamy—the warmth of his breath, the taste of his lips. He moved one of his hands from her waist to her lower back and Clarke shivered, suddenly acutely aware that she and Bellamy were standing in their underwear, dripping wet.

A cold breeze shuddered through the thick canopy of leaves and danced across the nape of Clarke's neck. She shivered again, and Bellamy slowly unlocked his lips from hers. "You must be freezing," he said, rubbing his hands up and down her back.

She cocked her head to the side. "You're wearing even less clothing than I am."

Bellamy ran his finger up her arm, then tugged playfully at her damp bra strap. "We can fix that, if it bothers you."

Clarke smiled. "I think it's probably a good idea to put on *more* clothes before we head off into the woods to follow those footprints." Even though she didn't think the tracks would vanish overnight, she knew Bellamy wouldn't want to stop now that he'd found the trail.

He looked at Clarke. "Thank you," he said, leaning over to kiss her again before he took her hand and led her toward the shore.

They dressed quickly, then grabbed their packs and headed back into the shadow-filled woods. The trail was fairly easy to follow, although Bellamy kept spotting the next print long before Clarke saw anything. Had his eyes grown that sharp from hunting? Or was it the by-product of his desperation? "Forget the gills. I think you've developed night vision," she called when he dashed toward yet another footprint she hadn't noticed. She'd meant it as a joke, of course, but then she frowned. The radiation levels on Earth clearly weren't as high as she'd once feared, but that didn't mean they were safe yet. Low-level radiation poisoning could take weeks to present, even if their cells had already begun to deteriorate. For all she knew, that was why no more dropships had arrived. What if the Council wasn't waiting to determine whether Earth was safe—because the hundred's biometric data had already proved that it wasn't?

Her heart racing, Clarke glanced down at the monitor clamped to her wrist and counted the days they'd been on Earth. She looked up at the moon, which was three-quarters full. It had been a pale sliver that first terrible night after they'd crashed. Her stomach plummeted as she remembered a pivotal moment in her parents' research. The day most patients grew sicker. Day twenty-one.

"I'm used to looking for things in the dark," Bellamy said ahead of her, oblivious to her anxiety. "Back on the Colony, I'd sneak into the abandoned storage areas. Most of them didn't have electricity anymore."

Clarke winced as a branch scraped her leg. "What were you looking for?" she asked, shoving aside her concern. If anyone did begin presenting signs of radiation poisoning, they had some medicine that might help, albeit a paltry amount.

"Old machine parts, textiles, the odd Earthmade relic—anything worth trading at the Exchange." His tone was casual, but she could hear a hint of strain in his voice. "Octavia didn't always get enough to eat at the care center, so I had to find a way to get extra ration points."

The admission pulled Clarke from her own thoughts. Her heart ached at the idea of a younger, slighter version of the boy in front of her, alone in a dark, cavernous storage area. "Bellamy," she started, searching for the right words, then cut herself off as she caught sight of something glinting from the shadowy depths behind the trees. She knew she should keep moving; they couldn't afford to lose any more time. Yet something about the way it shimmered brought Clarke to a stop.

"Bellamy, come look at this," she said, turning to walk toward it.

There was something on the ground, scattered among the roots of a large tree. Clarke bent down for a closer look and saw that it was metal. She inhaled sharply and reached out to run her finger along one of the long, twisted pieces. What could it have been part of? And how had it ended up here, in the middle of the woods?

"Clarke?" Bellamy shouted. "Where did you go?"

"I'm over here," she called back. "You need to see this."

Bellamy materialized soundlessly next to her. "What's going on?" He was breathing heavily, and there was an edge to his voice. "You can't just take off like that. We need to stick together."

"Look." Clarke picked up a piece of metal and held it in the moonlight. "How could this have survived the Cataclysm?"

Bellamy shifted from one foot to the other. "No clue," he said. "Now can we keep moving? I don't want to lose the trail."

Clarke was about to set the strange artifact back on the ground when she noticed two familiar letters carved into the metal. *TG*. Trillion Galactic. "Oh my god," she murmured. "It came from the Colony."

"What?" Bellamy crouched down next to her. "It must be part of the dropship, right?"

Clarke shook her head. "I don't think so. We have to be at

least six kilometers from camp. There's no way this is wreckage from the crash." *At least, not our crash.*

Clarke felt suddenly disoriented, as if trying to discern between a memory and a dream. "There are more pieces scattered around. Maybe they'll be something that'll—" She cut herself off with a cry as a jolt of pain shot through her right arm.

"Clarke? Are you okay?"

Bellamy's arm was around her, but she couldn't look at him. Her eyes were fixed on something on the ground.

Something long, dark, thin, and *wriggling.*

She tried to point the creature out to Bellamy, but found that she couldn't move. "Clarke! What's wrong?" he shouted.

Clarke opened her mouth, but no sound came out. Her chest was beginning to tighten. Her arm was on fire.

"Oh, *shit,*" she heard Bellamy say. She couldn't see him anymore. The world around her had begun to spin. Stars and sky and trees and leaves swirled in the darkness. The searing heat that had been shooting up her arm faded away. Everything was fading. She fell back against Bellamy, then felt herself being lifted into the air. She was weightless, just like she'd been in the lake. Just like her parents were now.

"Clarke, stay with me," Bellamy called to her from somewhere very far away. The darkness was rushing around her, wrapping her legs and arms in stars.

And then there was only silence.

CHAPTER *3*

Glass

Glass lifted her head from Luke's chest, trying not to be frightened by how much effort it required. He smiled as she pushed herself into a sitting position and let her long legs spill over the side of the couch. Glass wasn't sure whether the lack of oxygen was making her drowsy, or whether she was just tired from staying up most of the night. Lying in bed with Luke, the last thing she wanted to do was sleep. They didn't know how much time they had left, so every moment was precious. She and Luke had spent the last few nights wrapped in each other's arms: whispering their fleeting, half-formed thoughts, or just lying silently, memorizing the sound of each other's heartbeats.

"I should probably go out and look for more supplies." Luke spoke lightly, but they both knew the gravity of what he was proposing. Ever since the skybridge between the ships had closed, the chaos on Walden had reached a fever pitch. The Waldenites' desperate attempts to find and hoard food had turned violent. Armed with a meager handful of protein packets, Glass and Luke had barred themselves inside Luke's tiny flat, doing their best to ignore the sounds echoing from the corridors—the angry shouts of neighbors fighting over supplies, the frantic cries of mothers searching for lost children, the ragged wheezes of those struggling to breathe the increasingly thin air.

"It's okay," Glass said. "We have enough for a few days, and after that . . ." She cut herself off, looking away.

"You're really too good at keeping calm under pressure. It's a little scary. You should have been a guard." He tapped his finger under her chin. "I'm serious," he said in response to her look of skepticism. "I've always thought women make the best guards. It's a shame girls on Phoenix never really consider it."

Glass smiled inwardly, imagining her best friend Wells's surprise if she'd shown up to the first day of officer training. While he probably would've been too shocked to speak at first, she was sure he'd have supported her. Before she met Luke, Wells was the one person who'd always treated her seriously, who believed she had talents beyond flirting and styling her hair.

"I guess I could've given it a shot, as long as no one tried to make me spacewalk." The word alone was enough to make her nauseated as she imagined stepping into weightlessness.

Luke cleared his throat. "You know they don't let just *anyone* spacewalk," he said with mock grandiosity. Luke was part of the elite corps of guards who were also trained as engineers, responsible for making crucial—and dangerous—repairs to the ship. She would never forget how terrified she had felt a few weeks ago, when she'd watched Luke go outside the ship to examine a malfunctioning airlock. For twenty heart-racing minutes, a thin cord had been all that kept him from being lost in the emptiness of space. The cord, and Glass's fervent prayers.

"Not to mention, you would've looked pretty cute in the uniform."

"Want me to try on yours, to see?" Glass asked innocently.

He grinned. "Maybe later." But as soon as the words left his mouth, his face fell. They both knew there wasn't going to be a "later."

Glass jumped to her feet and tossed her long hair over her shoulder. "Come on," she said, grabbing Luke's hand. "I have an idea for dinner."

"Really? You managed to decide between two-day-old protein paste and three-day-old protein paste?"

"I'm serious. Let's make it special. Why don't we use the

plates?" Earthmade relics were rare on Walden, but Luke's family had held on to two beautiful plates an ancestor had carried onto the ship.

Luke hesitated for a fraction of a second, then rose to his feet. "That sounds like a nice idea. I'll go get them." He squeezed Glass's hand before disappearing into his room, where he kept the valuable relics hidden away.

Glass went into the tiny bathroom and looked at herself in the sliver of scratched mirror above the sink. In the past, she'd found the lack of grooming space endlessly frustrating, but now she was grateful not to know what she looked like after three days in the same clothes. She finger-combed her hair and washed her face with the tepid water.

She didn't think she'd taken very long, but when she stepped back into the living space, Glass found the flat transformed. The flickering lights near the table weren't flashbeams—they were candles. "Where did you get those?" Glass asked in surprise, padding over for a closer look. There weren't many candles left anywhere on the Colony, let alone on Walden.

"I was saving them for a special occasion," Luke said, coming out of his room. As Glass's eyes adjusted to the darkness, her breath caught in her chest. Luke had changed into dark pants and what seemed to be a matching jacket. Could it be a real suit? They rarely appeared in the Exchange. Even the men on Phoenix had trouble tracking them down.

Glass had seen Luke straight-backed and serious-faced in his guard uniform. She'd seen him casual and laughing in his civilian clothes, playing catch with the little kids in his corridor. In the suit, he looked as confident as soldier-Luke, but he held himself differently. More relaxed.

"I'm underdressed," Glass said, tugging at the sleeve of her slightly dingy shirt.

Luke tilted his head to the side and surveyed her for a long moment. "You look perfect." There was a note of admiration in his voice that made Glass grateful for the candles, for the flickering light that obscured her old clothes and her sudden blush.

She took a few steps forward and ran her finger along Luke's sleeve. "Where did you get this?"

"It was Carter's, actually."

The name made Glass snatch her hand away, as if she'd been burned.

"Are you okay?" Luke asked.

"Yes, fine," Glass said quickly. "I was just surprised. Carter never struck me as a suit guy." Carter was an older boy who'd taken Luke in after his mother died—out of charity, he'd claimed, but Glass had always suspected it was for the extra ration points. He was lazy, manipulative, and dangerous, and had once tried to assault Glass when she was waiting in their flat. Yet while Luke was generally far from naïve, his childhood admiration for Carter blinded him to his faults, and Glass had never been able to make him see the truth about the man he saw as a sort of mentor.

Luke shrugged. "He wasn't. He was short on points one month, so I bought the suit from him. It was pretty generous of him, actually. He could've gotten a lot more at the Exchange."

No, he couldn't have, Glass thought. *Because he would've been arrested for selling stolen goods*. But then she felt a pang of guilt. Carter had been a scumbag, but now he was dead—executed for a crime he hadn't committed.

And it was Glass's fault.

Last year, Glass had made the terrifying discovery that she was pregnant—a violation of the Colony's rigid population control law that was punishable by Confinement for minors . . . and death for anyone over eighteen.

Desperate to keep Luke safe, Glass had done her best to hide her condition. But when her pregnancy was discovered, she'd been arrested and forced to name the father. Glass knew that if she told the truth, nineteen-year-old Luke would be put to death. So, in a moment of panic, she gave the name of a man who made her skin crawl, a man she knew would be arrested sooner or later, anyway: Carter.

Luke didn't know what Glass had done. No one on Walden had any idea why Carter had been dragged away in the middle of the night. At least, that's what Glass had thought until two days ago, when Luke's best friend and ex-girlfriend, Camille, had threatened to expose Glass's secret if she didn't do anything and everything Camille asked.

"Should we eat?" Glass asked weakly, desperate to change the subject.

Luke placed the two plates on the table with a clink. "Dinner is served."

There was laughably little protein paste, but Glass noticed that Luke had given her a far larger serving. The upside to the meager portions was that they allowed Glass to admire the scenes painted on the plates—one depicted a couple in front of the Eiffel Tower, while the other showed the same couple walking a dog in a park. Luke didn't know the story behind the relics, but Glass liked to imagine that a real couple had bought the plates on their honeymoon, and then brought them up to the Colony as keepsakes.

"Is it strange to dress up to eat protein paste?" Luke asked as he scooped some up with his spoon.

"I don't think so. For a while, Wells was obsessed with this book about a famous boat crash. Apparently, everyone put on their best clothes and then listened to music while the ship was going down."

Glass was proud to know this little fact about Earth history, but instead of looking impressed, Luke winced. "You should've stayed on Phoenix," he said softly. "Coming here was like boarding a sinking ship." Although Walden and Arcadia had been abandoned by the Council—left to die as their oxygen supplies dwindled—Phoenix, the central ship, still had oxygen reserves. Glass had fled the safety of her home ship to come be with Luke on Walden.

"Do you think Camille made it across?" Luke asked as he used his spoon to trace a pattern in the protein paste.

Glass suppressed a wince of her own. When she'd arrived on Walden, Luke's ex-girlfriend Camille had demanded Glass show her how she'd snuck from ship to ship. And when Glass had hesitated, knowing that the guards would likely shoot a Waldenite trespassing on Phoenix now that the skybridge had been closed, Camille had whispered the most terrifying threat Glass could imagine: If Glass didn't help her, Camille would tell Luke about Carter. Glass had no idea how the other girl discovered her secret, but she hadn't wasted time trying to find out as she hurried Camille to the secret air vent that connected Walden to Phoenix.

"I hope so," Glass said in answer to Luke's question, turning away to avoid meeting his eye.

"It's not too late for you," Luke said carefully. He had begged Glass to return with Camille, but she refused. "You could climb through the vent and—"

Glass's spoon fell from her hand onto her plate. "*No*," she said, a little more sharply than she'd meant. "We talked about this."

Luke sighed. "Okay, how about this?" He took a breath to speak, but then he caught Glass's eye and let out a sputtering laugh.

"What?" Glass asked. "What's so funny?"

"You were *scowling* at me."

Glass sat up straighter. "Well, I'm upset. I'm not sure why you find it so amusing."

"Because I'm sure it was the exact expression you used to make when you were a little kid and didn't get your way."

"Luke, come on. I'm trying to be serious."

"So am I," he said, rising from his chair. "Come here." He took her hand and pulled her to her feet. "What if you go across through the vent and just look around? If it doesn't seem like the guards are patrolling Phoenix, you can come back and let me know."

Glass paused for a moment to scan Luke's face, trying to make sure he meant what he said. That it wasn't a ploy to get her to retreat to the safety of Phoenix and then shut the air vent for good, so she couldn't come back. "And then you'll go over with me?"

Luke nodded. "If there aren't guards near where the vent lets out, we can try to make it back to your flat without being spotted. And then . . ." His voice trailed off.

Glass took his other hand and gave it a squeeze. They both

knew sneaking onto Phoenix would only buy them a little more time. The Colony was breaking apart, and even Phoenix would lose oxygen eventually.

After a long moment, Luke broke the silence. "They might start sending people on the dropships."

"What? Before they know whether or not it's safe?" Glass shouldn't have been surprised. The Colony had lost contact with the hundred Confined teens who'd been sent down to Earth to test the radiation levels. Ninety-nine teens, actually, since Glass was supposed to be one of them but had escaped the dropship and snuck back onto the Colony. Her heart ached as she thought about Wells, who'd also been on the mission. He had always dreamed of going to Earth—Glass remembered how he'd made them play gladiator in the gravity gym when he was going through his Roman phase, or how she'd pretended to be a man-eating gorilla when they'd played jungle explorer behind his father's office.

She hoped he was still alive, that he wasn't being attacked by man-eating gorillas—or worse, dying slowly from radiation. She hoped that they'd made it to the ground at all.

"They don't have any other options," Luke said flatly. His eyes searched hers. "You should've stayed on that dropship when you had the chance."

"Yes, well, it turns out I'd left something pretty important behind."

Luke reached out and ran his finger along the chain of the locket he'd given her on their anniversary. "Of course. You can't go to Earth without your jewelry."

Glass swatted him playfully on the shoulder. "You know what I'm talking about."

Luke laughed. "I can't wait to see you scowl at me on Earth."

"Is that the only thing you're looking forward to?"

"No." Luke's hand moved to the back of her head as he lowered his face toward hers and kissed her gently. "I'm looking forward to a lot more than that."

CHAPTER 4

Wells

There was no way of keeping track of time at night, so Wells had to guess when it was time to change shifts. From the ache in his joints, he'd been patrolling the clearing for at least four hours. But when he went to fetch Eric, he found the Arcadian curled up next to Felix with such a peaceful look on his face, he couldn't stomach the thought of disturbing them.

With a silent groan, Wells stretched his arms over his head and switched the spear from one hand to the other. The weapon was a joke. The arrow that had killed Asher had been shot with deadly accuracy. If the Earthborns returned and took aim at Wells, he wouldn't stand a chance.

"Wells?" a girl called out.

He spun around, blinking in the darkness. "Priya? Is that you?"

"No . . ." There was a note of hurt in the girl's voice. "It's me. Kendall."

"Sorry," Wells said. "What's up? Everything okay?"

"Oh, yes, everything's fine!" she said, suddenly cheery. Way too cheery for the middle of the night. Luckily, it was too dark for her to see Wells cringe. "I just figured you could use some company."

The last thing Wells wanted right now was to make small talk. "I'm okay. I'm about to trade off with Eric," he lied. Even without seeing Kendall's face, he could sense disappointment radiating out from her. "Now go back to bed before someone steals your spot."

With a barely audible sigh, Kendall turned and traipsed back toward the cabin. When he heard the door close behind her, Wells returned his focus to the tree line. He was so tired, he had to use all his strength to keep his increasingly heavy eyelids from drooping.

Sometime later—it could have been minutes, it could have been another hour—a figure emerged from the shadows. Wells blinked, expecting it to disappear, but it only grew larger. He snapped to attention, raised the spear, and opened his mouth to shout a warning—but then the shape came into focus, and the words died on his lips.

Bellamy. He was lurching toward him, a limp figure in his trembling arms. For one brief moment, Wells thought it was Octavia—but even in the dark, there was no mistaking the rumpled, reddish-blond hair. He would know her anywhere.

Wells broke into a run and reached them just as Bellamy fell to his knees. His face was bright red and his breath came in ragged gasps, but he held on to Clarke long enough to pass her into Wells's outstretched arms. "She . . . she . . ." Bellamy wheezed, pressing his hand to the grass to steady himself as he struggled to speak. "She was bitten. By a snake."

That was all Wells needed to hear. Holding Clarke tight to his chest, he took off for the infirmary cabin. The tiny space was jammed with sleeping people—half a dozen were curled up on the few remaining blankets and cots. "Move it," Wells bellowed, senseless to the indignant murmurs and sleepy protests. "*Now.*"

"What happened? Are they back?"

"Is it the Earthborns?" someone whimpered.

"Is that *Clarke*? Is she okay?"

Wells ignored them and set Clarke down on one of the now-empty cots, inhaling sharply as her head fell to the side. "Clarke," he said, placing a hand on her shoulder and shaking her gently. "*Clarke!*" He knelt down and brought his face close to hers. She was breathing, but just barely.

Bellamy burst inside. "Get them out of here," Wells

ordered, gesturing to the remaining kids who were still staggering to their feet, gazing at Clarke in sleepy confusion.

Bellamy herded them toward the door. "Everybody out," he said, his voice ragged with exhaustion. When the last few had been unceremoniously removed, he stumbled over to Wells, who was tearing wildly through the medical supplies.

"What can I do?" Bellamy asked.

"Just keep an eye on her." Wells tossed bandages and vials over his shoulder, praying that they had antivenom, praying that he'd recognize it. He cursed himself for not studying harder during his biology tutorials. He cursed himself for not paying closer attention to Clarke when she spoke offhandedly about her medical training. He'd been too busy admiring the ways her eyes lit up when she talked about her apprenticeship. And now there was a chance those eyes would be closed forever.

"You'd better hurry up." Bellamy's voice came from the cot. Wells spun around to see him crouching next to Clarke, brushing the hair off her pale face. The sight momentarily resurrected the rage Wells had felt when he'd seen Bellamy kiss Clarke in the woods.

"Don't *touch* her." He winced at the sharpness of his tone. "Just . . . give her space to breathe."

Bellamy locked eyes with Wells. "She's not going to be breathing for much longer unless we figure out a way to help her."

Wells turned back to the medicine chest, willing himself to stay calm. When his eyes landed on a bright orange vial, his relief nearly knocked him to the ground.

A few years ago, a group of scientists had given a lecture on their research in Eden Hall. They were developing a universal antidote, a medicine that would give people a fighting chance of surviving when they finally returned to Earth. Not only had humans lost many of their natural immunities, but it was likely that many plants and animals had mutated, rendering the old medicines useless. The lecture felt like a lifetime ago, before Wells had met Clarke, before the Vice Chancellor forced her parents to study the effects of radiation on human test subjects. Wells had only gone because it fell under his responsibilities as the Chancellor's son. He'd never thought he'd ever set foot on Earth, let alone need to use such an antidote to save the girl he loved.

Wells grit his teeth as he attached a syringe to the vial and positioned it over a blue vein in Clarke's arm. He froze as his heart pounded a warning. What if he was wrong about the drug? What if he screwed up and injected a fatal air bubble into her blood?

"Give it to me," Bellamy snapped. "I'll do it."

"No," Wells said firmly. Though he hated to admit it, the thought of Bellamy saving Clarke was too much for him to bear. It was his fault she'd been sent to Earth in the first place, but it wasn't going to be his fault that she died.

In a single motion, he plunged the syringe into her skin and pressed the top down, watching the antidote empty into her body. "Clarke," he whispered, grabbing her hand. "Can you hear me?" He intertwined his fingers with hers and closed his eyes. "*Please*. Stay with me." He sat there holding her hand for a few moments in silence.

"Thank god," Bellamy breathed behind him.

Wells looked up to see Clarke's eyes flutter open. He exhaled and swayed slightly, woozy with relief. "Are you okay?" he asked, not caring that his voice cracked.

She blinked at him in confusion. Wells braced for the moment when she would remember everything that happened, and her face would harden with loathing. But Clarke's eyes closed again, and her lips curved into a small smile. "I found—" she murmured.

"What did you find?" Wells asked, squeezing her hand.

"I had no . . ." Clarke trailed off with a sigh as sleep overtook her.

Wells stood up, grabbed a blanket from one of the other cots, and spread it gently over Clarke. Bellamy was still standing stiffly behind him, his eyes fixed on the curled figure of the girl who, despite her immense strength, always looked younger—and somehow more fragile—when she slept.

Wells cleared his throat. "Thank you," he said, extending his hand. "For bringing her back."

Bellamy nodded slowly, still in shock. "I was so worried. I thought . . ." He ran a hand through his hair, then slid to the ground and sat with his back against Clarke's cot.

Wells bristled at the possessive gesture, but he found that he couldn't say anything. He was grateful to Bellamy for bringing Clarke back to the camp, but it hurt to think about what they might've been doing for the past two days.

Wells lowered himself to the ground with a sigh. "I guess this means you didn't find Octavia."

"No. We found a trail, but it was . . . weird." He spoke without looking up, and his voice was strangely flat. "The prints didn't look like she ran off. It looked like she was *dragged*."

"Dragged?" Wells repeated as the pieces of information clicked together, forming an even more troubling picture. "I can't believe it. They took her."

"They?" Bellamy's head shot up. "Who?"

Wells told him about everything that had happened since Bellamy and Clarke left camp—the surprise attack, Asher's death, the undeniable fact that there were other people on Earth.

When Bellamy finally spoke, his jaw was tight with anger. "And you think these people took Octavia during the fire?" Wells nodded. "Who are they? How did they survive the Cataclysm? And what the hell do these—these *Earthborns* want with my sister?"

"I don't know. They might be defending their territory. Maybe they took her as a warning, and then when we didn't show any signs of leaving, they killed Asher to make a stronger point."

Bellamy stared at him for a long moment. "So you think they're coming back?"

Wells opened his mouth to repeat the same vague response he'd been giving to the others in his attempt to prevent widespread panic. But when he met Bellamy's eyes, the canned reassurances fell away. "Yes. They'll be back." He told Bellamy about Graham's growing obsession with building an army, a move that would certainly lead to more deaths.

"It sounds like it hasn't been a walk in the park here either," Bellamy said with a snort. He glanced over his shoulder to check on Clarke, who still hadn't stirred, though her face was peaceful and her breath was steady. "You should get some rest. I'll keep an eye on Sleeping Beauty here, and let you know if there's any change."

Something in Bellamy's tone rankled Wells. "I'm fine," he said. "I have to stay up for guard duty, anyway. But you should definitely go to bed. You look exhausted."

The boys stared at each other wordlessly until Bellamy raised his arms over his head and stretched his legs out with a groan. "I guess we're both in it for the long haul, then."

They sat in silence, each avoiding the other's eyes, moving

only to look at Clarke the few times she rolled over, or sighed in her sleep. As the night wore on, a handful of people tried to come back inside the infirmary cabin, but Wells shooed them away. It was slightly unfair to make people sleep outside when there was space indoors, but he couldn't risk anything disturbing Clarke. Not after what she'd been through.

Wells wasn't sure how much time had passed, but light was streaming between the logs when a loud thud jolted him from his doze, sending him jumping to his feet. Bellamy's head snapped up. "What's going on?" he asked, drowsily. Without waiting to respond, Wells hurried outside.

The clearing was quiet and still. The people he'd kicked out of the infirmary cabin had joined the others around the fire pit. Everyone seemed to still be asleep.

Wells had started to turn back when a flash of movement near the tree line caught his eye. Something darted from behind a tree and ran deeper into the woods—a short, wiry figure dressed in black.

Without thinking, Wells started sprinting across the tree line, his feet flying over the uneven, root-tangled ground. He closed in on the intruder, lunging forward to tackle him with a shout. Wells grunted as a knee jabbed him in the stomach, but it didn't stop him from rolling over and pinning the stranger to the damp ground. He had one of them—an Earthborn.

Wells's blood was pumping so swiftly through his veins, it took him a moment to get a clear look at the person whose wrists he'd clamped, the owner of the green eyes staring furiously up at him.

It was a girl.

CHAPTER 5

Bellamy

Bellamy didn't care that the Earthborn was a girl. She was a spy. She was the enemy. She was one of the people who had killed Asher and taken his sister.

Fear flashed in her eyes, and her black hair flew across her face as she thrashed in the dirt, trying to wrench herself free. But Bellamy, kneeling next to Wells, only tightened his hold. They couldn't let her escape, not before she told them where Octavia was.

He helped Wells pull the girl to her feet and yanked her sharply forward. "Where the hell is she?" he shouted. His face was so close to hers, his breath sent wisps of her hair flying. "Where'd you take my sister?"

The girl winced but said nothing.

Bellamy twisted her arm behind her back, just like he used to do to the boys in the care center he caught teasing Octavia. "You'd better tell me *right now*, or you'll wish you never crawled out of whatever cave you came from!"

"*Bellamy*," Wells said sharply. "Calm down. We don't know anything yet. She might have nothing to do with—"

"Like hell she doesn't," Bellamy said, cutting him off. He reached over and yanked on the girl's hair, bringing her face up to his. "You tell me right now, or this is going to get really unpleasant, really fast."

"*Knock it off*," Wells shouted. "For all we know, she doesn't speak English. Before we do anything, we need to—"

Wells was cut off once again, this time by a thunderstorm of shouts and footsteps as the rest of the group, drawn by the noise, came to investigate. "You caught one," Graham said, shoving his way to the front. His voice was tinged with something close to admiration.

"So she's from Earth?" asked a Walden girl, awestruck.

"Can she talk?" another asked.

"She's probably a mutant. You might catch radiation poisoning just by touching her," a tall Arcadian boy said, craning his neck for a better look.

Bellamy didn't care if the girl was radioactive, or if she had goddamn *wings*. All he cared about was finding out where she and her friends had taken his sister.

"What are we going to do with her?" a girl asked as she shifted her spear from one hand to the other.

"We kill her," Graham said, as if it were the most obvious thing in the world. "And then we put her head on a spike to let the others know how we deal with people who threaten us."

"Not before she and I have a little conversation," Bellamy growled. The girl's eyes narrowed as Bellamy stepped forward, and she raised her knee in an attempt to jab him, but he danced aside.

"Bellamy, back *off*," Wells ordered, struggling to hold her still.

Graham scoffed. "Want to have a little fun with her first? I can't say I've ever understood your taste in girls, mini-Chancellor, but I guess we all have needs."

Wells ignored Graham, and turned to ask a Walden boy for rope. "We'll tie her up and keep her in the infirmary until we figure out what to do with her."

Bellamy glared at Wells as rage bubbled up from his stomach into his chest. That wasn't good enough. The longer they stood here, the farther away her people could be dragging Octavia. "She needs to tell us where to find my sister," he snapped, daring Wells to challenge him. As if it were his decision to make. Bellamy hadn't really cared when the others started deferring to Wells. Better him than Graham.

But that didn't mean Wells got to decide what to do about this girl—the only link to Bellamy's sister.

The Walden boy came running over with the rope. Wells bound the girl's hands behind her back, then deftly tied her feet together so she could only take short, shuffling steps. His smooth, practiced moves reminded Bellamy that Wells wasn't just a spoiled Phoenician. Before his arrest, he'd been training as a guard. As an officer, in fact. Bellamy's hands tightened into fists at his side.

"Clear a path," Wells shouted, escorting his prisoner toward the cabin. Her long black hair had fallen away from her face, and Bellamy was able to really look at her for the first time. She was young, maybe Octavia's age, with almond-shaped green eyes. Her furry black top wasn't even the strangest thing about her. It was something about her skin, Bellamy realized. The Colonists' skin came in a wide array of shades, but the hundred had all burned their first week on Earth, before Clarke started urging people to limit their sun exposure. But the captive's skin had a sort of glow, and a smattering of freckles across her high cheekbones. Unlike the rest of them, she had grown up in the sunlight.

His anger turned to nausea as he thought about how her people might be treating Octavia. Did they have her tied up? Locked in a cave somewhere? She hated small places. Was she terrified? Was she crying for him? At that moment, he would've taken the ax and chopped off his hand if he thought it would help his sister.

Bellamy followed Wells and the Earthborn into the infirmary cabin, which was now empty except for the still-sleeping Clarke. He watched as Wells directed the girl to sit on the other cot, checked that her hands were tied securely behind her, then took a step back, surveying her with an expression he must have picked up during officer training.

"What's your name?" he asked.

She glowered and tried to rise to her feet, but her bound hands threw her off-balance. It was easy for Wells to push her back on the cot. "Do you understand what I'm saying?" he continued.

A troubling thought took shape amid Bellamy's haze of fury. What if she *didn't* speak English? They might've landed in North America, but that didn't mean the Earthborns spoke the same language as they had three hundred years ago.

Wells crouched down so he was eye level with the girl. "We didn't know anyone was still living here. If we've done something to offend you, we're sorry. But—"

"*Sorry?*" Bellamy spat. "They took my sister and killed Asher. We're not apologizing for anything."

Wells shot him a warning look, then turned back to the Earthborn. "We need to know where you took our friend.

And you're going to stay here until you give us some useful information."

She turned to Wells, but instead of responding, she simply pressed her lips together and glared.

Wells rose to his feet, rubbed his head in frustration, then started to turn away.

"That's it? *That's* your idea of questioning her?" Bellamy said, torn between fury and bewilderment. "Do you know what your father and his Council friends do when they need information from someone?"

"That's not how we're doing things here," Wells said with infuriating self-righteousness, as if half the people in camp hadn't been interrogated by his father's guards at some point. He walked over to Clarke's cot, adjusted her blanket, then headed toward the door.

"You're just going to *leave* her there?" Bellamy asked incredulously, his eyes darting between the prisoner and Wells.

"We're going to have people guarding the cabin round the clock. Don't worry, she's not going to escape."

Bellamy took a step forward. "Yeah, she's sure as hell not going to escape because *I'm* staying in here with her. With both of them." He tipped his head toward the sleeping Clarke. "You think it's a good idea to leave her in here with a killer?"

Wells leveled his gaze at Bellamy. "She's tied up. She's not going to hurt anyone."

The condescension in his voice was enough to make Bellamy's blood boil. "We don't know *anything* about these people!" he shot back. "What kind of mutations they've undergone. Remember the two-headed deer?"

Wells shook his head. "She's a human being, Bellamy, not some kind of monster."

Bellamy snorted and turned to the girl. She was staring at them, wide-eyed, her gaze flitting back and forth between Wells and Bellamy. "Well, I'd still feel more comfortable if I kept an eye on her personally," he said, trying to sound relaxed. He knew Wells wouldn't let him stay in here if he thought he was going to hurt her.

"Fine." Wells shot one final look at Clarke before turning back to Bellamy. "But leave her alone for now. I'll be back in a little bit."

When Wells left, Bellamy walked to the other side of the cabin and lowered himself to the ground next to Clarke. The Earthborn girl had shifted on her cot so she was facing the other wall, but Bellamy could tell from the tension in her shoulders that she was aware of his every move.

Good, he thought. Let her worry about what he might do next. The more terrified she became, the better the chances she'd tell them where to find Octavia. Bellamy was going to rescue his sister, no matter what it took. He'd spent the past fifteen years risking his life to keep her safe, and he had no intention of stopping now.

Bellamy loved Remembrance Day. Not because he particularly enjoyed listening to the care center tutors drone on about how *lucky* they all were that their ancestors had made it off Earth. If Bellamy's great-great-grandfather had known that his descendants would have the privilege of cleaning bathrooms in a floating can filled with recirculated air, he probably would have been like, "You know what, guys, I'm good here." No, Bellamy looked forward to Remembrance Day because the storage decks were nearly empty, which made it an ideal time for scavenging.

He slipped behind an outdated generator that had been shoved carelessly against a wall. Spots like this could conceal valuable stuff for decades. Last Remembrance Day, he'd found an actual pocketknife inside a grate on C deck. Bellamy grinned as his fingers closed around something soft and pulled out a piece of pink fabric. A scarf? He shook it out, ignoring the dust motes. It was a small blanket, with a trim of darker pink. Bellamy folded it carefully and slid it inside his jacket.

As he made his way back to the care center, Bellamy toyed with the idea of giving his find to Octavia. She'd recently been moved from the small bedroom where the five- and six-year-olds slept to the larger dorm for older girls. While she liked being thought of as a big kid, the dorm was still frightening to her, and a pretty blanket would go a long way toward making the new space feel like home.

But as he readjusted the blanket under his arm and felt the soft wool against his skin, he knew it was too valuable to keep. Life in the care center was difficult. Although food was meant to be distributed evenly, the orphans had developed an elaborate system based on bribes and intimidation. Without him, Octavia would never get enough to eat. Bellamy was a good scavenger, and he traded everything he found for ration points, or to bribe the kitchen staff for extra food. Over the past few years, he'd done a pretty good job of making sure Octavia had enough to eat. She never got that feral, hungry glint in her eye so common in the care center.

He slipped in through the rarely used service entrance and hid the blanket in his usual spot, a grate in the wall too low for anyone to notice. He'd come back for it tonight and trade it on the black market. The dim, narrow hallways were deserted, which meant that everyone was still shoved into the cramped gathering room for Remembrance Day, being force-fed fun facts about radiation poisoning and the Cataclysm.

Bellamy turned the corner. To his surprise, there were noises coming from the girls' dorm, high-pitched laughter that wasn't quite loud enough to mask the sound of—was that crying? He picked up his speed, and burst inside without knocking. The long room was mostly empty, but there were a few older girls standing in a circle, so absorbed with whatever they were doing that they failed to notice his arrival.

A tall blond girl was holding something in the air, giggling as a smaller hand stretched out in a futile attempt to grab it. *Octavia*. Even in the dim light, Bellamy caught sight of her tearstained cheeks and huge eyes through the gaps between her tormentors' bodies.

They had her red ribbon, the one Octavia wore every day in her dark hair. "Give it back," she pleaded, in a trembling voice that made Bellamy's heart cramp.

"Why?" one of the older girls taunted. "It makes you look like an idiot. Is that what you want?"

"Yeah," the third girl said. "We're doing you a favor. Now people aren't going to ask, 'Who's the weird little kid with the ugly ribbon?'"

The girl holding the ornament made a show of examining it. "I don't even think it's a real ribbon. I bet it came off a garbage bag or something."

Her friend giggled. "I bet that's why she smells like the recycling deck."

"And you're going to smell like a rotting corpse when they finally find you," Bellamy interrupted, striding forward and snatching the ribbon out of the blond girl's hand. He shoved them out of the way and knelt down next to Octavia. "Are you okay?" He reached out to wipe away her tears.

She nodded with a sniffle. He handed her the ribbon, which she clutched in a tiny fist, as if it was a living thing that could escape.

Bellamy rose and, keeping a hand on his sister's shoulder, turned to face the girls. His voice was tight. "If I hear one word about you bothering her again, you'll wish you'd been floated."

Two of the girls exchanged nervous glances, but the blond only raised her eyebrows and smirked. "She's not even supposed to be here. She's a waste of oxygen who was only born because of your stupid slutty mother. And your *sister*"—she said the word like it was something disgusting—"is going to turn out just like her."

Bellamy's muscles reacted before his brain did. Before he realized what he was doing, he'd grabbed the girl by the throat and shoved her against the wall. "If you ever talk to my sister again, if you do so much as *look* at her, I will *kill* you," he hissed. He squeezed her neck tighter, overcome with a sudden and terrifying desire to shut her up for good.

In the distance, he heard someone cry out. He released the girl and staggered backward just as a pair of arms wrapped around him and dragged him away.

It wasn't the first time Bellamy had been sent to the director's office, although he'd never shouted quite so many obscenities en route. The minder who'd grabbed Bellamy shoved him into a chair and told him to wait there for the director. "Stay away from this one," the man said, addressing a girl in the chair across from Bellamy.

Bellamy scowled as the minder waved his hand in front of the scanner, waited for the door to open, and strode back out. Part of him wanted to make a run for it now. Did trying to choke that piece of space trash who'd been bullying his sister count as an Infraction? He'd already had so many warnings, it was only a matter of time before the director wrote a report that landed him in Confinement. But he wouldn't last more than a few days as an outlaw, and then who would take care of Octavia after he was captured? Better he stay here and try to make his case.

He looked up at the girl. She was about his age, but he'd never seen her before; she had to be a new arrival. She was sitting with her feet tucked under her while she fiddled nervously with the buttons on her sweater. Her wavy blond hair was neat and shiny, and he felt an unexpected pang of pity as he imagined her getting dressed in her room for the last time, carefully arranging her hair for the trip to this hellhole.

"So what did you do?" she asked, interrupting his thoughts. Her voice was slightly hoarse, as though it had been a long time since she'd spoken—or like she'd recently been crying. He wondered how she'd wound up here, if her parents had died or perhaps committed Infractions and been floated.

There was no point in lying. "I attacked a girl," he said in the light, careless tone he generally used when discussing his various indiscretions. The girl's eyes flickered, and suddenly, he wanted to explain. "She was hurting my sister."

Her eyes widened. "Your *sister*?" Unlike the blond girl, she made the word sound like something rare and precious. Okay, she was definitely new; everyone at the care center knew about him and Octavia. With the strict population laws, there hadn't been siblings on the ship in at least a generation.

"Well, technically she's my half sister—but we're the only family each other's got. Her name's Octavia." He smiled, just like he did whenever he said her name. "So did you just get here?"

She nodded. "I'm Lilly," she said.

"That's a pretty name." The words slipped out before he realized how stupid they'd sound. "I'm Bellamy." He tried to think of something else, to prove that he wasn't a complete doofus, but the door slid open and the director trudged in.

"Not you again," she said, shooting Bellamy a look of disapproval before turning her attention to Lilly. "Lilly Marsh?" she asked, in a voice Bellamy had never heard directed at him. "It's very nice to meet you. Let's go into my office and I'll tell you a little more about how things work here." As Lilly rose slowly to her feet, the director turned back to Bellamy. "One month of probation, and if you so much as step a toe out of line, you're out of here. For good."

Relief and confusion washed over Bellamy, but he wasn't

going to stick around long enough for the director to change her mind. He jumped from the chair and hurried toward the door. As he waited for it to open, he glanced over his shoulder to look back at Lilly.

To his surprise, she was smiling at him.

CHAPTER *6*

Clarke

Whatever you do, don't go inside the lab.

The anguished cries reached out to her, until Clarke couldn't tell what was coming from the other side of the wall, and what was echoing in the shadowy depths of her own brain.

The experiments use dangerous levels of radiation. We don't want you to get hurt.

The lab was nothing like she'd imagined. It was full of hospital beds instead of workstations. And in each bed was a child.

It's our job to determine when Earth will be able to support human life again. Everyone is counting on us.

Clarke glanced around the room, looking for her friend Lilly. She was lonely. And scared. Everyone around her was dying. Their small bodies withered away until they were hardly more than wisps of skin and bone.

We never wanted you to find out this way.

But where was Lilly? Clarke came to visit her often, whenever her parents weren't in the lab. She brought her friend presents, books she took from the library and candy she stole from the pantry at school. On Lilly's good days, their laughter drowned out the sounds of the heart-rate monitors.

It wasn't our idea. The Vice Chancellor forced us to experiment on those children. They would've killed us if we'd refused.

Clarke moved from bed to bed, each of them containing a sick child. But none of them were her best friend.

And then, suddenly, she remembered. Lilly was dead. Because Clarke had killed her.

They would've killed you too.

Lilly had begged her to make the pain go away. Clarke hadn't wanted to, but she knew that Lilly had no chance of getting better. So eventually she'd agreed, and gave her friend the fatal drugs that ended her suffering.

I'm sorry, Clarke tried to tell her friend. *I'm sorry. I'm sorry.*

"It's okay, Clarke. *Shhh*, it's okay. I'm right here."

Clarke's eyes snapped open. She was lying on a cot, her arm wrapped in bandages . . . why? What had happened?

Bellamy was sitting next to her, his face dirty and haggard. But he was smiling in a way Clarke hadn't seen before, a wide, beaming grin without any hint of amusement or mockery. There was something startlingly intimate about it, as if this smile exposed more of Bellamy than she'd seen when they went swimming in their underwear.

"Thank god you're okay. Do you remember getting bitten by the snake?" he asked. Clarke closed her eyes as fragments of memory shot through her mind. The slithering movement on the ground. The blinding pain. Yet at the moment, the only sensation she was aware of was the warmth of Bellamy's hand on hers. "We gave you the universal antidote thing, but I wasn't sure you got it in time."

Clarke sat up, suddenly alert. "You *carried* me all the way back to camp?" Her cheeks flushed at the thought of being unconscious for that long in Bellamy's arms. "And you figured out about the medicine?"

Bellamy shot a quick glance at the door. "That part was all Wells."

The name landed with a thud in Clarke's chest. After Wells stopped her from rushing into a burning tent to save her friend Thalia, she'd fled the camp in a haze of grief and rage. But as she looked around this new infirmary cabin, all she felt was sadness. Thalia was gone, but she couldn't really blame Wells for what he'd done. He'd saved her life—twice now.

On the other side of the small cabin, a girl was curled up on a cot. Clarke pushed herself onto her elbows for a better look, but when Bellamy noticed the direction of her gaze, he sat down on the edge of Clarke's cot, as if shielding her. "So," he said, shooting a glance over his shoulder. "About that."

In a strangely detached voice, he told Clarke about the attack that had killed Asher, and the girl Wells had taken prisoner.

"What?" Clarke sat bolt upright. "You're telling me that girl over there was born on *Earth*?" Some small part of her had expected this since the orchard, but waking up to find an Earthborn meters away was almost too much to process. Thousands of questions exploded in every sector of her brain. How had they survived the Cataclysm? How many of them were there? Were there pockets of people all over the planet, or just in this area?

"Keep your voice down," Bellamy whispered, placing a hand on Clarke's shoulder and gently guiding her back down on the cot. "I think she's asleep, and I want her to stay that way as long as possible. It's creepy as all hell having her in here."

Clarke shook off his hand and rose to her feet. The excitement and shock pulsing through her veins left her whole body trembling. "This is unbelievable. I have to talk to her!"

Before she could take another step, Bellamy grabbed her wrist. "That's not a good idea. Her people took Octavia and killed Asher. We caught her spying on us." His mouth twisted into a sneer. "She was probably trying to decide who to take next."

Clarke stared at him in confusion. Why would they speculate about the girl's motives instead of *asking* her? "Has anyone tried talking to her?" There was no danger in trying, especially since her hands and ankles were bound. Clarke rose onto the balls of her feet for a better look. The girl was curled up on her side, with her back to Bellamy and Clarke. It didn't look like she'd moved at all.

Bellamy pulled Clarke back onto the cot with a tug. "I think the girl speaks English. She hasn't said anything, but it seems like she understands what we're saying. As soon as we get some useful information from her, I'll head out to find Octavia."

His voice was calm, but he couldn't hide the note of anxiety when he said his sister's name. For a moment, Clarke's thoughts left the girl on the cot and returned to the woods where she and Bellamy had been following Octavia's footprints. She felt a stab of guilt that he had abandoned Octavia's trail in order to carry her all the way back here.

"Bellamy," she said slowly as another thought took shape. "That wreckage we found. Did you see the logo on it? It said

TG." Every child on the Colony knew that TG, Trillion Galactic, was the company that had originally built their ship.

"I know," he said. "But that could mean anything."

"It's not from our dropship," she said quickly, her voice rising in excitement. "Which means it has to be from something else the Colony sent down. Maybe some kind of drone? Or what if . . ." She trailed off, suddenly hesitant to share the spark of an idea forming in the back of her mind. "I think it's important that we figure out what it is," she finished vaguely.

Bellamy squeezed her hand. "As soon as we get Octavia back, we'll go check it out."

"Thank you," she said quietly. "For everything. I know you lost a lot of time bringing me back here."

"Yeah, well, it would have been a shame to lose the only doctor on Earth, even if you were arrested before you finished training. Can you remind me again which body part I should avoid injuring?" he said with a smile. "Are you better with elbows or ankles?"

Clarke was glad to see him in a playful mood, but it wasn't enough to shake the guilt building up in her chest. She lowered her voice, glancing again at the girl across the infirmary. "It's just . . . if you need to leave again, you should go. I feel terrible that you already lost a day because of me."

His teasing smile softened. "It's okay." He reached up and absentmindedly began twisting a strand of her hair around his finger. "I think for now, my best chance is to see what this girl knows, before I go back looking for the trail."

Clarke nodded, relieved that Bellamy didn't resent her, and relieved that he wasn't planning on leaving right away. "Octavia's lucky to have you," she said, then cocked her head to the side and surveyed Bellamy with a smile. "You know, I remember when I heard there were *siblings* on Walden."

Bellamy raised an eyebrow. "My reputation precedes me? I guess I shouldn't be surprised. How could you *not* talk about someone this good-looking?"

Clarke knocked against him, digging her elbow into his ribs. He made an exaggerated grimace, then laughed. "It's true," she continued. "My friend Lilly remembered you guys from the care center. I think her exact words were, 'There's a girl with an older brother. It's great that she has a sibling, but he's so spectacularly attractive, no one can look directly at him. It's just too blinding, like staring at the sun.'"

Instead of smiling, Bellamy's face went pale. "Lilly? It wasn't Lilly Marsh, was it?"

Clarke's chest tightened as she realized what she'd just let slip. Of course Bellamy and Lilly had known each other. There couldn't have been that many children in the Walden care center, could there? Lilly had rarely volunteered information about her life on Walden, and Clarke hadn't asked. It hadn't been a conscious decision, but she realized now that it was easier to think about Lilly as a girl without a past, without people who cared about her.

"How did you know Lilly?" Bellamy was staring at her, searching her eyes for the information she was desperately trying to hide.

"I met her at the hospital, during my apprenticeship," Clarke said, not bothering to count the number of lies in the short sentence. "Were you friends?" She prayed he'd shrug and say something about knowing her vaguely from the care center.

"We were—" Bellamy paused. "We were more than friends. Lilly was the only girl I ever cared about. Until you."

"What?" Clarke stared at him in shock. Lilly, her friend and her parents' test subject, had been Bellamy's—

"Are you okay?" Bellamy asked. "Does it bother you that I had a girlfriend back on the ship?"

"No. Of course not," she said. "I'm fine. Just tired." Her heart racing, Clarke rolled onto her side before she could see the look on Bellamy's face. Better he think she was irrationally jealous and possessive than do anything to hint at the truth.

"Okay," he said, clearly unconvinced. "Because it was a long time ago."

She didn't turn around. Lilly's death may have felt like a long time to Bellamy, but Clarke relived her friend's final moments every day. She still saw Lilly's face whenever she closed her eyes and tried to go to sleep. She still heard her voice echoing in her head.

Lilly's death was never far from her thoughts. Because Clarke had been the one who killed her.

CHAPTER 7

Glass

Glass and Luke were silent as they left his flat for the very last time. As they stepped into the eerily empty corridor, Glass reached for Luke's hand, shocked by the silence. The chaos that had overwhelmed the ship for the past few days seemed to have died down, washed away by a heavy tide of despair. The dim ceiling lights flickered wearily, like an exhausted child trying to keep his eyes open.

They took the main stairs quietly, finally reaching the lower levels of the ship, which were used to house the electrical and plumbing systems. Neither spoke until Glass pulled Luke to a stop in front of the air vent, then reached up to remove the grate.

"Please," Luke said. "Allow me." He pulled the grate from the wall and placed it on the ground with exaggerated delicacy. "And to think, all those hours I spent worrying what kind of date to take you on, it turns out we could've gone on a romantic crawl through the ventilation system."

"It's all your influence," Glass said, managing a smile despite the prickle of tears she could feel building behind her eyes.

"What?" Luke reached out and ruffled her hair. "Slumming it?"

Glass rose up onto her toes to give him a kiss. "Being adventurous."

Luke pulled her into a hug. "I love you," he murmured into her ear. Then he boosted her into the vent, waited for her to climb inside, and replaced the grate.

Glass paused for a moment to wipe away the tears threatening to obscure her vision. "I love you too," she whispered, knowing that Luke wouldn't be able to hear it. Then she gritted her teeth and began to crawl down the narrow metal chute.

As she slowly made her way forward, straining to see in the dim light, Glass tried to imagine the look on her mother's face when she opened the door. Would she be overwhelmed with relief? Or would part of her still be furious that Glass had risked her life by sneaking onto Walden? The thought of all the pain she'd caused her mother over the past year made Glass's heart cramp. If this was the end, then she needed one last chance to apologize, one final opportunity to tell her how much she loved her.

Glass winced as her ankle knocked against the metal wall. If someone had told her two years ago that she would someday crawl through an air vent from Walden to Phoenix, she'd have laughed in their face. Things had been different then—*she* had been different. She smiled in the darkness. Now her life might be in danger, but it was finally one worth fighting for.

". . . when the Cataclysm struck, there were one hundred and ninety-five sovereign nations, although the vast majority had joined one of the four major alliances."

Glass yawned, covering her mouth halfheartedly. Their tutor had dimmed the lights to make the holograms easier to see, so there was little chance that she would notice that Glass wasn't paying attention.

"In the first six weeks of World War Three, nearly two million people were killed . . ."

"Cora," Glass whispered, leaning over the desk. "*Cora.*"

Cora lifted her head and blinked sleepily at Glass. "What?"

". . . and in the next six months, more than five million died of starvation."

"Did you get my messages?"

Cora rubbed her eyes, then blinked again, activating her cornea slip. She squinted as she scrolled through her unread messages, including one from Glass asking if she wanted to go to the Exchange after tutorial.

A few seconds later, there was a flash in the top right corner of Glass's vision field. She blinked as a message from Cora appeared. *Sure, if we're fast. I have to meet my mother at 3.*

Why? Glass blinked back.

Greenhouse duty ☺

Glass smiled. "Greenhouse duty" was Cora's family's code for when they took an extra visit to the solar fields. It was totally illegal, but the guards turned a blind eye because Cora's father was the Resources Chief and no one wanted to risk upsetting him. Glass didn't really care that Cora's family got the best produce this way—her family had perks of their own—and Cora let her come over for fresh berries every now and then.

"Yes, Clarke?" The tutor gestured toward a girl in the front row who had her hand raised. Glass and Cora rolled their eyes. Clarke *always* had a question, and the tutors were so delighted by her "intellectual curiosity" that they let her babble on, even after class was supposed to have ended.

"Had any species already gone extinct? Or did that all happen after the Cataclysm?"

"That's an interesting question, Clarke. By the middle of the twenty-first century, at least a third of the . . ."

"I wish *she'd* go extinct," Glass muttered, not bothering to blink it to Cora as a message.

Cora laughed, then sighed and placed her head back on her desk. "Wake me up when it's over."

Glass groaned. "That girl needs to get a life," she whispered. "If she doesn't shut up, I'm going to float her."

After their tutor finally dismissed them, Glass jumped to her feet and grabbed Cora's hand. "Come *on*," she whined. "I need to find buttons for that dress."

"Are you going to the Exchange?" Clarke asked eagerly, looking up from her desk. "I'll come with you. I'm trying to find a pillow for my friend."

Glass ran her eyes up and down Clarke's ensemble of pants and a shirt so dowdy, they could've come from the Arcadia Exchange. "You can burn those pants, stuff the ashes into the shirt, and *voilà*, a new pillow for your *friend* and one less eyesore for us."

Cora burst out laughing, but the thrill of accomplishment Glass was expecting never came. Clarke's eyes widened with hurt and surprise, then she pressed her lips together and spun away without a word.

Whatever, Glass thought. *That's what she gets for being a suck-up and ruining everyone else's day.*

Since they'd been kept late, Cora didn't wind up having time for the Exchange, so Glass went home. She hated shopping by herself. She didn't like the way the guards stared at her when the officer in charge wasn't looking. Or the way men stared at her when their wives weren't looking, for that matter.

On the walk back, she thought about ways to make her father give her more of their ration points. The Remembrance Day Celebration was coming up, and for once, Glass was determined to have a prettier dress than Cora.

She scanned into the flat and tossed her school bag on the floor. "Mom?" she called. "Mom, do you know where Dad is?"

Her mother wandered out from her bedroom. Her face was pale under her artfully applied blush, and her eyes glistened strangely, though it might've just been a trick of the light. "What's wrong?" Glass asked, looking over her shoulder. She wished her father would get here. She never knew what to do when her mother was in one of her moods. "Where's Dad? Is he still at work? I want to talk to him about my allowance."

"Your father's gone."

"Gone? What do you—?"

"He left us. He's moving in with"—she closed her eyes for a moment—"that *girl* from the committee." Her voice was flat, as if she'd tucked her emotions away as neatly as one of her elaborate dresses.

Glass froze. "What do you mean?"

"It means your allowance is the least of our problems," Sonja said, sinking onto the couch and closing her eyes. "We have nothing."

Her feet were cramping and her hands were raw by the time Glass crawled around the corner of the vent that led onto Phoenix. She prayed there wouldn't be guards on the other side, that she'd be able to turn right around and bring Luke back with her. With everything that was going on, surely she could keep Luke out of sight until they made it to her mother's flat, and then figure out how to get onto one of the dropships.

Back when she first thought of going to Earth—when she was pulled from her Confinement cell and told that she and ninety-nine others would be sent to the surface on a dropship—the idea of the planet had filled her with terror. But now, a different image of life on the ground began to take shape. Holding hands with Luke as they walked through the woods. Sitting on the top of a hill in perfect, contented silence as they watched a real sunset. Perhaps some cities had survived—what if they could go to Paris like the couple on Luke's plates?

She was smiling as she reached forward to grasp the grate on the Phoenix side, but she couldn't take hold. Her fingers scratched around for purchase and found nothing. She could feel the edges of the vent; something flat was covering it, sealing it shut from the other side.

Glass rolled over so her feet were facing the end of the air shaft. She took a deep breath and kicked. Nothing happened. She kicked again, this time crying out in frustration when the grate rattled, but stayed in place. "No!" she exclaimed, wincing as her voice echoed through the vent. Camille must've blocked it off from the other side to keep anyone from following her. It made sense—one Walden stowaway had a much better chance of staying hidden than a whole stream of them. But in doing so, she'd sentenced Glass and Luke to die.

Glass hugged her knees to her chest, trying not to imagine the look on Luke's face when she told him the path was blocked. How he'd use every ounce of self-control to look stoic and brave, but wouldn't be able to keep the despair from flickering in his eyes.

She'd never get to see her mother. When the oxygen finally ran out on Phoenix, Sonja would be all alone, huddled in her tiny flat as she wheezed a last good-bye to the daughter who'd disappeared without a word.

But just as Glass turned around to start the long crawl back, an idea flitted into her head. An idea so reckless and insane that it might actually work.

If there was no way to get from Walden to Phoenix *inside* the ship, she would just have to go *outside*.

CHAPTER 8

Wells

Molly wasn't any better after breakfast. Her fever had grown worse and she couldn't stop shivering, no matter how many blankets Wells covered her with.

By midday, Molly was still curled up in one of the now-empty cabins, where she'd been since dawn. Wells surveyed her with a frown. Sweat beaded her pale forehead, and her eyes had an odd, yellowish tinge.

Wells had been avoiding facing Clarke for the first time, but now he had no choice. He bent down, scooped the small girl into his arms, and walked out into the clearing. Most of the camp was too busy whispering about the Earthborn or sparring with Graham's new spears on the far side of the clearing to notice, though a few people watched curiously as Wells pushed open the door to the infirmary cabin and carried Molly inside.

The Earthborn girl was lying with her back to the door, either asleep or pretending to be. But Clarke was sitting up, staring at her so intensely that she didn't notice Wells at first.

He stepped over Bellamy, who'd apparently fallen asleep on the floor next to Clarke's cot, then gently lowered Molly onto one of the other empty beds. When he straightened up, Clarke had turned from the Earthborn, and was now looking at Wells, her eyes wide.

"Hey." He took a few steps forward. "How are you feeling?"

"Better," Clarke said hoarsely, then cleared her throat. "Thank you . . . for giving me the antidote. You saved my life." She sounded sincere. There was no trace of lingering anger in her voice, no sign that she still resented Wells for what he'd done during the fire. But her vague, polite tone was almost worse than fury, as if he were a stranger who'd performed some kind service. Was this what it would always be like between them now, he wondered, or could this maybe be a fresh start?

As Wells searched for the right response, Clarke's eyes drifted to Molly. The detached expression on her face slid away, replaced by a penetrating gaze that was much more familiar. "What's wrong with Molly?" she asked, her voice sharp with concern.

Grateful to have something else to talk about, Wells told Clarke how the younger girl had suddenly fallen ill. Clarke frowned and started to rise from her bed. "Wait," Wells said, hurrying over. He placed a hand on Clarke's shoulder before he had time to think better of it, then snatched it away. "You need to rest. Can you look at her from here?"

"I'm okay," Clarke said with a shrug. She lowered her feet to the ground and stood up shakily. Wells fought the urge to offer her his arm.

She walked slowly over to Molly, then knelt down for a better look. "Hey, Molly. It's me, Clarke. Can you hear me?"

Molly only whimpered in response, thrashing against the blanket Wells had wrapped her in. Clarke frowned as she placed her fingers on the girl's wrist to check her pulse.

"What do you think?" Wells asked, taking a hesitant step toward them.

"I'm not sure." She'd moved her hand to Molly's neck to feel her glands, then twisted around to glance up at Wells. "Hey, how long have we been here? I seem to have lost track of time with the snakebite and everything."

"Just over three weeks." He paused, calculating in his head. "I think it was three weeks yesterday."

"Day twenty-one," Clarke said quietly, more to herself than to him.

"What's that? What are you talking about?"

Clarke looked away, but Wells could see the fear in her eyes. He knew what that haunted look meant. He remembered the anguish he'd felt when Clarke had finally confided in him about her parents' experiments. "You don't think it has something to do with radiation, do you?" he asked. "But . . . wouldn't people have gotten sick much earlier?"

Clarke pressed her lips together, scrunching her mouth to the side like she always did when giving her body time to catch up to her racing brain. "If it was in the air, yes, we wouldn't have been able to breathe. But if it was just trace amounts in the water, then this would be the time. But I don't think that's what's wrong with Molly," she said quickly. "It doesn't *look* like radiation poisoning." A shadow of pain flickered in her eyes, and Wells knew she was thinking about her friend, the one who'd died. "I think she might be having a bad reaction to something. Is the rest of the universal antidote still in the medicine chest?"

"The rest of it?" Wells repeated. "There was just the one vial."

Clarke stared at him. "Please tell me you didn't use the whole thing on me. That was probably twelve doses!"

"And how exactly was I supposed to know that?" Wells asked, indignation tugging at the guilt that had begun to coil around his stomach.

"So it's all gone?" Clarke turned back to Molly and cursed under her breath. "This isn't good."

Before Wells could ask Clarke to elaborate, the door flew open, and Eric hurried inside, leading Felix by the hand. "Clarke? Thank god you're awake. We need you." Startled to see the normally stoic Eric so agitated, Wells hurried toward him and helped Eric settle Felix in one of the remaining empty cots.

"He passed out on our way back from the stream," Eric said, looking anxiously from Clarke to Felix. "And he said he hasn't been able to keep any food down."

By this point, Bellamy had woken up. He rose to his feet slowly, rubbing his eyes as he yawned. "What's going on? Clarke, what the hell are you doing out of bed?"

She ignored him as she took a few shaky steps in order to begin examining Felix. His eyes were open, but he had trouble focusing on Clarke, and didn't seem able to answer any of her questions.

"What's wrong with him?" Eric asked, searching Clarke's face with an intensity that reminded Wells of the guards in the command center back on the ship, the ones in charge of scanning the monitors for asteroids or debris.

"I'm not sure," she said, her voice a mix of confusion and irritation. Clarke hated being stumped. "But it's probably nothing to worry about. It could be dehydration caused by the stomach flu. We'll hydrate him and see what happens. Bellamy, can you bring us some more water?"

Bellamy hesitated and looked at Wells, as if about to suggest that *he* go, but then he nodded and hurried out the door.

Wells crouched down next to Clarke, close enough that he could speak softly, but far enough that there'd be no danger of brushing against her. "It's weird, isn't it? That Molly and Felix fell ill at pretty much the same time?"

"Not really. With a hundred people living together in such a small space, it's a wonder there hasn't been some sort of outbreak sooner."

Wells glanced at Eric, who was busy stroking Felix's hair, and lowered his voice. "But what if it isn't the flu? What if it's the radia—"

"It isn't," Clarke said as she tilted her head toward Felix's chest to listen to his lungs as best she could without a stethoscope.

"But if it was. Is there anything in the medicine chest that would help?"

"My parents were developing something," Clarke said softly. "There's a bottle of pills that could slow the effects of radiation poisoning."

"Shouldn't we give it to them, then? To be safe?"

"Absolutely not."

Clarke's tone brooked no arguments, but Wells pressed on, anyway. "Why?"

Clarke jerked her head toward Wells and gave him a look of frustration, mingled with fear. "Because if it's not radiation poisoning, then the pills will kill them."

CHAPTER 9

Clarke

"You sure you'll be okay for a few hours?" Bellamy asked, examining Clarke's still-swollen arm with a frown. "I'll try not to go far, in case—"

"I'm *sure*," she interrupted. "Go hunting. It's fine, I promise." They were low on food, and when Wells had returned that afternoon to check on Molly and Felix, he'd swallowed his pride and asked Bellamy for help replenishing their supplies.

Bellamy jerked his head toward the sleeping girl on the other side of the cabin. "Promise me you won't talk to her," he said. "I don't trust her alone with you."

"I'm not *alone*," Clarke said. "Molly and Felix are here."

"Unconscious people don't count. Just keep your distance, okay? And try to get some rest."

"I will. I promise." Clarke tried to keep her voice steady so Bellamy wouldn't suspect how eager she was for him to leave. But the moment he was gone, she rose onto her knees to peer over at the Earthborn girl.

She was wearing all black, but Clarke didn't recognize most of the materials. The pants were tight and made out of something smooth and slightly shiny—maybe animal skin?— while the fabric draped over the top of her body looked softer. What was woven animal hair called? Wool? The bulky wrap around her shoulders was unmistakably animal fur. Clarke was desperate to find out what sort of creature it came from. So far, the only mammal she'd seen was a deer; the fur on the girl's wrap was much thicker and darker.

Across the room, Felix moaned in his sleep. Clarke hurried over and placed her hand against his forehead. His fever was also getting worse. She bit her lip as she thought about what she'd told Wells. It was true that radiation poisoning presented differently; after the nausea and fever came sores, bleeding gums, and hair loss. That's what had made watching Lilly so terrible. Clarke had known what was in store for her friend before each new wave of suffering.

As she headed back to her own cot, Clarke thought about the pills in the medicine chest. If Felix and Molly's illness had nothing to do with radiation, the drug would kill them. But if Clarke was wrong, she'd be sentencing them to a long and painful death. The pills had to be administered in the early stages of radiation poisoning.

She sat down and placed her head in her hands, wondering for the umpteenth time why the Council hadn't bothered talking to her before they sent the hundred to Earth. Yes, she'd been a convicted criminal, but she was also the only person intimately acquainted with her parents' research.

"So who's Lilly?" an unfamiliar voice called from the other side of the cabin.

Clarke gasped and jerked her head toward the Earthborn girl, shocked into silence. So she *did* speak English. She was sitting up now, facing Clarke. Her long black hair was matted but still shiny, and her skin had a warm glow to it that made her eyes appear startlingly green.

"What—what do you—?" Clarke stammered. Then she took a deep breath and forced herself to regain some semblance of composure. "Why do you want to know about Lilly?"

The girl shrugged. "You said that name in your sleep, when you were having the fever dreams." Her accent and cadence were different from what Clarke was used to, slightly more musical. Hearing it was thrilling, like the first time she had listened to a heartbeat during her medical training. "And then that boy acted so strange when you mentioned her," the girl added.

"Lilly was a friend of mine, back on the ship," Clarke said slowly. Did the Earthborns even know about the Colony? A million questions jostled for dominance in Clarke's brain, one rising to the surface quicker than the others. She decided to start small. "How many of you are there?"

The girl looked thoughtful. "Right now, three hundred and fifty-four. Maybe three hundred and fifty-five if Delphine had her baby. She's due any day."

A baby. Would it be born in a hospital? Was it possible they had any functioning equipment from before the Cataclysm? Had the Earthborns rebuilt any of the major cities? "Where do you live?" Clarke asked eagerly.

The girl's face darkened, and Clarke regretted her lack of tact. She was being kept prisoner; of course she didn't want to tell Clarke where her friends and family were. "What's your name?" she asked instead.

"Sasha."

"I'm Clarke," she replied, though she had a feeling the girl already knew that. She smiled and rose slowly to her feet. "This is insane. I can't believe I'm talking to someone from *Earth*." Clarke walked across the cabin and sat down next to Sasha. "Did you know there were people living in space? What did you think when you saw us?"

Sasha stared at Clarke for a long moment, as if unsure whether she was being serious. "Well, I didn't expect you to be so young," she finally said. "The last ones were much older."

The words knocked the breath out of Clarke's chest. *The last ones?* It couldn't be. She must have misunderstood. "What do you mean?" she asked. "Are you saying you've already met people from the *Colony*?"

Sasha nodded, sending Clarke's heart into overdrive. "A group came down about a year ago. We'd always known that people were living in space, but it was still a shock, meeting them face-to-face. Their ship landed badly, just like yours did." She paused, apparently debating how much to share with Clarke. "The first time, we didn't know any better, and we tried to help them. We brought them into our—we let them stay with us. We gave them food and shelter, even though their ancestors left ours behind during the Forsakening. My people were willing to put the past behind us in the name of peace and friendship." An edge had crept into her voice, and she raised her chin slightly, as if defying Clarke to challenge her.

Clarke fought the urge to defend the Colonists, or to ask more questions. In this case, the best way to gain the girl's trust was probably to remain silent. Sure enough, after a long pause, Sasha continued. "We were foolish to trust them. There was . . . an incident." Her face contorted in pain at the memory.

"What happened?" Clarke asked softly.

"It doesn't matter," Sasha snapped. "They're all gone now."

Clarke sat back, struggling to sort through the staggering information.

Could there really have been a mission to Earth last year? She thought of the debris she had found, the TG logo, and it suddenly seemed possible. But who were these older Colonists on the mission? Why had they sent the hundred, if another mission had already gone before them?

"Do you know . . . do you know anything about them?" Clarke asked, doing her best to keep her voice neutral. "Did they volunteer to come, or were they forced to?"

"I have no idea," Sasha said dismissively. "We weren't exactly spending a lot of time having personal conversations. Not after they . . ." She trailed off.

Clarke frowned as her brain raced to fill in the rest of the sentence. She couldn't imagine what the Colonists had done to offend the Earthborns so badly. But it didn't sound like Sasha was going to tell her much more, and she couldn't keep this news to herself for another minute.

"I'll be back," Clarke said, rising to her feet. "Don't go anywhere."

Sasha lifted an eyebrow, extending her legs so that Clarke could see her bound ankles.

Clarke's cheeks burned with shame. She hurried over to Sasha, knelt down, and began untying the rope. Wells had made the knot extremely complicated—something he'd learned in officer training, no doubt—but she'd spent enough time tying off stitches to figure it out. Sasha flinched when Clarke's hand first brushed against her, but she didn't protest.

Clarke unwrapped the final loop and threw it to the ground. "Come on," she said, offering her hand to Sasha. "Come with me. They'll never believe me otherwise."

Sasha stared at Clarke's hand warily, then stood up unaided. She shook one foot, then the other, wincing as the circulation returned to her feet.

"Let's go," Clarke said as she took Sasha's elbow and guided her outside.

CHAPTER *10*

Bellamy

It had only been ten minutes since he'd returned with the rabbits, and they were already roasting over the fire. The tantalizing smells had brought most of the camp running toward the campfire, where they now stood waiting, their eyes wide and hungry.

They reminded Bellamy of the youngest kids at the care center, who had approached him every time he returned from one of his foraging trips, hoping he'd found them something to eat. But he'd never been able to feed all of them, just as he wasn't able to feed all of them now.

"You only brought two?" Lila asked, trying to exchange a disdainful look with her friend Tamsin, a reedy blond girl who struck Bellamy as a quieter, and somehow even stupider, version of Lila. A week ago, they, along with a few of the other girls, had cut their standard-issue gray pants into shorts of varying lengths, ignoring Clarke's warning that they'd regret it once the weather changed.

And now they did. They were both shivering, though Lila was doing her best to hide it. Tamsin just looked miserable.

"Good counting, Lila," Bellamy said slowly, as if praising an accomplished toddler. "You'll make it all the way to ten soon."

Lila narrowed her eyes and folded her arms across her chest. "You're an asshole, Bellamy."

"Ever hear the saying 'Don't bite the hand that feeds you'?" he shot back with a grin. "Or, why don't I put it to you this way? There are *two* rabbits, as you so astutely pointed out, and there are way more than two of us." Ninety-three to be exact, though no one needed to be reminded of the fact that they had already lost so many members of their group. "Not everyone is going to get a bite. And you just made that decision a little easier for me. So, thank you." He extended his hand as if offering it to Lila to shake. "I'm very grateful for your help."

She smacked his hand away and spun on her heel, tugging on the uneven edges of her shorts as she strode away. *Typical Wal-ditz*, Bellamy thought, using the term Octavia had coined for the girls on Walden who purposefully acted like airheaded Phoenicians. But the thought of Octavia banished his smile, unlocking the ache he'd been trying to contain in his chest. God only knew what kind of suffering she was enduring right now, while Lila and the rest of her friends flounced around the camp in their short shorts.

Two Arcadian boys had taken charge of roasting the rabbits, which Eric and Priya had skinned. Bellamy was eager to get back to the infirmary and check on Clarke, but he knew that if he left now, the meat would have vanished by the time he returned. He didn't need any for himself, but he wanted to make sure Clarke got a few bites. "There's not nearly enough for everyone," Priya was saying to Wells, who'd just returned from a trip to the stream. "How many protein packets do we have left?"

Wells frowned and shook his head, then leaned over to whisper something to Priya. They were obviously trying to be discreet, but at least twenty people were watching them nervously.

Bellamy thought of the days after they first landed, when the group was full of explosive, almost dangerous energy. Now exhaustion and hunger had made them far less talkative. Even the chatty faux-Phoenix girl, Kendall, was quiet as she stared at Wells and Priya, although the small smile on her face made her seem more amused than suspicious.

For a few minutes, the only sounds in the clearing were the crackle of the logs and the thud of wooden spears as they bounced off tree trunks and landed on the grass. The people Graham had recruited to his "security force" had been practicing all day, and even Bellamy had to admit some of them were getting pretty good. If they were as focused on hunting dinner as they were on imaginary Earthborns, then there was a chance the Colonists wouldn't starve after all.

Kendall was the first to break the silence. "So, Wells, when's the next dropship coming?" Bellamy snorted at her transparent attempt to lure Wells into a conversation. A number of girls had been paying a lot of attention to Chancellor Junior lately.

"Who cares?" Lila interjected as she rejoined the group, making a show of stretching her arms over her head. "I'm not in any rush to have guards around here, acting like they own the place."

Bellamy silently agreed, although he'd never give Lila the satisfaction of saying it aloud. He had the most to lose of any of them. While his insane plan of posing as a guard had gotten Bellamy onto the hundred's dropship, the Chancellor—Wells's father—had been shot in the ensuing chaos, taking a bullet meant for Bellamy. Even if the other members of the mission were pardoned for their Infractions, Bellamy would be considered a criminal. For all he knew, the guards had orders to shoot him on sight.

"But the Council has to know it's safe by now," Kendall said, gesturing to the monitor on her wrist, the one that was meant to send vital signs back up to the ship.

"Safe?" Lila repeated with a bitter laugh. "Yeah, Earth seems real *safe* to me."

"I meant the radiation levels," Kendall said, shooting a look at Wells, clearly hoping he'd back her up. But he was just staring out into the trees. Something had caught his attention.

Bellamy jumped to his feet, grabbed his bow, and jogged over toward Wells. A triumphant cry filled the clearing, and Bellamy exhaled. It wasn't the Earthborns. It was Graham.

He crashed through one of the bushes that grew near the tree line with a spear in one hand, and something dark and bulky in the other. Something dark, bulky, and *furry*. The bastard had actually killed something, Bellamy realized, not sure whether he was more relieved or annoyed. It would be great to have help hunting; he just wished it could've come from anyone besides Graham. "Look what I have," he crowed, letting his kill fall to the ground with a thud.

"Graham, it's still *alive*," Priya said, stepping forward while the others backed away in fear and disgust.

She was right. The creature was twitching. It was larger than the rabbits Bellamy had brought back, but smaller than a deer. It had a long snout, slightly rounded ears, and a bushy, striped tail. He peered over for a closer look and saw that the creature was bleeding from a deep wound in its stomach. It would die eventually, but its death would be long and painful. Wells reached into his pocket and pulled out the small knife he always carried with him.

"You need to shoot it through the heart," Bellamy said to Graham. "That way, it's a clean kill, and the animal dies right away. Otherwise, slit its throat."

Graham shrugged, as if Bellamy were chastising him for not closing the supply tent properly. "It's a *fox*," he said, nudging the animal with his toe.

"Actually, it's a raccoon," Bellamy said. At least, he thought it was. It looked similar to the raccoons he'd seen in photos, except this creature had something growing out of his head, something that *glowed*. A circle of light danced on the dark grass as the animal thrashed from side to side. It almost looked like it was wearing a headlamp, like the engineers used to repair the outside of the ship. Bellamy had a vague recollection of watching a video of a fish with a similar apparatus, a light it used to attract prey at the bottom of the ocean.

"Hold on. Were you hunting by yourself?" Lila asked, her voice a mixture of pride and censure. "What if the Earth people are still out there?"

"I hope they're out there. I'll make them wish they *had* gone extinct during the Cataclysm." Graham laughed as he tossed his spear into the air and caught it one-handed. "We'll be *their* Cataclysm."

"Don't be an idiot," Wells snapped, his patience evidently wearing thin. "There could be hundreds of them. *Thousands*. If it comes down to a real battle, we don't stand a chance."

Graham lifted his chin. "I think that all depends on who's leading us, don't you?" he said, his voice suddenly quiet. He and Wells stared at each other for a moment, then Graham broke away with a grin. "Now, who's going to skin this thing? I'm starving."

"Step one, wait until it's actually *dead*," Bellamy said. He looked over to Wells, who was still holding his pocketknife in his hand.

"It's dead," Kendall piped in cheerfully. She was crouched on the ground next to the raccoon. "I just broke its neck."

Bellamy thought she was joking, but then he noticed that the creature was still and the strange glowing light had gone out. He turned to Kendall, slightly startled, but before he could ask where she'd learned to do that, the sound of footsteps pulled his attention toward the middle of the clearing.

Clarke was running toward them, dragging the Earthborn girl by the arm. "Guys!" she shouted, breathless. There was a light in her eyes Bellamy had seen only a few times before, when she encountered something new about Earth that set her scientist mind ablaze. "You're not going to believe this!"

Everyone jumped to their feet, clustering around Clarke and the girl. "What is it?" Bellamy asked.

Clarke's eyes darted to him, before turning to the prisoner. "Tell them," Clarke urged her. "Tell them what you told me."

So, he thought, the girl *did* understand English.

It was the first time most of the group had seen the girl since they'd captured her. Some were staring at her in fascination, jostling their neighbors for a closer look, while others backed away nervously. Bellamy noticed that Wells had quietly returned to the campfire and was watching Clarke and the Earthborn girl with interest.

The girl said nothing, her eyes wide with fear as she surveyed the crowd. "It's okay, Sasha," Clarke prodded.

Sasha? Bellamy bristled. Clarke knew her *name*? What the hell had happened while he'd been out hunting?

Sasha cleared her throat, and the whispers that had been rising up from the crowd vanished. "I . . . I told Clarke that you're not the first group to come down from the Colony."

A stunned silence descended over the clearing. "That's impossible," Wells said, stepping forward. "How would you even know?"

Sasha's face hardened, and she raised her chin to look directly into Wells's eyes. "Because," she said, her voice calm, "I met them."

The group erupted in chaos, everyone muttering their own theories and fears all at once. Wells put his fingers to his lips and whistled sharply, an uncomfortable reminder of the painful years Bellamy and his mother spent hiding Octavia from the guards. A whistle had been her signal to hide. Finally, the group quieted down. "You met other people from the *Colony*?" Wells prompted, clearly skeptical.

"Yes. I *knew* them. We let them live with us after their ship crashed." Sasha gestured toward the remains of the hundred's charred dropship. "You people haven't really figured out graceful landings, have you?"

Bellamy couldn't take this anymore. "Why don't you save the history lesson for later and tell me where I can find my sister?"

"I don't know anything about your sister," Sasha replied. "I'm sorry."

"We're not idiots, you know." Bellamy saw Clarke flashing him a look of warning, but he ignored it. "You killed Asher, and you took my sister. You'd better start talking, *now*."

"Bellamy, let her finish," Wells said, sounding more like the Chancellor than he had any right to. He turned back to Sasha. "Just tell us what happened," he went on in a gentler voice.

Sasha shot a quick glance at Clarke, who nodded encouragingly. "Another group came down, a little over a year ago.

They lost most of their supplies when they crashed. We took them in."

"How many people were there?" Graham asked, surveying Sasha suspiciously.

"Ten. Although only seven survived the crash."

"And how many of them did you shoot through the neck?" Graham added under his breath, but loud enough for everyone to hear.

Sasha flinched, but continued. "Everything was okay at first, though it was strange having new people around. The rest of us have known each other our whole lives, and it was our first time meeting outsiders. But we did our best to make them feel welcome." Her face darkened, and her voice grew cold. "They didn't treat us with the same courtesy, so they had to leave."

Something in her tone ignited Bellamy's anger. "What the hell does that mean?" he snapped. He was sick of this girl and her vague responses. "Where are they?"

She took a deep breath. "They're dead."

"*Dead?*" Wells repeated, momentarily losing his composure as murmurs rose up from the crowd. "*All* of them?"

Sasha nodded.

Murderers, Bellamy thought. The Earthborns were insane killers. They'd shot Asher without warning. He shuddered as the thought he'd been trying to suppress for days rose to the surface: *What if Octavia was already dead?* He clenched his fists, digging his nails into his palms. If he didn't get her back, he was going to make every single one of them pay. With their lives.

"So what, you killed them?" Graham asked. "And since that wasn't enough, you decided to kill Asher too?"

"No, that's not what happened. We—"

But Graham cut her off, turning to Wells with a sneer. "It's not too late to kill her, you know."

"Will you just *listen*?" Clarke said angrily. "She says they didn't kill Asher!"

"Then who did?" Bellamy demanded. It took every ounce of his willpower not to shout the question at Clarke. Why the hell was she taking the Earthborn girl's side?

"None of us ever thought another group would come down. But then you arrived." Sasha looked between Clarke and Wells, as if it had been their idea to come down to this god-damn planet. "There was all this arguing, and fighting, and then a faction of us split off. They're the ones who killed your friend." She pressed her lips together and turned to Bellamy. "I bet they're the ones who took your sister too."

"So where are they?" he challenged.

"I wish I knew. None of us have seen them since they took

off. You've seen them more recently than I have. But the rest of us aren't like that."

"And why should we believe you?" Graham asked with a sneer. A chorus of agreement rose among the others. "There are ways of finding out if she's telling the truth."

"Cut it out, Graham," Wells snapped, stepping forward to stand between Graham and the girl. "Clarke, take Sasha back to the infirmary and keep an eye on her until we figure out what to do."

"I know what to do," Bellamy interrupted, anger and frustration beginning to boil dangerously in his blood. "We grab our weapons and go after the bastards who took Octavia."

"Don't!" Sasha said, her voice suddenly shaky. "They'll kill you. There are a lot more of us than there are of you."

"So we'll bring you with us, as leverage." Graham pushed past Wells and grabbed Sasha's arm.

"Let *go* of her!" Clarke shouted. But Sasha didn't need any assistance. In a single smooth move, she kneed Graham in the stomach, freed herself from his grasp, and twisted his arm behind his back.

"Don't touch me," she hissed. She released Graham and sent him stumbling forward, then staggered back a few steps herself, as if the act had required all her strength.

"Are you okay?" Clarke asked, taking Sasha's elbow as the girl's knees started shaking.

"Fine," Sasha said hoarsely.

"How long has it been since you've eaten anything?" Wells asked.

"A while."

When Bellamy saw Wells glance over his shoulder toward the fire, where the two rabbits were already being devoured, he bristled. "No way are you feeding her what I hunted," he said to Wells, his voice cold.

"I agree," Graham interrupted. "We're not *feeding* that little bitch." About three-quarters of the group nodded in agreement. The others were already busy fighting for the last scraps of meat clinging to the rabbits' bones.

Before anyone had time to respond, a shriek rose up from the shadows on the far side of the campfire. Bellamy ran toward the sound, a dozen others at his heels. They all slammed into him as he skidded to a stop.

Tamsin stumbled into the clearing, then collapsed on the ground with a shriek. Blood gushed from a wound in her thigh, just below the jagged hem of her shorts.

"Holy shit," said Graham, standing next to Bellamy, too stunned to do more than stare at the arrow sticking out of Tamsin's leg.

As Clarke rushed over, Bellamy turned to look at the Earthborn girl. She was being held in place by a grave-faced Azuma and a sneering Dmitri, her eyes wide with horror as she looked from the injured girl to the shadowy forest. But Bellamy knew better than to be fooled by her act.

The next time blood was spilled in the camp, it was going to be hers.

CHAPTER *11*

Wells

"Wells?" Someone was prodding his arm. "Hey, Wells?"

Wells's eyes snapped open, draining the last droplets of a dream from his mind. He'd been floating down a canal in Venice. No, wait, he'd been riding a horse into battle alongside Napoleon.

Kendall was standing over him, but Wells ignored her as he scrambled to his feet. The Earthborn—Sasha—was just where he'd left her; she hadn't moved all night. Not that there was much opportunity for her to move with her ankles bound together. She was still sitting up against the tree, staring off into the distance with an inscrutable expression on her face, as if she'd trained herself not to betray her thoughts.

In the end, his only option had been to spend the night outside with the prisoner. The three cabins were packed with the nearly one hundred people who'd sprinted for safety in the chaos after the second attack. There was barely room for everyone to sit down, let alone sleep.

Wells and Bellamy had carried the sobbing but lucid Tamsin to the infirmary cabin, followed by Clarke, who'd shoved people out of the way to make room for her newest patient. Luckily, the wound hadn't been life threatening, and even with a dozen terrified people surrounding her, Clarke had managed to stitch up and bandage Tamsin's leg. But when Eric and Graham had come in, dragging Sasha between them, the cabin had erupted in a frenzy of angry shouts.

"I say we kill her now," Graham had bellowed, transforming a number of the shouts into cheers.

"Absolutely not," Bellamy growled. "Not before she tells us where to find my sister."

Graham's mouth twisted into a sneer. "I hate to be the one to tell you this, but they've probably killed Octavia by now. Our only shot at justice is cutting this little bitch's head off and leaving it in the woods for her friends to find."

There'd been no chance at a peaceful solution, not when everyone was half-crazed with fear and adrenaline. And so Wells had volunteered to spend the night outside with the prisoner—keeping her safe but separate from the group until they figured out what to do with her.

A few people had objected to that plan as well, saying that it was too dangerous for Wells to be in the clearing by himself, but when they realized it was either that or keep Sasha inside with them, they'd fallen silent.

Wells knew he should've been terrified after seeing what had happened to Asher and Tamsin, but as he settled against a tree a few meters away from Sasha, curiosity soon swept his fear aside. He couldn't quite believe he was looking at someone born on Earth, someone who'd be able to answer all the questions that had kept him up late into the night as a kid. What did snow feel like? Had she ever seen a bear? Were there still cities standing? What was left of New York? Chicago? But he must've lulled himself to sleep with his questions, and turned them into the stuff of dreams.

"Um, Wells?" Kendall said again. "Are you okay?"

Wells turned to her and rubbed his eyes. "Yes, fine. What's going on?"

"I said I'd come ask you about breakfast. What are the rations today?"

Wells sighed. "No breakfast today, I'm afraid." Bellamy's rabbits and Graham's raccoon were long gone, and they had to be extremely careful with their protein packets—no more than one per person per day.

"Oh, that's a shame," Kendall said. "I've been up since dawn carving Asher's name into his marker. It looks pretty good. Want to come see?"

"Maybe later," Wells said. "And, um, thanks."

When it became clear that Kendall wasn't going to leave on her own, he asked for her help spreading the bad news about breakfast. She seemed disappointed that Wells didn't want to come see her handiwork, but set off with a smile, pleased at being useful to Wells.

After Kendall had trudged back to the cabin to relay the bad news, Wells reached into his pocket for the crumpled protein packet left over from the day before. He glanced at Sasha. Her skin was paler than it'd been when they'd captured her the day before, though Wells wasn't sure whether that was from stress or hunger. Still, they couldn't let her starve. She'd done nothing wrong, and it was cruel to treat her like a prisoner of war.

"Hey," Wells said cautiously, holding out the protein packet. "Do you want some of this? You must be pretty hungry by now."

Sasha stared at it for a moment, then looked up at Wells. "What is it?" she asked hoarsely.

"It's protein paste. Haven't you seen it before?" She shook her head. "Try it," he insisted. "Hold out your hand." He squeezed the rest of the paste into Sasha's palm, then smiled as she dipped a finger into the paste and brought it to her mouth, wrinkling her nose.

"It's not as bad as it looks," she admitted, taking another dab. She finished the protein paste, then wiped her hands together. "But I know where you can find food—real food."

Wells eyed her suspiciously. "Really?"

Sasha nodded. "I'll take you there, if you'll let me out of your camp."

He paused. Strategically, they needed to keep her prisoner until they got Octavia back. Even if she was telling the truth about the rogue Earthborns, Sasha could turn out to be an important bargaining tool. He couldn't risk losing her by falling into a trap. "What's to keep you from running away?" Wells asked.

"You can tie my hands again, if it'll make you feel better," she said. "Listen, I'm only trying to help. And eat," she added. Her stomach growled loudly in agreement.

"Okay," Wells said slowly, surveying her face for any sign of treachery. "I'm just going to round up a few people to come with us."

"No!" She locked eyes with Wells. "It's not going to be a free-for-all. I'm trusting you to take only what you need, and just this one time. Deal?"

Wells hesitated. The others would be furious if they knew he'd let Sasha leave the camp, even if it was to help them find food. But then again, being a leader sometimes meant doing what you knew was right, even if it made you unpopular. That was one lesson his father had never let him forget.

"Happy birthday!" Wells's mother singsonged, walking out of the kitchen carrying what looked suspiciously like a cake.

"How did you do that?" Wells asked, his voice full of wonder as he watched his mother place the white, frosting-covered confection on the table. There were even candles on it—twelve of them—although they were unlit. Candles were even more difficult to find than sugar and egg essence. If his mother lit them at all, it would only be for the briefest moment.

"Magic," she said with a smile. "Don't worry about it. I didn't do anything illegal. Your father will have nothing to worry about."

Unlike some of the other Council members, Wells's father was incredibly strict about adhering to every detail of the Gaia Doctrine, the set of laws the Colony had laid out when they first launched into space. Just a few minutes earlier, while hurrying home from tutorial, Wells had seen Councilor Brisbane walking along A deck carrying two bottles of what was clearly black-market wine.

Wells stared longingly at the cake. Maybe there would even be enough left over to bring a piece to Glass. "You're sure he won't mind?" He didn't know what the Chancellor would object to more: wasting resources on something with questionable nutritional value like a cake, or recognizing a birthday at all. The ancient tradition made too much fuss over one person, exaggerating the importance of the individual when, really, it was the species that mattered. A new life was always something to celebrate, but in the Chancellor's eyes, there was no reason to give someone a false sense of their own importance once a year.

"Of course not." His mother sat down in the chair next to him. "Although, there's no reason this needs to be a birthday cake. It could be a 'congrats for being the highest-ranked student for the third year in a row' cake. Or a 'hooray, you finally cleaned your room' cake."

Wells grinned. "Is Dad going to be home soon?" The Chancellor generally worked late, coming home after Wells was already in bed. He'd hardly seen him at all the past week and was excited that the three of them might get to spend the whole evening together.

"He should be." She leaned over and kissed him on the forehead. "I told him we were having a special dinner in honor of his very special son."

As she scooped salad into bowls, his mother asked him about his tutorials. He told her a funny story about a boy in his class who'd asked how many dinosaurs died during the Cataclysm. "Why don't you start eating," his mother said, when Wells's stomach growled loudly.

Through the windows, the circadian lights were beginning to

dim. His mother didn't say anything, but her smiles became a little tighter, her laughter a little more forced. Finally, she reached over and squeezed Wells's hand. "I think your father must've gotten held up. Let's dig in to that cake now, okay?"

"Sure," Wells said, doing his best to keep his voice cheerful, although he purposefully avoided his mother's eyes. The cake was rich and sweet, but Wells was so focused on keeping his disappointment from his face that he hardly tasted it. He knew it wasn't his father's fault. As the Chancellor, he wasn't just in charge of the well-being and safety of everyone in the Colony. He was responsible for the future of the human race. His primary duty was ensuring that the species survived long enough to make it back to Earth. Whatever was keeping him at work took precedence over his son's birthday.

He felt a pang of guilt as he imagined his father sitting alone in his office, his face weary as he pored over the latest round of troubling reports, unable to appreciate the priceless relics that made the room Wells's favorite place on the whole ship. He wouldn't stop to look at the stuffed eagle, or take a moment to admire the painting of the dark-haired woman with the mysterious smile. The only relic he might catch a glimpse of was the pen holder inscribed with the ancient phrase *Non Nobis Solum Nati Sumus*. "We are not born for ourselves alone," a quote from a Roman writer named Cicero.

The door opened, and Wells's father walked in. Even though

he was clearly exhausted, his back was straight and his stride purposeful. He looked from Wells's mother to the half-eaten cake on the table and sighed. "I'm sorry. The Council meeting ran later than expected. I couldn't get Brisbane to sign off on the new security measures on Walden."

"That's okay." Wells rose to his feet so quickly, he jostled the table and sent the dishes teetering. "We saved you some cake."

"I still have some more work to do." He kissed Wells's mother on the cheek and gave Wells a curt nod. "Happy birthday."

"Thank you," Wells said, wondering if the hint of sadness in his father's eyes was just his imagination.

The Chancellor disappeared into his study before another question arose, uninvited, in Wells's mind. If his father had been tied up with Brisbane, why had Wells seen the Council member hours earlier on A deck?

Wells's stomach twisted as an unfamiliar and uncomfortable realization passed over him.

His father was lying.

"Okay," Wells said, nodding at Sasha. "But if it's just the two of us, I'll need to tie you to me, so you can't bolt once we're in the woods."

"Fine." She stood up and extended her hands.

Wells winced when he saw the red sores on her wrist where the rope had rubbed her skin away. "I'll use the metal cuffs this time. They'll be less irritating." He fetched the cuffs from the supply tent, then took some bandages, which he wrapped around Sasha's right wrist before locking one of the cuffs to it. He paused a moment, then snapped the other cuff to his own left wrist, taking care to tuck the key deep inside his pocket. "Ready?" he asked. She nodded, and after glancing around the clearing to make sure no one was watching, he led her across the tree line, shortening his step when the bite of the metal let him know he was moving too quickly.

Walking together became trickier once they were in the woods. While Wells had to slow down to navigate exposed roots and moss-covered rocks, Sasha sped up, springing lightly over the same obstacles. Wells couldn't take a step without making a noise, but Sasha moved as gracefully and silently as a deer. This was clearly land she had crossed many times. He wondered what it was like to know a section of forest as intimately as you knew another person, lifting your foot over a fallen log as naturally as you might take someone's hand.

Soon, she was leading Wells down a hill he'd never seen before, where the trees were thinner and the grass grew higher, almost up to their knees. Her long braid had come loose, and her dark hair rippled down her back.

"Do you think they're worried about you?" he said finally.

At first, he wasn't sure Sasha had heard him, because she didn't turn around or break stride. But the chain connecting them trembled slightly. "Worried . . . and furious," she said. "We were ordered to stay away from you, but I had to see for myself."

Wells lengthened his step so they were walking side by side for the first time. "I've spent my whole life imagining what it was like in space, what *you* were all like. I didn't really get to know the people in the first group. I barely got to talk to any of them. So then when you all came down, I wasn't going to miss my chance."

Wells laughed, then winced as the chain went taut. Sasha had stopped in her tracks and was glowering at him. "What's so funny?" she asked.

"Nothing. It's just crazy to think about you imagining us when I've spent my whole life wondering about Earth."

Sasha gave him a strange look but started walking again. "Really? So what do you want to know?"

Wells barely missed a beat. "How many people survived the Cataclysm? Are there still cities standing? What kinds of animals are there? Have you ever seen the ocean? What happens when . . ." He trailed off when he saw Sasha grinning at him. "What?"

"Why don't we do one at time?"

"Okay," Wells said with a smile. "The first one, then. Who survived? What happened after the bombs fell?"

"We're not sure," Sasha admitted. "Our ancestors made it to a self-sustaining bomb shelter deep underground, where the limestone kept them safe from radiation. It was only about fifty years ago that they emerged to the surface again. There's been no other sign of human life—to the best of our knowledge, we're the only ones who survived. But who knows? There may be others around the world."

"And where are we exactly?" Wells asked.

"Really?" She furrowed her brows as though wondering if he were joking. "We're in North America, in what used to be called Virginia. Did they really not tell you where they were sending you? Why all the secrecy?"

Wells hesitated, unsure how much to reveal about the mission. Admitting that they'd all committed crimes and been sentenced to die on their eighteenth birthdays probably wasn't the best way to seem trustworthy. "The dropships don't have the most sophisticated navigation systems. We weren't entirely sure where we were going to end up."

Sasha looked skeptical. "Yet you landed within ten miles of the other dropship. You must have been sent to this area for a reason. You were probably meant to find us, right?"

The thought gave Wells chills. No one on the Colony could have known about the existence of Sasha's people—could they? "If we're in Virginia, are we near Washington, D.C.?" he asked, eager to change the subject. "Did any of the buildings survive?" His heart sped up as he thought about exploring the remains of the White House, or better yet, a museum. There had been famous ones in Washington, he recalled.

Disappointment swept through him as Sasha shook her head. "No, the city was razed. Just a few buildings are still standing, and only parts of them. Here, watch your head," she said, ducking under a branch.

She led him over a small stream and then into a grove where the trees grew so close together, the branches almost knit into a roof overhead. Wells suddenly felt foolish, letting her take him in a direction the hundred hadn't really gone before. What if it was a trap?

Something sticky and soft brushed against the back of his neck, and he let out a shout, swatting at it. Strands of a gossamer-like material broke apart in his fingers. "What is this?" he said, trying to wipe it away.

"Relax." Sasha laughed, and Wells couldn't help smiling, realizing how foolish he probably looked. "It's just a spider-web. See?"

She pointed, and Wells looked up to see that one of the trees was draped in finely woven, glistening threads that stretched across the branches, creating a sort of net.

Sasha started to tug him forward, but Wells couldn't pull his eyes away. The web was unexpectedly captivating, its geometric shapes oddly beautiful against the wild tangle of branches and leaves. "I thought spiders were tiny."

"Sometimes. But the ones that live in the woods are bigger." She held up her arm. "Their legs can be this long."

Wells suppressed a shudder and sped up to walk next to Sasha. They were quiet as they continued through the grove, the leaves on the ground absorbing the sound of their footsteps. Something about the silence and shadows made Wells hesitant to disrupt the stillness. It had been the same back on the ship: People lowered their voices whenever they set foot in Eden Hall, a gathering space on Phoenix dominated by what they'd all believed to be the only tree left in the universe, brought onto Phoenix as Earth burned. That is, until Wells set fire to it, seeking arrest in order to be sent to Earth with Clarke.

After another ten minutes, the forest thinned out again, and Sasha led him up a steep slope. When they reached the crest of the hill, she stopped and raised her hand. "Here we go," she said, pointing to a group of trees up ahead.

At first, Wells didn't notice anything remarkable about them. But then he squinted and realized that there was something solid hanging from the branches.

Sasha led him toward the closest tree. The boughs were sagging under the weight of dozens of long, green, oblong pods. She rose onto the balls of her feet and stretched her arm above her head, but her fingers only barely grazed the lowest pod.

"Allow me." Wells extended his own arm and just managed to grab the one she'd been reaching for. He snapped it off the branch and handed it to Sasha, marveling at the bumpy texture.

With expert movements, she began peeling away the outer layer, revealing bright pink seeds. "What is that?" Wells asked.

"You don't have corn up in space?"

"We grow some vegetables in the solar fields, but nothing like that." He paused. "Doesn't corn grow out of the ground?"

Sasha shrugged. "Maybe it used to, but it grows on trees now. Just watch out for the blue ones. They're really spicy." She raised her cuffed hand. "If you undo these, we can climb up and pick as much as we can carry."

Wells paused. He wanted to trust her, and somehow felt he *could* trust her, but it could also be a monumentally stupid risk.

Finally, he reached into his pocket and removed the key. "Okay. I'll undo the cuffs, but if you run off, you know we'll all come after you."

Sasha was quiet for a moment, then raised her shackled wrist. Wordlessly, Wells inserted the key into the lock and turned it until her cuff sprang open. She clenched and unclenched her fingers, then shook her hand and smiled. "Thanks."

In a flash, she'd scrambled up the trunk and was pulling herself onto a branch. She made it look easy, but when Wells tried to follow, he found it difficult to get a good hold. The bark was rough, but the moss covering it was slippery, and it took him a few tries before he got enough leverage to get off the ground.

He was out of breath by the time he pulled himself onto the third-lowest branch, where the corn grew the thickest. Sasha had climbed nearly to the end of the branch, straddling it like a bench, and was using both hands to snap off ears of corn and toss them to the ground, which suddenly looked very far away.

Wells took a deep breath and forced himself to look up. The view was breathtaking. Wells had seen innumerable photos of picturesque spots on Earth, but none of them captured the beauty of the orchard before them. The meadow stretched out below, and provided a stunning contrast to the hazy purple outlines of the mountains in the distance. He felt his skin tingle when his eyes settled on their jagged white tops. *Snow.*

"I'll have to show this to my father when he gets here," Wells said before he had time to think better of it.

Sasha whipped her head around. "Your father? There are *more* of you coming?"

Wells wasn't sure why the accusation in her voice made him feel guilty. The Colonists had spent the past three hundred years figuring out how to bring the human race back home. They had just as much right to the planet as the Earthborns. "Of course," he said. "The ships weren't built to last forever. Eventually, everyone will come down." *And by eventually, I mean in the next few weeks*, Wells thought. *All thanks to me.* After Clarke's arrest, he'd been desperate to make sure she was sent to Earth instead of facing execution. He knew that the Council was considering sending Confined teenagers, and he knew the mission needed to happen before Clarke's eighteenth birthday—so he'd done something drastic, and dangerous. He purposely worsened the existing airlock breach. Now the remaining Colonists had little time left in space, and would be forced to come to Earth. He still felt sick thinking about what he'd done—but it had saved Clarke's life.

"Didn't your father want to come with you?"

Wells's chest tightened as he thought about the last time he'd seen his father, the blood staining the Chancellor's uniform as the door to the dropship had closed. He'd spent the past few weeks trying to convince himself that the bullet wound was superficial, that his father would recover in time to come down with the next wave of Colonists. But he had no way of knowing what had really happened, or if his father was even still alive.

"He has a lot of responsibilities on the ship," Wells said instead. "He's the Chancellor."

Sasha's eyes widened. "So, he's in charge of everybody? Is that why you're the leader of the group that came down?"

"I'm not the leader," Wells protested.

"They all seem to listen to you."

"Maybe." Wells sighed. "But I always feel like I'm letting someone down, no matter what I do."

Sasha nodded. "I know. My father . . . well, he's actually in charge down here too."

Wells stared at her in surprise. "Really? Your father is the Chancellor?"

"We don't use that term, but it sounds like the same kind of thing."

"So you know what it's like to . . ." He trailed off with a frown. It was strange trying to put his feelings into words, feelings that he'd spent the past sixteen years trying to ignore.

"What? To be held to a higher standard than everyone else? To have everyone assume that you know the answers, when most of the time you don't even know what questions you're supposed to be asking?"

Wells smiled. "Yeah. Something like that."

Sasha tossed another ear of corn to the ground, biting her lip. "I feel bad for my dad, but honestly, I'm sick of it too. They turn everything I do into some kind of political statement."

"What did you do?"

Sasha laughed mischievously. "Some things I shouldn't have. Including coming here." She caught Wells's eye, and the playfulness disappeared from her face. "What about you? Your father must really trust you to send you to Earth on your own."

Wells hesitated. It was best to let her believe that. Sasha would be more likely to treat the hundred with caution if she thought they were specially trained, handpicked for the mission, as opposed to useless criminals sent to possibly die.

A gust of wind swept through the tree, whipping Sasha's wild black hair into her face.

"Hardly," Wells said, wondering what it was about Sasha's bright green eyes that made him feel reckless. "You wouldn't believe me if I told you the truth."

Sasha raised an eyebrow. "Try me."

"I was arrested a few weeks ago. For setting fire to the only tree in the Colony."

She stared at him for a long moment, then to his surprise, laughed and slid one leg over the branch. "I guess I'd better hurry up before you take a dislike to this one." Sasha lowered herself into the air, then let go, landing lightly on the ground. "Come on," she called. "We have enough corn. Or are you scared?"

Wells shook his head. It didn't matter that he had no idea how the hell to get out of the tree. For the first time since they'd landed on Earth, he didn't feel afraid of anything.

CHAPTER *12*

Glass

"You can't do this," Luke said, finally breaking the silence that filled the small repair room. They were in the now-abandoned guard station that stored the suits Luke and his fellow engineers used for spacewalks. "It's beyond dangerous—it's suicidal. If anyone goes out there, it will be me. I'm *trained* to do it."

Glass placed her hand on Luke's arm and was surprised to feel him trembling. "No," she said, looking him in the eye for the first time since she'd told him her plan. "It would be insane to have you risk your life on a spacewalk, only to be shot once you get to Phoenix."

"There aren't exactly going to be guards waiting for me at

the airlock. I doubt they think anyone would be crazy enough to try to get across on the *outside* of the ship," Luke said. Not only were spacewalks performed exclusively by Luke and the rest of his highly trained team, they only did so when absolutely necessary, and only with everyone running support, monitoring oxygen and pressure levels, keeping an eye out for debris, providing backup in case of equipment failure. Glass tried not to think about the fact that she would be crossing without any of that.

"Opening the airlock will set off alarms. They might arrest me, but they're not going to shoot me on sight," she insisted.

"Glass." Luke's voice was hoarse. "I can't let you do this."

"I'm not just doing it for us." She looked up at him, willing herself to stay calm. "By closing the skybridge, Phoenix left all of Walden and Arcadia to *die*. I can't let innocent people suffer, not if there's something I can do to help. I need to open the skybridge."

Luke sighed and closed his eyes. "Okay," he said, taking a deep breath. "Then let's get started." He began methodically reviewing the equipment, explaining how everything worked—the pressurized suits, the clamps, the cord that would keep her tethered to the ship. His tone was calm and businesslike, as if he'd convinced himself that he was briefing a new guard, and not the only person he loved left in the universe.

He led Glass to the large window next to the airlock and pointed out the handholds that stretched all the way across. "The airlock on Phoenix can be opened from the outside— just untwist the big wheel; that will let you into the airlock chamber. Once you're inside, I'll head to the skybridge and meet you there."

"It's a date," Glass said, managing a smile.

Luke pulled out one of the guards' thermal jumpsuits and handed it to Glass. "Sorry," he said. "This is the smallest one." It was clearly made for someone much larger, but it would have to do.

Glass quickly pulled off her shirt and stepped out of her pants, shivering as the cold raised goose bumps along her arm. As she fumbled with the thermal, she looked up to see Luke staring at her with an intensity she'd never seen before, like he was trying to commit every line of her body to memory.

"You're getting it all bunched up," he said, his voice thick. "It won't work if it's not right next to your skin. Here." Glass stood perfectly still as he ran his hands over the fabric, smoothing out all the wrinkles, his fingers traveling deftly across her shoulders, down her back, over her hips. She shivered. Each time his hands moved to a new spot, she felt a tiny pang of loss. What if he was touching her for the very last time?

Finally, he stepped away and reached for the space suit, checking various pieces of equipment before carrying it over to her.

Neither of them spoke as Luke helped her step into the bottom part of the suit, fastening it tightly around her waist. He instructed her to raise her arms and pulled the top portion over her head. His face pale, he locked the two sections into place. There was an audible click, and Glass inhaled sharply. "Are you okay?" Luke asked, taking her hand.

She nodded. He opened his mouth to respond, then changed his mind and reached for the gloves, which he pulled, one at a time, over Glass's hands.

Only the helmet was left. "I should've put my hair up first," Glass said, holding up her gloves.

"I'll do it." He reached into her pocket to remove the elastic band for her, then stepped behind her and smoothed her hair back into a ponytail, gently tucking a few stray strands behind her ears and wrapping the band around it tight.

Luke smiled shakily as he stepped back. "I guess it's go time." He wrapped his arms around her, and even though she couldn't feel the pressure through the suit, Glass felt warmer inside. "Be very, very careful out there, okay?" he said, his voice muffled. "If anything happens, come straight back. Don't take any risks."

Glass nodded. "I love you." She couldn't count the number

of times she'd said those words, but they seemed different now. She could hear the echo of every past *I love you* in them, and the promise of a lifetime more.

Luke lowered his head and kissed her. For a moment, Glass closed her eyes and allowed herself to pretend that this was just a normal kiss, that she was a regular seventeen-year-old kissing the boy she loved. She leaned forward eagerly—and felt the weight of the bulky space suit jar her back to reality.

Luke pulled away and picked up the helmet. "Good luck," he said, bending down to kiss her forehead. Then he lowered the helmet over her head and locked it into place.

Glass gasped as the world became dark and suffocating. She was back in Confinement. She couldn't see, couldn't breathe. But then she felt Luke squeeze her hand through her glove, and she relaxed, taking a deep breath as air from her tank streamed directly into her nose.

After days of oxygen deprivation, being able to breathe like this felt euphoric. She was suddenly wide awake, able to do anything. She gave Luke a thumbs-up sign to let him know that she was ready, and he walked over to the control panel. There was a crackling sound in her helmet, and then Luke's voice was in her ear. "How you doing in there, spacewalker?"

"I'm okay," she said, not sure where she was supposed to speak. "Can you hear me?"

"Loud and clear," he said. "Radio's all set. Feel like a stroll?"

Glass nodded, and he led her to the airlock. The suit was lighter than she'd expected, but walking still required a great deal of thought, almost like she was a toddler, experimenting with each limb before she tried to move it. Luke punched a code into the panel next to the heavy metal door, and it opened, revealing the tiny airlock chamber. On the other side was the door that led outside, to a minus-270-degree vacuum.

He fastened a cable to the front of her suit, then checked again to make sure it was secure. Luke showed her where it attached to the ship, and how it extended and retracted to follow Glass's movements. "Okay," he said, his voice coming from somewhere behind her right ear. "I'm going back inside to close the first door. Then I'll let you know when it's safe to open the second door. You'll have ten seconds to make it through before it closes automatically. Just grab on to the first handhold and swing yourself out."

"Sounds like a breeze."

Luke gave her gear a final check, then squeezed her hand. "You'll be great." He tapped the front of her helmet. "See you soon."

"See you soon," she echoed.

He disappeared back through the door, leaving her alone,

with nothing between her and the vast emptiness of space except a metal door and a three-hundred-year-old space suit.

"Okay," Luke's voice came from the speaker again. "Get ready. I'm going to open the second door."

Glass dragged herself forward, her legs suddenly heavy. After the longest eight steps of her life, she reached the door. "I'm ready."

"All right. I'm entering the code now." There was a loud beep, and the door in front of Glass slid open.

For a moment, all she could do was stand there and stare as she got a clear view of space for the first time. Now she understood what Luke meant, when he said that it was beautiful. The darkness was rich, like the velvet her mother had made into a skirt once, and the stars sparkled against it, so much brighter than she'd ever seen them through a window. For once, the hazy gray sweep of Earth looked more mysterious than frightening. It was incredible to think that Wells was down there, walking around, breathing . . . *if he's still alive*, the cynical part of her brain added.

"Go for it," Luke's voice whispered in her ear.

She took a deep breath and reached out for the first handle, forcing her gloved fingers to wrap around it and pulling herself through the door.

And then she was in space, grasping a single handhold while she stared into the dizzying sea of stars and gas just waiting to swallow her whole. Behind her, the door closed with a thud.

Glass swung herself around, briefly reveling in the thrill of weightlessness. Then she saw the path to Phoenix, and her mouth felt suddenly dry. It had never seemed that long when she was running to see Luke, but from this perspective, it looked endless. She would have to make her way around the entire side of Walden before she could even see the skybridge.

You can do this, she reminded herself, gritting her teeth. *You* have *to do this. One at a time.* She moved her left hand to the next rung, then pulled her body across. In the absence of gravity, it required minimal effort, but her heart was pounding at an unsustainable rate.

"How are you doing out there?" Luke's voice echoed in her helmet.

"It's beautiful," Glass said quietly. "Now I understand why you were always so quick to volunteer for this."

"It's not as beautiful as you."

Glass swung from handhold to handhold, falling into a rhythm. "I bet you say that to all the girls from mission control."

"Actually, if I remember correctly, I've used that line on you before," Luke said. Glass smiled. Back when they used to sneak to the solar fields, they would look at the stars through the window, and Luke would always tell Glass that she was prettier.

"Hmm. It sounds like you need some new material, my friend." She swung to the next handle and risked a glance back. She couldn't see the release door anymore. "How much farther?" she asked.

"You're coming up on the skybridge, which means you'll have to be careful not to let anyone see you. There's a second set of handles under the bridge. Use those, just to be safe."

"Got it."

She moved steadily along, trying not to think about what would happen if something went wrong with her suit, which suddenly felt very fragile, a flimsy protection from the vacuum of space.

The skybridge appeared in the corner of her eye. It was still barricaded, with an airtight barrier between the Walden and Phoenix sections. Crowds of people still swarmed the barrier from the Walden side, helplessly pounding on it, hoping to break through. As she got closer, Glass saw the second set of handholds Luke had mentioned, the ones that led under the bridge instead of along the side. There was a significant gap between the last rung of the set she was on and the first rung of the next set—much too far for her to reach.

Glass paused. If she pushed off the side of Walden with enough force, she could throw herself in the direction of the handhold. Even if she missed, the worst that could happen was that she'd float for a few seconds until Luke retracted the wire and pulled her back toward the ship.

"Okay, I've got to jump to the next handhold," Glass said. She twisted her body so both feet were against the side of the ship and stretched her left arm out so she'd be ready. She took a deep breath, tensed her muscles, and pushed off, grinning at the brief sensation of soaring through space.

But she'd apparently overestimated the force she'd needed, because she flew right past the handhold, her fingers grasping at nothing but empty space.

"Luke, I missed it. Can you pull me back in?" She'd started to spin and was losing her sense of direction. "Luke?"

His voice never came.

All Glass could hear was the sound of her own breath. She kept spinning, farther and farther from the ship, the wire rapidly uncoiling behind her. "Luke!" she screamed, flailing her arms.

"*Luke!*" she called again, wheezing as the oxygen seemed to vanish from her helmet. She'd taken too big a breath, and needed to wait for the ventilation system to readjust. *Don't panic*, she told herself. But then she caught a glimpse of the Colony, and gasped. She'd already drifted too far—Walden, Phoenix, and Arcadia were in view, and growing smaller by the second. The wire seemed far too long. Should it have caught and snapped her back toward the Colony by now? Then another thought hit her, sharp as a knife. What if the cord had broken? Glass knew enough about momentum to know that unless she collided into something, she would keep spinning in the same direction. In ten minutes, her oxygen would run out, and she would die. And then her body would keep floating, forever and ever, into the distance.

She felt herself crying and bit her lip. "Luke?" she asked, trying not to use too much breath. Her head hurt from the disorienting spinning. Every time the Colony flashed into view, it was smaller. This was it.

Then there was a sharp, violent tug on the front of her suit, and the cord went taut. "Glass? Are you there? Are you okay?"

"Luke!" She had never been so happy to hear his voice. "I tried to jump, and I missed the rung, and then—what happened?" The wire began to slowly retract, pulling her back toward the ship.

"We had some . . . unexpected visitors in the control room, people scavenging for supplies. Don't worry, I took care of it."

"What do you mean?"

Luke sighed. "I had to knock them out. There were four of them, Glass, and they wanted to—" He paused. "They weren't being friendly. You were in danger, and I couldn't take the time to explain what was going on."

"It's okay. I'm okay." Then she caught sight of the sky-bridge, and the series of handholds. She flexed her fingers in anticipation. There was no way she was missing it this time.

"I'm almost there," she told Luke. The handhold was approaching rapidly. Glass stretched out her arm, fixed her eyes on it, and reached out—"Got it!" she shouted as her fingers locked onto the metal rung.

"That's my girl!" She could hear the smile in Luke's voice.

Glass exhaled loudly and then swung her other hand over the adjacent rung. It didn't take her long to traverse the underside of the skybridge and make her way up toward the Phoenix airlock.

When she finally reached the entrance, she planted her feet against the side of the ship and used all her strength to rotate the heavy handle. The door slid open with a satisfying hiss. "I'm here!" She grabbed the edge and pulled herself into a small antechamber, almost identical to the one on Walden.

Luke gave a joyful whoop. "Okay, I'm on my way. Meet you at the skybridge."

"See you there."

Glass waited for the outer door to slide back into place, then unhooked herself and hurried toward the second door, which opened automatically. Without missing a beat, she took off the helmet, and began struggling with the suit. It took her longer to get out of it than it had taken Luke to put it on, but she managed.

There didn't seem to be any guards in the corridors. There didn't seem to be any people at all. Glass's exhilaration gave way to concern as she imagined what her mother might be doing. Was she alone and panic-stricken? Or were the Phoenicians pretending that everything was business as usual, ignoring the fact that two-thirds of the Colony had been abandoned to die?

There were only two guards at the skybridge, neither of whom was paying any attention to the controls. They were both about a third of the way down the bridge, their hands on the guns at their hips, watching the partition at the middle of the skybridge. So many people were pressed against the clear wall that it almost seemed to be made of human flesh.

Men and women were pushing their faces against it, screaming, holding blue-faced children up for the guards to see. No sound came through, but their anguish echoed in Glass's head nonetheless. She watched palms grow red from the banging. An elderly man was being crushed against the wall by the surging crowd, his face white with panic as he slid down the barrier toward the ground.

There wasn't a choice. She had to let them through. Even if it meant less oxygen for her, for her mother, for Luke.

Glass scrambled over the side of the unmanned control

booth. The switch looked simple enough. There wasn't a great deal of nuance to the technology. The bridge was either open or closed. She took a deep breath and flipped the main switch.

By the time the alarm started ringing, it was too late. The guards spun around and looked at Glass in shock and horror as the partition began to rise into the ceiling.

An old man was the first to slide under, pushed by the frenzy of the crowd. Then a few of the smaller women crawled underneath on their stomachs. Within seconds, the partition had completely retracted, and the skybridge was flooded with people—shouting, weeping with joy and relief, taking huge lungfuls of air.

Glass rose up onto her toes, looking through the sea of bodies for the only one who mattered to her. There he was, at the other end. As Luke came toward her, a proud smile on his face, she hoped they had done the right thing.

She'd just saved hundreds of lives—and drastically shortened hundreds more. Including their own.

CHAPTER *13*

Clarke

By midmorning, the cabin had mostly cleared out. After twelve hours spent jostling for room in a densely packed space that reeked of fear and sweat, everyone had apparently decided that the Earthborns weren't so threatening anymore.

But the mood in the camp was still tense. A large group was already hard at work building a fourth cabin, so they could shelter more comfortably. Wells was nowhere to be found, so Bellamy had taken over. She could hear his voice in the distance as he gave orders about foundations and support beams.

Clarke smiled, but then felt it slip away as she walked over to check on Molly and Felix. They weren't improving. Even worse, two others—an Arcadian boy and a Walden girl—had begun showing the same symptoms of fatigue, disorientation, and nausea.

Priya was inside the infirmary cabin, helping a half-awake Molly take a few sips of water. She nodded at Clarke, then gently lowered Molly's head back down. She walked over, still holding the metal cup. "I thought we'd use this one for the sick people," she said softly. "In case whatever they have is contagious."

"That's a good idea," Clarke said. "Though you don't seem to be afraid of catching anything."

Priya shrugged, then pushed a piece of her thick black hair behind her ear. "If we can't take care of each other, then it means they were right about us all along."

"They?"

"The people who sentenced us to die on our eighteenth birthdays. They took me from the execution room, you know. The doctor had the needle ready and everything. He was just about to inject me when he got a message on his cornea slip telling him I was being sent to Earth instead."

"What were you Confined for?" Clarke asked softly, sensing that it was okay for her to ask Priya the one question that was strictly taboo in their camp.

But before Priya had time to respond, the door swung open and Eric trudged inside, worry and exhaustion etched on his face. "I think we should give them the pills," he said, abandoning any pretense of civility. Clarke opened her mouth to ask what he was talking about, but Eric cut her off. "I know about the radiation pills. I think you should give them to the sick people. Now."

Clarke gave him what she hoped was a confidence-inspiring look. "It's not radiation poisoning," she said, calling on whatever reserves of patience were left after their horrific night. "And those pills will *kill* them if they're used for anything else."

"How can you be so sure? You didn't even finish your medical training. What do you know about radiation poisoning?"

Clarke blanched, not from the insult—she knew Eric was just worried about Felix—but from the secret festering inside of her, far more toxic than any wound. Only two people on the planet knew why Clarke had been Confined. No one else knew anything about her parents' experiments, or the children who'd suffered under their watch.

She tried another route. "If there were toxic levels of radiation, all the Earthborns would be dead."

"Not if they evolved to be immune to it, or something."

Clarke had no answer for that. She was desperate to ask Sasha more about the other Colonists, the ones who'd come a year ago. A theory had been percolating in her mind ever since she stumbled across the wreckage. The bits of metal were the missing link, she was sure of it. She just needed to find out more. "Don't worry," she said, placing her hand on Eric's shoulder. "We're going to figure this out. They're going to be okay. Can you and Priya just keep an eye on everyone for a little bit? I'll be right back."

Eric nodded, then slid to the ground next to Felix's cot with a sigh. Priya watched him for a moment, then sat beside him and gave his arm a squeeze. "Go ahead, Clarke. We'll be fine."

Clarke squinted as she stepped into the sunlight. The pain in her arm was mostly gone, and her head was clear for the first time in days. But while she felt better physically than she had since the snakebite, anxiety pooled in her stomach as she searched for Sasha. Had she somehow managed to escape under Wells's watch? Or worse, had Graham and his buddies taken her somewhere?

She scanned the clearing, which was abuzz with activity, most of which revolved around the new cabin. A bunch of people were dragging huge pieces of wood toward the new site, while others carved notches into smaller logs so they'd fit together. A few of the older boys had begun to roll the largest logs into the ditches they'd dug for the foundation. Bellamy was among them.

He had taken off his shirt, and his skin was slick with sweat. Even from a distance, Clarke could see his back muscles contracting as he used all his weight to drag the log into position.

A curly-haired girl approached him, trailed by two giggling friends. This trio had taken the cutoffs trend to the extreme, and were now tugging at the frayed edges of shorts that barely skimmed the tops of their thighs. "Hey," the first girl said. "We need a tall person to help us fix the roof on the north cabin. It's caving in already."

Bellamy barely glanced at her. "Build a ladder."

Clarke suppressed a laugh as a shadow of irritation flitted across the girl's face before she resumed her coy smile. "Can you show us how?"

Bellamy looked over his shoulder and made a beckoning motion. "Hey, Antonio. Get over here." A short, stocky kid with acne and a good-natured smile came jogging over. "These ladies need help with the cabin. Can you give them a hand?"

"With pleasure," Antonio said, his eyes widening as he looked from Bellamy to the girls, who were trying, with various degrees of success, to hide their disappointment.

Clarke smiled to herself, secretly pleased by how little interest Bellamy demonstrated toward the other, very pretty girls. He was so cocky, and so charming when the mood struck him that it was hard to believe he'd only ever had one girlfriend.

It was even harder to believe that that girlfriend was the person whose face Clarke saw every night before she went to sleep. Whose voice she could still hear when everything was quiet.

She shook her head and started toward Bellamy. "Such a gentleman," she teased, watching the girls trudge off with a visibly elated Antonio.

"Well, hello there." Bellamy pulled her into a hug. "How are you feeling?"

"Like I need to shower." Clarke pushed Bellamy away, laughing. "Now I have your sweat all over me."

"Well, consider it payback for when I carried you *six kilometers* while you were unconscious. I didn't know it was possible for a human being to drool that much without dying of dehydration."

"I didn't *drool* on you," Clarke protested.

"How do you know? You were passed out. Unless . . ." He narrowed his eyes and looked thoughtful. "Unless you just faked the whole snakebite thing so you wouldn't have to walk anymore. That would be pretty crafty."

Clarke just smiled. "Do you know where Sasha went?" she asked.

Bellamy's face hardened. "I think Wells might've taken her somewhere. They've both been missing for hours." He shook his head. "The idiot."

"Oh," Clarke said, trying her best to keep her voice neutral. There was no reason for her to care that Wells had gone off with Sasha. He had just as much right to talk to her as Clarke did. But for some reason, the idea of them alone in the woods made her uncomfortable.

"Yeah, I know," Bellamy said, mistaking her surprise for disapproval. "I don't know what the hell he was thinking. I can't force her to help me find Octavia, but Wells can go off on a picnic with her. Makes sense."

"Listen, will you come with me? I want to go back and look at that wreckage we found."

Bellamy frowned. "I'm not sure that's a good idea."

"We'll be on the lookout for the Earthborns. It'll be fine," she said.

"It's just . . . I don't want to stray too far from camp, in case Octavia comes back. I don't want to miss her."

Clarke nodded guiltily. Here she was, caught up with her ridiculous theory, when Bellamy still didn't know where his sister was or if she was even alive. When her campmates might be dying in the infirmary cabin, and she had pills that could possibly save their lives. "You're right. I'll go by myself."

"What?" Bellamy shook his head. "No way. I'd rather cover myself in Graham's drool than let you go out there on your own."

"*Let* me?" Clarke repeated. "I'm sorry. Last time I checked, no one was in charge of me."

"You know what I mean. I'm just worried about you."

"I'll be *fine*."

"Yeah, I know you'll be fine, because I'm coming with you."

"Okay," Clarke said, forcing herself to sound more annoyed than she felt. She knew Bellamy wasn't trying to control her. He cared about her, and the thought brought a flush to her cheeks.

They slipped away without telling anyone where they were going, and a few minutes later, were deep in the stillness of the woods. They walked mostly in silence, both of them relieved to escape the constant questioning of their needy campmates. But after nearly an hour, a prickle of concern prompted Clarke to speak.

"Are you sure this is the right way?" she asked, after they passed a moss-covered rock for what seemed to be the second time.

"Positive. There's the spot where I almost dropped you," he said, pointing vaguely into the distance. "That's where I stopped to make sure you weren't choking on your own vomit. And, oh, look, that's where you regained consciousness for a few seconds and told me that I had the biggest—" He cut himself off with a yelp as Clarke jabbed him in the stomach with her elbow.

Bellamy laughed, but then something in the distance caught his attention, and his face turned serious. "I think we're close."

Clarke nodded and began scanning the ground for anything metallic. She was determined to figure out what the wreckage was from. A dropship? A shelter the first Colonists had built?

But instead of the glint of metal, her eyes settled on a series of shapes that sent her heart rushing into her throat.

Three large stones stuck out of the ground. They might've once been straight, but now two were tilted toward each other, while a third teetered precariously away from the group. They were approximately the same size, and there was no mistaking that they'd been placed there on purpose. Even from a distance, Clarke could make out crude markings on the stones—letters, hastily carved with inadequate tools. Or, Clarke realized as she deciphered the shapes, carved by someone shaking with fear and grief.

REST IN PEACE.

Clarke had never heard the words spoken aloud, but she could feel them in her chest, as if the memory was stored somewhere inside her bones. Her hand reached out for Bellamy's, but her fingers grasped nothing but air.

She turned and saw him crouching in front of one of the markers. She walked over and placed her hand on his shoulder. "They're graves," he said quietly, without looking at her.

"There really *was* another mission, then. Sasha was telling the truth."

Bellamy nodded and ran a finger along the stone. "It's nice, you know, having a place to visit the people you've lost. I wish we had something like that on the Colony, something more personal than the Remembrance Wall."

"Who would you have wanted to visit?" Clarke asked quietly, wondering if there was any way he could know that Lilly had died.

"Just . . . friends. People I never got to say good-bye to." Bellamy rose to his feet with a sigh, then wrapped his arm around Clarke.

She leaned in to him, then turned her attention back to the graves. "Do you think they died in the crash? Or later, after whatever happened with the Earthborns?"

"I'm not sure. Why?"

"I just wish we'd come down sooner. Maybe we could've done something to help them."

Bellamy gave her a squeeze. "You can't save everyone, Clarke," he said quietly.

You have no idea, she thought.

CHAPTER 14

Wells

"Careful," Wells called out as he watched one of the younger boys reach toward the fire. "Use the stick."

"I got it," he said, carefully removing the corn from the red-hot stones Wells had piled on top of the flames, the way Sasha had told him to.

The corn had, quite literally, been a lifesaver. Now instead of furtive whispers and weary complaints, the camp was filled with the sound of crackling flames and reinvigorated chatter. Everyone sat around the fire, gnawing at the strange but welcome food.

After returning with as much as they could carry, Wells and Sasha had grabbed two empty water containers and headed back to the orchard for more. By the time they'd staggered back, smiling and weary from their efforts, Wells had almost forgotten that Sasha was their prisoner. He'd felt exceedingly awkward when, after thanking her for her help, he'd had to sneak her back to the infirmary cabin. Luckily, Clarke had been gone, and the sick people asleep, so no one saw him apologizing to Sasha as he retied her hands.

You caught her spying *on you*, he reminded himself as he watched a group of girls challenge some Walden boys to a corncob-throwing contest. Wells started to protest—Sasha had warned them not to leave the cobs in the clearing, lest they attract unwelcome animal visitors—but he swallowed the words. He'd have an easier time sneaking some food to Sasha if he didn't make a scene.

Wells gingerly plucked a few cobs from the embers, stretching out his shirt so he could carry them without burning his hands, then headed back to the infirmary cabin.

"Hey," he whispered as he moved quietly toward her cot. "I brought you one." He handed her one of the corncobs, which had cooled enough to touch, then placed the others next to Molly, Felix, and Tamsin so they'd have something to eat when they woke up. It was becoming hard to find volunteers to bring food and water to the sick people. Rumors about their illness were spreading, and now it was rare for anyone besides Clarke, Wells, Bellamy, Priya, and Eric to set foot inside the infirmary cabin.

"Thanks," Sasha said, shooting a wary glance toward the door before taking a small bite of the corn.

"How is it?" Wells asked, returning to sit on the edge of her cot. "Better than the protein paste?"

She smiled. "Yes, definitely better. Although still pretty bland. Why didn't you season them with those pepper leaves like I told you?"

"I figured the corn was suspicious enough. Revealing some fancy cooking tricks might've caused more trouble than it was worth."

He expected her to tease him about his culinary skills, but instead her face grew serious. "They really don't trust me, do they?" There was an edge to her voice as she shifted on the cot. "What can I do to convince you all that I had nothing to do with the attacks?"

"It'll just take some time," Wells said, though he still wasn't entirely sure whether *he* believed her. He knew Sasha was kind and rational, but that certainly didn't mean her people—her *father*—weren't capable of violence. If, somehow, the Colony were threatened by some hitherto unimagined enemy, Wells's father wouldn't have thought twice before launching an attack.

The door opened and Kendall walked in. Wells jumped to

his feet as Kendall stared at them, an inscrutable look on her face. "Sorry to disturb you," she said, glancing between Wells and Sasha. "I was just coming to take a quick nap. I didn't get much sleep last night, obviously."

"It's fine," Wells said. He gestured toward the empty cots. "There's plenty of room." Apparently, Kendall wasn't worried about catching the mysterious illness.

"No, it's okay. I'll try one of the other cabins." She gave Wells one more lingering look before she turned around and walked back into the clearing.

"See? No one even wants to be in the same room as me. They all think I'm a murderer."

Wells glanced over at Tamsin, whose heavily bandaged leg might as well have been emblazoned with a warning about the Earthborns. To say nothing of the newly dug grave in the cemetery. Until Sasha could prove that there really was a rogue band of Earthborns, people who had nothing to do with her, it'd be impossible for the hundred to see her as anything but a threat. "Do you want to go for a walk?" he said suddenly. "It's silly for you to be locked in here all day."

Sasha gave him a long, searching look before raising her bound hands from her lap. "Okay. But no more handcuffs. You know I'm not going anywhere."

Wells untied her and then, while Sasha rearranged her fur wrap, went over to check on Molly. "Hey," he whispered, crouching next to her cot. "How are you feeling?" She murmured something but didn't open her eyes. "Molly?" With a sigh, Wells pulled her blanket up over her thin shoulders, then tucked a strand of sweat-dampened hair behind her ear. "I'll be back soon," he said quietly.

Wells peeked into the clearing. Most of the camp was still gathered around the fire, or putting the finishing touches on the new roof. If they hurried, they'd be able to leave unseen. Wells chose not to dwell on the fact that, for the second time that day, he was doing something secret, hiding his actions from the rest of the group. He turned around to gesture to Sasha, and then they quickly darted outside and across the tree line.

Sasha led Wells in a different direction this time, one he hadn't taken before. Unlike Bellamy, he hadn't spent a great deal of time in the woods, and was only familiar with the path they usually took to fetch water from the stream. "Watch out," Sasha called over her shoulder. "It gets pretty steep here."

Steep was a bit of an understatement. The ground suddenly fell away, and Wells was forced to creep down sideways, grabbing on to the thin, flexible trees that grew out of the hillside to keep himself from tumbling down. The incline was so sharp that some of their roots grew out into the air instead of down into the ground.

Sasha didn't seem bothered by the grade. She'd barely slowed down and was now several meters ahead of Wells.

She'd extended her arms to the side, using her outstretched fingers for balance, looking like the birds he'd seen swooping above the clearing.

A loud crack sounded from behind. Startled, Wells whipped his head around. The movement was enough to send his feet flying out from under him, and he fell, sliding down the slick grass. He tried to dig his fingers into the ground to slow himself down, but he kept gaining speed until something jerked him to a stop. Breathless, he looked up to see Sasha grinning at him as she held the collar of his jacket. "You're going to have to wait a few months for sledding," she said as she helped pull him to his feet.

"Sledding?" Wells repeated as he brushed off the back of his pants and tried not to think about how much of an idiot he must've looked. "You mean there's going to be snow?"

"If you're still alive that long," Sasha said, grabbing Wells's elbow as he slipped again.

"If I die before seeing snow, it'll be because I have one of your friends' arrows in my back. Not because I keep falling on my ass."

"How many times do I have to explain this? Those people are most definitely not my *friends*."

"Yeah, but don't you know them well enough to ask them to stop trying to kill us?" he replied, searching her face for a hint of whatever she was hiding from him.

"It's a little more complicated than that," she said, pulling him along the slope.

Wells gestured downward. "You seem to like complicated."

She rolled her eyes. "Trust me, space boy. This will be worth it."

When they were almost at the bottom, Wells pushed off the hill to jump down the last few meters. But instead of landing on grass, his feet struck something hard. The impact was enough to send a jolt of pain shooting up his legs, though fortunately, he managed to stay upright this time. He winced, but when he glanced down, surprise chased away all thoughts of discomfort.

The ground wasn't grass or dirt. It was rock. He bent down and brushed his fingers along the rough gray surface. No, not rock—this was a *road*. Wells jumped back and looked from side to side, half expecting to hear the rumble of an engine.

"Are you okay?" Sasha asked, coming to stand next to him. Wells nodded, unsure how to explain. When he'd found Clarke stranded in the ruins of the church, he'd been too terrified to focus on anything besides getting her out. Now he leaned over to study the cement, the way its fissures cracked and grew, small plants growing in the gaps.

On the Colony, it had been easy to think about the Cataclysm in the abstract sense. He knew how many people had died when it'd happened, how many metric tons of toxins had been released into the air and so on. But now, he thought about the people who'd driven, ran, or maybe even crawled down this road in a desperate attempt to escape the bombs. How many people had died in this very spot as the earth shook and the sky filled with smoke?

"It's just over here," Sasha said, placing her hand on his shoulder. "Follow me."

"What's just over there?" he asked, turning his head from side to side. The air felt different here than it did in the clearing, heavy with memories that made Wells shiver.

"You'll see."

They walked in silence for a few minutes. With each step, Wells's heart began to beat a little faster. "You have to promise me you won't tell anyone about this," Sasha said. Her voice grew quiet, and she glanced nervously over her shoulder.

Wells hesitated. He'd learned the hard way what happened when you made promises you couldn't keep. "You can trust me," he said finally.

Sasha stared at him for a moment, then nodded. As they turned around a bend in the road, Wells's skin began to tingle, his nerves buzzing with energy as his body braced for whatever awaited them.

But when the road straightened out again, there was nothing. Only more cracked pavement veined with plants.

"There," Sasha said, pointing toward the trees that bordered the side of the road. "Do you see it?"

Wells started to shake his head, then froze as a geometric outline took shape among the tangle of branches.

It was a house.

"Oh my god," Wells whispered as he took a few steps forward. "This is impossible. I thought there was nothing left!"

"There's not much. But these mountains protected a few structures from the blasts. Most of the people around here survived the bombs, but died later from starvation or radiation poisoning."

As they got closer, Wells saw that the house was made of stone, which he supposed had a better chance of weathering the destruction, although much of the right side had collapsed.

There was no glass left in any of the windows, and thick vines covered a large portion of the surviving walls. There was something almost predatory about the way they wrapped up the sides, snaking through the gaping windows and up out of what had once been a chimney, as if the earth were trying to erase all evidence of human life.

"Can we go inside?" Wells asked when he realized he'd been staring at the house in shocked silence.

"No. I think it'll be more fun to stand here all day and watch you gaping like a fish."

"Cut me some slack. This is the craziest thing I've ever seen."

Sasha blinked at him incredulously. "You lived in *space*. You've seen *Mars*!"

He grinned. "You have to use a telescope to see Mars, and even then it just looks like a red dot. Now come on. Are we going inside or what?"

They walked toward the side of the house farthest from the collapsed wall, where there was a window about two meters from the ground with an inviting ledge beneath it. Wells watched as Sasha climbed up onto the ledge with ease, then lowered herself through the window, disappearing into the darkness inside.

"You coming?" she called back to him.

He grinned again and climbed through the window, landing with a soft thud that jolted all other thoughts from his mind. He was standing in a house, an actual *home*, where people had lived before the Cataclysm.

He turned his head from side to side. It seemed like they were in what had once been a kitchen. The floor was covered in cracked yellow and white tiles, and there were white cabinets hanging slightly askew over a deep sink, the largest Wells had ever seen. The only light came from the broken window, which, filtered through the surrounding trees, gave the room a faint, greenish glow, as if he were looking at an old photograph. But this was undeniably real. He took a few steps forward and gingerly ran his finger along the counter, which was covered in generations of dust. He reached up, and even more gently, opened one of the cabinets.

There were stacks of plates and bowls inside. Although they'd slid to the side when the cabinet came loose, it was clear they'd been arranged with care. Some seemed to belong to a set, others were one of a kind. Wells removed a plate from the top of the pile. This one had an illustration on it, though it looked like it'd been done by a child. There were four stick figures with oversize, smiling faces, standing in a line holding one another's misshapen hands. I LOV ARE FAMLEE was printed in wobbly letters above their heads. Wells replaced the plate carefully and turned to see Sasha staring at him out of the silent, dusty gloom.

"It happened a long time ago," she said quietly.

Wells nodded. The words *I know* formed in his brain but got lost somewhere on the way to his mouth. His eyes began to prickle and he turned away quickly. Eight billion. That's how many people had died during the Cataclysm. It'd always seemed as abstract as any huge figure, like the age of Earth, or the number of stars in the galaxy. Yet now, he'd give anything to know that the people who'd eaten dinner together in this kitchen, with those plates, had somehow made it off the burning planet.

"Wells, come look at this." He turned and saw Sasha kneeling next to a pile of rubble on the far side of the room, where the wall had caved in. She was brushing dust and bits of debris off something on the floor.

He walked over and crouched down next to her. "What is it?" he asked as Sasha pulled at what looked like a clasp. "Careful," he warned, remembering Clarke's snake.

"It's a suitcase," Sasha said, her voice a mix of surprise and something else—apprehension? Fear?

The case fell open, sending a new cloud of dust into the air, and they both leaned forward for a better look. There were only a few items inside. Three small faded shirts that Wells examined one at a time, carefully replacing each exactly as he'd found them. There was also a book. Most of the pages had rotted away, but enough remained for Wells to tell it was about a boy named Charlie. He hesitated before putting it back inside the suitcase. He would've loved to examine it in the sunlight, but for some reason, it didn't seem right to take anything away from the house.

The only other recognizable item was a small stuffed bear. Its fur had probably been yellow at one point, though it was hard to tell with all the dust. Sasha picked it up and stared at it for a moment before pressing a finger against his black nose. "Poor bear," she said with a smile, although she couldn't quite keep her voice from catching.

"It's just so sad," Wells said, running his finger along one of the T-shirts. "If they had left sooner, maybe they would've made it out in time."

"Where were they supposed to go?" Sasha asked, shooting him a look as she rubbed dust off one of the bear's paws. "Do you have any idea how much it cost to get to one of the launch sites during the Forsakening? The people who lived around here didn't have that kind of money."

"That's not how it worked," Wells said, an edge creeping into his voice. He took a deep breath to regain his composure. It felt terribly wrong to shout in a place like this. "People didn't have to *pay* to go on the ship."

"No? Then how were the Colonists selected?"

"They came from the neutral nations," Wells said, suddenly feeling like he was back in a primary tutorial. "The ones that weren't greedy or foolish enough to get caught in nuclear war."

The look Sasha gave him was unlike anything he ever saw on his tutors' faces, even when he was wrong. They never stared at him with a mixture of pity and scorn. If anything, Sasha looked more like his father. "Then why does everyone on the ship speak English?" she asked quietly.

He didn't have an answer for that. He'd spent his whole life imagining what it'd be like to see real Earth ruins, and now that he was here, thinking about all the lives that had been extinguished during the Cataclysm made it difficult to breathe.

"We should get back," he said, rising to his feet and reaching out to help Sasha. She glanced at the suitcase for a long moment, then tucked the bear under her arm and took Wells's hand.

CHAPTER *15*

Bellamy

It had taken a while to convince Clarke to head back to camp. She'd insisted on looking for more pieces of wreckage, for anything that would provide some information about the other Colonists. But as the shadows lengthened, Bellamy's skin prickled in a way that had nothing to do with the chill creeping into the air. It was foolish to spend too much time in the woods with the Earthborns lurking about. Once their little spy told him where to find Octavia, Bellamy would go after them—spears and arrows be damned. But he didn't want to face them until he was prepared, and certainly not with Clarke by his side.

After an hour of fruitless searching, Clarke had finally

agreed that it was time to leave. "Just—one more second," she said now, and hurried over to the edge of the clearing.

She stopped before a tree covered with white blossoms. It was fragile-looking, and seemed somehow too small for all the flowers dropping off it. Bellamy was reminded of how Octavia used to look when she put all their mother's clothes on, layers upon layers of fabric, and paraded in front of Bellamy.

Clarke rose up on her toes, plucked a few of the blossoms from the tree, and knelt down to arrange them in front of each of the grave markers. She stood there in silence for a moment, her head bowed. Then she came and took Bellamy's hand, leading him away from the lonely cemetery the rest of the world had forgotten.

Clarke was unusually quiet as they made their way back to the camp. Finally, Bellamy broke the silence. "Are you okay?" He extended his hand to help Clarke over a fallen tree, but she didn't even notice.

"I'm fine," she said, clambering over the log and landing neatly on the other side.

Bellamy didn't reply. He knew better than to push. Clarke wasn't the type of girl who played mind games. She would talk when she wanted to talk. But as he glanced at her again, something in her face tugged at his chest, fraying his resolve. She didn't just look serious, or even sad—she looked haunted.

He stopped in his tracks and wrapped his arms around her. She flinched for a moment, not returning the embrace.

Bellamy started to draw back, but thought better of it and tightened his hold. "Clarke, what's wrong?"

When she spoke, her voice was quiet. "I can't stop thinking about those graves. I just wish I knew whose they are, how they died . . ." She trailed off, but Bellamy knew she was thinking about the sick people she'd left behind at the camp.

"I know," Bellamy said. "But, Clarke, whoever those people were, they've been dead for over a year. There's nothing you could have done to help them." He fell silent for a moment. "And think of it this way—at least they got to be here, on Earth, even if it wasn't for very long. They were probably really jazzed about that."

To his surprise, Clarke smiled—it was a small smile, but enough to chase away some of the sadness lurking in her eyes. "*Jazzed?* What does that mean? Like you're so happy, you'd be willing to listen to jazz music?"

"*Willing* to listen to jazz music? You must mean 'happy because you *get* to listen to jazz music.' So happy that your heart starts beating a jazz riff."

"Like you know jazz," Clarke shot back, still smiling. "Most of that music was lost centuries ago."

Bellamy smirked. "Maybe on Phoenix. I found an old MP3 player with some jazz songs on it once." He shrugged.

"At least, I assumed it was jazz." It had sounded the way he'd always expected jazz to sound—playful, soulful, free.

"So what does a jazz riff sound like?"

"It's more about what it *feels* like," Bellamy said, reaching for Clarke's hand. He began tapping a rhythm up and down her arm.

She shivered as his fingers danced on the inside of her elbow. "So jazz feels like some weirdo tickling your arm?"

"Not your arm. Your whole body. You feel it in your throat . . ." He brought his fingers to her neck and tapped along her collarbone. "In your feet . . ." He knelt down and tapped along the side of her boot, and Clarke laughed. "In your chest . . ." He stood up, bringing his hand to rest lightly on top of her heart, and was very still.

She closed her eyes as her breathing grew shallow. "I think I feel it now," she said.

Bellamy stared at Clarke in wonder. With her eyes closed and lips slightly parted, the afternoon light dancing over her reddish-blond hair like a halo, she looked like one of the fairies he used to describe to Octavia in her bedtime stories.

He bent his head down and brushed his lips against hers. She kissed him back for a moment, then pulled away with a frown. "Didn't you want to get going?" she asked. "I know we've been gone for a while."

"It's a long walk back. Maybe we should rest first." Without waiting for her to reply, Bellamy slid his arm down her back and scooped Clarke up in his arms, the way he'd carried her back last time. But now, her eyes were bright and focused on his, her arms laced around his neck. Slowly, Bellamy guided them both to the ground, which was covered in moss and damp leaves. "Better?" Bellamy whispered.

Clarke responded by twining her hands in his hair and kissing him. Bellamy closed his eyes and pulled her closer, forgetting everything but the feeling of Clarke's body against him.

"Are you cold?" she asked, and he realized that at some point she had pulled his shirt over his head.

"No," he said softly. He knew in an objective sense that it was cold out, but he didn't feel it. He leaned back and looked at her, her hair spilling out over the grass. "Are you?"

He ran his hand lightly along her side, and Clarke stiffened. "Bellamy," she whispered. "Have you ever . . . ?"

She didn't finish the sentence, but she didn't need to. Bellamy took his time answering, kissing her forehead, then her nose, then her delicate pink lips. "I have," he said finally. He could tell from Clarke's telltale flush that she hadn't, and was a little surprised, given her history with Wells. "But just with one person," he added. "Someone I really cared about."

He wanted to say more, but his voice faltered. All those memories of Lilly were wrapped up in pain. And the only thing he wanted to think about right now was the beautiful girl next to him: a girl he would never, ever let go of, no matter what happened.

"Seriously? You took the whole thing?" Bellamy asked, surprised and more than a little impressed. They were in the emergency staircase behind the care center—technically it was past curfew, but no one ever really kept tabs on the older kids, so it was easy for Bellamy and Lilly to meet here.

Lilly held up the platter of cakes she'd stolen from the distribution center. They were meant for some Commitment Ceremony on Phoenix, but now they were about to be committed to Bellamy's and Lilly's stomachs.

Bellamy grinned. "I've really been a bad influence on you, haven't I?"

"Please. Don't give yourself too much credit." Lilly popped an apple tart into her mouth. She picked up a vanilla cake—Bellamy's favorite—and handed it to him. "I always had it in me."

Lilly raised her eyebrow in a way that was so adorable, Bellamy was seized by a sudden, mad desire to kiss her. But he knew better. He'd kissed girls before, and it had never done anything except scramble their brains, turning them into a walking mass of giggles who always wanted to hold his hand. Lilly was his best friend. Kissing her would most definitely be a mistake.

"Save this one for Octavia," Lilly said, handing him a cake garnished with Venus berries.

Bellamy set the cake carefully on the step next to him, then went back to devouring his own. He knew from experience that it was always best to get rid of stolen goods as quickly as possible.

Lilly laughed, and he looked up at her with a grin. "What?" Bellamy asked, wiping his mouth with the back of his hand. "Don't you dare criticize my table manners. We're nowhere *near* a table."

"I'm actually curious," she asked with faux sincerity. "How did you manage to get so much cake on your face?" He swatted at her, and she laughed. "I don't think I could get that much cake on my face if I *tried*."

"Challenge accepted." Bellamy reached over, scraped the frosting off one of the cakes, and smeared it across her chin and mouth. She shrieked and pushed him away, but not before he managed to put a second dollop on the tip of her nose.

"Bellamy!" she exclaimed. "Do you know how much we could have sold that for?"

Bellamy smirked. It was hard to take someone covered in icing very seriously. "Oh, trust me, this visual is priceless."

Lilly's expression shifted to something he couldn't quite identify. "Is it?" she asked softly. He closed his eyes, bracing himself for icing all over his face—and felt Lilly's lips on his. He froze for a moment in surprise, then kissed her back. Her kiss was soft, and tasted like sugar.

When she finally pulled away, he searched her face,

wondering what had just happened. "Oh," she said. "I think I forgot something."

"What?" Bellamy shifted awkwardly. He knew it was a bad idea to kiss his best friend, he never should have—

"I missed a spot," Lilly murmured, pulling him forward and kissing him again.

Clarke sat up so quickly, her head bumped against Bellamy's chin. "Whoa," he said, taking her by the shoulders. "Clarke, it's okay. We don't have to do anything right now." He rubbed his hands in slow circles on her back. Her skin was cold through her thin T-shirt.

"It's not that," Clarke said quickly. "I just . . . I have something I need to tell you."

Bellamy took Clarke's hand and interlocked her fingers with his. "You can tell me anything," he assured her.

She pulled her hand away, bringing her knees to her chest and hugging them tightly. "I don't really know how to say this," Clarke began, almost more to herself than to him. She stared straight ahead, unwilling—or unable—to meet his eyes. "I've only told one person before, and it didn't end well."

He knew instinctively she was talking about Wells. "It's okay." He reached an arm around her shoulders. "Whatever it is, we can figure it out."

She finally turned to face him, her expression stricken. "I

wouldn't promise that." She exhaled, seeming to deflate, and then, haltingly, began to speak.

At first, Bellamy thought Clarke's story about the testing was some kind of joke. He couldn't believe what she was telling him—how her parents were researching radiation, how they were forced by the Vice Chancellor to conduct experiments on unregistered children. But one look in Clarke's eyes and he knew that this was all terrifyingly real.

"That's *monstrous*," Bellamy finally interrupted, praying that she'd say something to make it all make sense, to explain why she was telling him all of this now. Suddenly, another thought made his blood run cold. "*Octavia* was unregistered," he said slowly. "Was she next in line for your little experiments?" He shuddered in horror, imagining his sister locked in a hidden lab where no one would hear her cry—where no one would know she was slowly being poisoned to death.

"I don't know," Clarke said. "I don't know how the children were selected. But it was terrible. I hated myself every day."

"Then why didn't you stop it? Why did your parents *kill* innocent children? How evil were they?"

"They weren't evil. They didn't have a choice!"

She was on the verge of tears, but Bellamy didn't care. "Of course they did," he spat. "I made a choice to do everything I could to protect Octavia. But you made a choice to stand by and watch a bunch of kids *die*."

"I didn't always stand by." Clarke closed her eyes. "Not with Lilly."

It took a moment for Bellamy to understand what Clarke was saying. "Lilly? That's how you knew her? Lilly was one of your . . . subjects?" Clarke nodded, wincing, and Bellamy's voice rose in anger. "She didn't die from some mysterious illness. She died because your murderer parents performed *experiments* on her." Lilly. The only person on the ship who'd cared about him, aside from Octavia. The only person he'd ever loved.

He paused as Clarke's words sank in. "What do you mean, you didn't always stand by?" When Clarke said nothing, he pressed on. "You mean you helped her escape? Is she still alive?"

"She was my friend, Bellamy." Tears were streaming down Clarke's cheeks, but Bellamy ignored them. "She told me how to talk to boys, and made me promise to wear my hair down once a week. I used to bring her books, and she would read them aloud in all these funny voices, until she got too sick, and then I read them to her. And then, when she asked me to help her, I did it, I *had* to, she didn't give me a choice . . ."

"Help her how?" Bellamy asked, his voice low and dangerous.

"I . . . She begged me to make the pain go away. She asked me—" Clarke sniffed and wiped her nose with the back of her hand, her voice breaking. "To help her die."

"You're lying," Bellamy said, feeling nauseous. An hour ago he would have insisted that Clarke was incapable of something like that, would have defended her honor to the death. But now the girl in front of him looked like a monstrous stranger. Lilly, though, he knew. "She would never have said that," he snarled, rising to his feet. "She would've done everything possible to survive your sick game."

"Bellamy," Clarke started weakly. "You don't understand—" She broke off as a sob rose in her throat.

"Don't you *dare* tell me what I understand," Bellamy cut her off. "I never want to see you again. Maybe you can offer yourself up to the Earthborns. Wouldn't that be fun? A whole new population of children to experiment on." He spun around and strode off, leaving Clarke alone and trembling in the woods.

He tore through the forest blindly, blinking back tears. He never should have trusted Clarke, never should have let himself get close to her. He'd learned long ago that the only person he could rely on was himself. And the only person who mattered to him was Octavia.

He'd wasted too much time already. It was time to get his sister back.

He was done playing nice with the Earthborn girl. He was done playing at all.

CHAPTER *16*

Wells

He'd been worried about how to sneak back into camp without being spotted, although at least this time, he and Sasha weren't carrying food—only the memories of the ruined house that clung to his mind like a fine film of dust.

When Wells saw Clarke step around from behind a large tree, he exhaled with relief. They were close enough to the clearing that he could pass Sasha to Clarke, and let her pretend that she'd been escorting the prisoner to the bathroom. She wouldn't mind covering for him. Of all people, Clarke saw the foolishness of trying to keep Sasha tied up in the cabin.

Wells raised his hand in greeting, then noticed that something was wrong. Clarke always moved with such purpose—whether reaching for a book in the library at home, or striding forward to examine a plant that caught her eye. It was a shock to watch her trudge through the woods as if dragging some invisible weight behind her.

"Clarke," Wells called. He exchanged a look with Sasha, who nodded a silent agreement to stay where she was, then he broke into a jog. As he got closer, he saw that her eyes were red. Clarke, who'd sat through her parents' trial in stony silence, had been crying? "Are you okay?"

"I'm fine," she said, looking straight ahead to avoid meeting his eyes. Even without the tears, he'd know she was lying.

"Come on, Clarke," Wells said, glancing over his shoulder to make sure Sasha was still safely out of earshot. "After everything we've been through"—*after all the pain we've caused each other*, Wells wanted to say, but didn't—"don't you think I know when something's wrong?" She nodded, sniffing, but said nothing. Wells frowned. "Did something happen with Bellamy?"

He expected her to brush him off, but to his surprise, Clarke looked up at him, her eyes shiny with tears. "I'm sorry," she said. "I'm so sorry, Wells. I punished you for so long. I should have forgiven you . . ." Her voice broke and she turned away.

"It's okay," Wells said hesitantly, wrapping one arm around her. Somehow, he knew her apology had more to do with Bellamy than it did with him. "What can I do to help?" he asked. "Want me to go beat him up for you?"

"No," Clarke sniffed, but at least she was smiling.

Before he could say anything else, Clarke's eyes widened as she caught sight of something over Wells's shoulder. For a moment, he thought she was looking at Sasha, but as he turned to follow Clarke's gaze, his discomfort turned to horror.

Something was hanging from the branch of a tall, thick tree, rotating slowly, wobbling from side to side as it bumped against the trunk.

It's a person, Wells thought, before realizing that was impossible. No one's head could hang at that angle. No one's face could possibly be that blue.

Behind him, Clarke made a sound he'd never heard before, half shriek, half moan.

Wells took a few steps forward, waiting for his brain to offer another explanation, but nothing came.

"No," he said aloud, blinking rapidly to dispel the image, like he used to do with his cornea slips.

But the rotating shape remained.

It was a small girl, and although her face was bloated almost beyond recognition, he knew her by her shiny dark hair. Her delicate wrists and small hands that had always surprised Wells with their strength.

"*Priya*," Clarke gasped behind him. She staggered next to Wells and clutched his arm. For the first time since they'd landed on Earth, Clarke was too horror-struck to do more than stare.

The rope that was wrapped around Priya's neck was digging into her skin—skin that had been golden brown hours ago, and was now a mottled blue. "We have to get her down," Wells said, although he knew she was beyond help.

He took a shaky step forward, then realized that Sasha was already scaling the tree. "Pass me your knife," she said as she began creeping along the branch. "Now," she ordered when Wells didn't move.

He took a few lurching steps forward while he fumbled for the knife in his pocket, then tossed it up to Sasha, who caught it one-handed.

Silently, Sasha cut the rope tying Priya to the tree, and lowered her carefully down. "Do you think . . . did she do this to herself?" Wells asked, turning away as Clarke felt the bruised neck for a pulse they all knew she wouldn't find. Quiet, helpful, steadfast Priya. Why would she have done something like this? Was it terrible homesickness? Or had she sensed the hundred were beyond saving? Threads of guilt began to wind their way through his horror. Could he have done more to make her feel safe?

"No," Sasha said, her voice shaking. She'd climbed down from the tree and was now standing a few meters behind Wells.

"I'm not sure yet," Clarke said without taking her eyes from Priya. "I'd have to think more about the marks on her neck, the position of the rope . . ." She trailed off. Wells knew she didn't relish the role of coroner.

"She didn't kill herself," Sasha said, more firmly this time.

"And how do you know?" Clarke asked, finally tearing her eyes from Priya to face Sasha. Wells couldn't tell whether Clarke disliked having her medical authority questioned, or if she resented the outsider's intrusion into their private pain.

"Her feet," Sasha said softly, pointing.

Until this moment, Wells hadn't realized that Priya was barefoot. He stepped forward and squinted in an attempt to see what Sasha was talking about. There were marks on her soles that, at first, looked like streaks of dirt. But as he got closer, Wells realized they were cuts—cuts in the shapes of letters.

"Oh my god," Clarke gasped.

There was a message carved into Priya's flesh. One word on the sole of each small foot.

Go. Home.

He didn't have to worry about returning Sasha to the cabin. Once the sound of footsteps and muffled shouts made it clear that people were coming to investigate Clarke's cries, Wells sent Sasha back into the woods with instructions to sneak back into the clearing when the coast was clear. As word about Priya spread, the clearing would fill with enough commotion that no one would notice the Earthborn girl had gone missing.

About ten minutes later, Eric and an Arcadian girl were carrying Priya's body back down the hill, while Antonio escorted the wide-eyed, shaking Clarke. Wells wished he could help her himself—especially considering how upset she'd been about Bellamy earlier—but someone needed to investigate the crime scene, such as it was, before the sun set.

He watched as the others trailed after the body. Once the impromptu funeral procession had disappeared behind the trees, he began scanning the ground, trying to determine whether Priya had been seized in the forest, or dragged from another location. Wells tried not to think about how terrified she must've been, or what the Earthborns had done to keep her from screaming. He tried not to think about whether she'd felt the knife digging into the soles of her feet, or if they'd waited until she was already dead to carve her flesh.

He climbed up onto the branch to examine the frayed pieces of rope. It turned out to be one of the thin, nylon cords that had secured the supply containers in the dropship. That meant that the Earthborns had been in their *camp*.

As more grim thoughts began to overpower his resolve, another scream echoed through the trees, making his heart lurch in his chest.

Sasha.

In one smooth movement, he dropped from the branch and broke into a sprint.

The scream came again, louder this time. Wells sped up, cursing every time he skidded on a patch of mud or tripped over a hidden stone. He tore past the path that had been formed by frequent trips to the stream, following the sound deeper into the woods.

When he crashed through a clump of bushes and saw Sasha with Bellamy, his first reaction was relief. Bellamy had heard the screams too and come running. But then two details of the scene clicked into focus—the fear in Sasha's face, and the glint of metal at her throat.

Bellamy had his arm wrapped around Sasha's neck from behind, and was pressing something sharp and silver to her skin. "Tell me where your friends took my sister," he was saying, his eyes wild. "Where do your people live? What are they doing with her?"

Sasha gasped and whispered something Wells couldn't hear. With a shout, he hurtled forward and knocked Bellamy to the ground.

"Are you crazy?" Wells shouted, kicking the piece of metal—a twisted remnant of the dropship—out of Bellamy's hand. He turned to Sasha, who had her arms wrapped around her sides, trembling. "Are you okay?" he asked, more gently.

She nodded, but when she reached up to touch her neck, her hand came away smeared with blood. "Let me see." Wells pushed back her hair to get a closer look—there was a small puncture wound at the base of her throat, but just a scratch. She would be fine. Wells didn't want to think about what would've happened if he'd arrived any later.

"What the hell?" he spat, turning to Bellamy, who was rising shakily to his feet. When Bellamy caught sight of the blood on Sasha's neck, he seemed to pale slightly, but his tone was indignant.

"I was doing what I had to do, to get Octavia back. It's clear that I'm the only one who still cares what happens to her." Bellamy glanced at Sasha. "I wasn't going to hurt her. I just wanted to show her that this isn't a game. It's my sister's *life*."

"You need to stay the hell away from her," Wells said, stepping in front of Sasha.

Bellamy's mouth twisted into a sneer. "Are you serious? Whose side are you on, Wells? Every day that passes, my chances of finding Octavia alive grow smaller. What do you think she's doing, having a tea party with the Earthborns? They could be *torturing* her for all we know." The pain in his voice unlocked something inside Wells's chest. He knew how Bellamy felt, terror and desperation pushing him to the brink—because it was exactly how he'd felt when he learned that Clarke was going to be executed, back on the Colony.

"I know," Wells said, struggling to keep his voice level. "But no more trying to hurt anyone, okay? That's not how we do things."

"*Please*," Bellamy shot back. "If I was actually *trying* to hurt her, there would be a pool of her Earthborn blood on the ground right now."

"That's *enough!*" Wells shouted, his voice raw. "I'm taking Sasha back to camp. I suggest you stay here until you're ready to have a rational discussion."

Wells grabbed Sasha by the wrist and began leading her back toward the clearing. "Traitor," he heard Bellamy mutter under his breath. Wells tried to ignore him, but he couldn't help wondering if Bellamy was right. Was he foolish to trust Sasha? He glanced over at her face, which was completely closed off, her eyes looking straight ahead. His brain flashed, unbidden, to an image of Priya's hanging body. *They'd been inside the camp.* They'd used the hundred's own rope to kill her.

"I'm sorry about what happened back there," Wells said quietly. "Are you okay?"

"Yes, I'm fine." But her voice was still shaky, and he could feel her trembling against him. Then her forearm shifted in his wrist, and she slipped her palm into his, still looking straight ahead and revealing nothing.

Wells was silent as they walked back toward camp, hand in hand.

CHAPTER *17*

Glass

"Don't look," Luke said as he pulled Glass away from the body on the ground. She averted her eyes before she had a chance to see whether it was a guard or a civilian. She didn't even know if it was a man or a woman.

Glass wasn't sure what she'd expected. Had she really thought the skybridge would open, and all the Waldenites and Arcadians would file onto Phoenix in a calm and orderly fashion, bidding polite *hello*s to the people who'd left them all to die?

No, she'd known it wouldn't be simple, or organized. But she hadn't expected the noise that filled the skybridge when the barrier raised—an earsplitting chorus of sobs and shouts and cheers and screams.

She hadn't expected a male voice to come blasting out of the speakers. For the past seventeen years, Phoenix's PA system had been used for inane, prerecorded announcements read by the same slightly robotic-sounding woman. "Please remember to abide by all curfew restrictions" and "All signs of illness must be reported to a health monitor."

But as the first wave of people surged across the skybridge, a very different voice rang out over the chaotic clamor. "All residents of Walden and Arcadia must return to their own ships immediately. This is your only warning. All trespassers will be shot."

Hearing a man's voice coming out of the speakers was as disconcerting as seeing the skybridge closed, almost as if the ship had been possessed. But even that wasn't as troubling as the sight of a dozen guards marching toward the bridge, guns raised.

Even then, Glass hadn't expected them to actually shoot anyone.

She was wrong.

The guards had opened fire on the first wave of Waldenites who crossed the bridge, but even that wasn't enough to deter the crowds who rushed forward to overpower the guards and take their weapons. Within minutes, Phoenix was filled with Waldenites and Arcadians. At first, most had just seemed relieved to be able to breathe, taking huge gasps of oxygen-rich air. But then they began to spread out throughout Phoenix, carrying whatever they could find as weapons and breaking down doors to steal from the Phoenicians. It had rapidly gotten violent and out of hand.

Luke pulled Glass to the side as two men ran past, each holding an enormous container of protein packets. Then another pair of Waldenites turned the corner, but these weren't carrying supplies—they were dragging an unconscious guard.

Glass covered her mouth in horror as she watched the young guard's head roll from side to side. There was a deep purple bruise on his cheek, and he was bleeding from a gash in his shoulder, leaving a trail of blood behind him. She could feel Luke tense next to her, and she grabbed his arm to restrain him. "*Don't,*" she whispered. "Let them go."

Luke watched the Waldenites drag the guard around a corner and disappear, although they could still hear their laughter echoing in the corridor. "I could have taken them," he said with a huff.

In another situation, Glass might've smiled at Luke's indignation, but she felt only a growing panic. All she could think about was finding her mother and heading to the launch deck. She could only hope that her mother was safe at home, that she'd known better than to venture out into the chaos.

Glass loved her mother, but she had never been particularly good in a crisis. Over the years, Glass had realized that there were some battles Sonja simply couldn't face.

And so Glass had learned how to fight for both of them.

It felt odd walking back from the Exchange by herself, without Cora or Huxley next to her chattering about their purchases, or scheming of ways to keep their parents from discovering how many points they'd spent. Their absence made Glass all the more aware of the lightness of her pocket. Just minutes ago, it had held her mother's last necklace.

Huxley's mother had appeared at the jewelry booth just as Glass began haggling with the vendor about how many points the necklace was worth. "It's a lovely piece, dear," she murmured, giving Glass a pitying smile before leaning over to say something to a woman Glass didn't recognize. Glass had flushed, but kept arguing. She and her mom needed those ration points.

Moving through the Exchange, Glass had felt everyone's eyes on her. Phoenix was in a state of delighted shock at the scandal surrounding her family. Affairs were nothing new, but moving out was a drastic step given the housing shortage. And according to regulations, two people couldn't occupy a flat meant for three, which meant that Glass and Sonja had been forced to move to a smaller unit on an inconvenient deck. Now, without her father's seemingly endless supply of ration points, they'd had to sell practically everything they owned at the Exchange just to keep from living on water and protein paste.

Glass turned down their hallway and sighed with relief when she saw that it was empty. The one benefit of living in such an undesirable location was that she wouldn't run into people she knew. Or, used to know. It had been weeks since Cora had done more than give her a curt nod in the corridor, grabbing Huxley's elbow when she smiled at Glass. Wells was the only one of her friends who acted like nothing had changed—but he'd recently started officer training, which kept him so busy, he barely had time to visit his mother in the hospital, let alone hang out with Glass.

She pressed her hand against the door's sensor and stepped inside, wrinkling her nose. Their old flat had always smelled like a combination of expensive greenhouse fruit and her mother's perfume, and she still hadn't gotten used to the stale, stuffy scent that choked the smaller unit.

It was dark inside, so Sonja couldn't be home. The lights were connected to motion sensors. But when Glass stepped inside, they didn't turn on. That was strange. She waved her hand up and down, but still nothing happened. She groaned. Now she would have to send a maintenance request, which always took forever. In the past, her father simply would've messaged his friend Jessamyn—the head of the repairs unit—and it would be fixed right away. But Glass couldn't stomach the thought of asking for any favors from her father.

"Glass? Is that you?" Sonja rose from the couch, an amorphous shape in the dim light. She started to walk toward Glass, but yelped as she bumped into something that clanked to the floor.

"Why are you sitting in the dark?" Glass demanded. "Did you send a message to maintenance?" Sonja didn't answer. "I'll do it myself," Glass said, annoyed.

"No, don't. That won't work." Sonja sounded weary.

"What are you talking about?" Glass snapped. She knew she should try harder to be patient with her mother, but she'd been so infuriating lately.

"The sensor isn't broken. We went over our power quota, and I don't have the ration points to cover it."

"What?" Glass said. "That's ridiculous. They can't do this to us."

"We don't have a choice. We'll just have to wait until—"

"We're not waiting," Glass said indignantly.

She spun on her heel and strode out of the dark flat.

Cora's father's office was at the end of a long corridor where most of the department heads worked. The hall wasn't particularly busy—from her experience, most of the Council-appointed heads spent very little time in their offices—but her stomach still twisted at the thought of running into one of her dad's friends.

Mr. Drake's assistant, a young man Glass didn't recognize, was sitting at a desk, fiddling with some numbers in a holograph. He looked up and raised an eyebrow. "Can I help you?"

"I need to talk to Mr. Drake."

"I'm afraid the Resources Chief is busy at the moment. Why don't I take a message and I'll let him know—"

"It's okay. *I'll* let him know." Glass gave the boy a patronizing smile and swept past him into the office.

Cora's father looked up from behind his desk when Glass walked in. For a second, he just stared at her in surprise, but then his face broke out into a big, insincere smile. "Glass! What a nice surprise. What can I do for you, sweetheart?"

"You can turn my lights back on," she said. "I'm sure it was just a mistake, of course. You would never knowingly let me and my mother spend the next month sitting in the dark."

Mr. Drake frowned as he tapped on his desk, opening a file on the screen. "Well, you went over your quota, so unless you have points to transfer to your account, I'm afraid there's nothing I can do."

"We both know that's a lie. You're the Resources Chief—you can do whatever you want."

He gave Glass a cold, appraising look. "I have the well-being of the entire Colony to consider. If someone takes more than their fair share, it would be irresponsible of me to make exceptions."

Glass tilted her head to the side. "So bribing your way into the greenhouse and selling fruit on the black market doesn't count as an exception?" she said with feigned innocence.

Mr. Drake's cheeks grew red. "I have no idea what you're talking about."

"Sorry. I must've misunderstood Cora. I'll have to get my friend Wells to explain it to me. He knows much more about all this than I do, since he's the Chancellor's son and all."

Mr. Drake was silent for a moment before clearing his throat. "I suppose I can make an allowance this *one* time. Now, you should be on your way. I have a meeting."

Glass flashed him a too-bright smile. "Thank you so much for your help," she said, then swept out of the office, pausing only to nod at the glaring assistant.

When she arrived home, the lights were already back on. "Did you do this?" Sonja asked, gesturing to the lights in amazement.

"I just cleared up a little misunderstanding," Glass said, going to the kitchen to assess their options for dinner.

"Thank you, Glass. I'm very proud of you."

Glass felt a thrill of satisfaction, but as she turned around to smile at Sonja, she realized her mother had already disappeared back into her bedroom.

Glass's smile faded as she stared at the spot where Sonja had been standing. She'd spent her whole life believing that she'd never be as beautiful as her mother, never be as charming. But perhaps Glass could succeed where her mother had failed.

She would figure out how to get what she wanted—what she needed—even when her long lashes failed to convince, when her body was no longer young and beautiful.

She'd be more than pretty. She'd be strong.

Glass's hallway was startlingly quiet. Glass wasn't sure whether this was a good or a bad sign. Her heart racing, she walked up to their door and pressed her thumb to the scanner, Luke placing a hand on her shoulder in silent reassurance. But before the machine had even read her print, the door flew outward.

"Oh my god, Glass!" In a flash, her mother's arms were around her. "How did you get back? The skybridge is closed . . ." She trailed off as she caught sight of Luke.

Glass braced for Sonja's relief to curdle into disdain at the sight of him—the boy she blamed for ruining Glass's life. But to her surprise, her mother stepped forward and clasped Luke's hand in her own. "Thank you," she said with quiet dignity. "Thank you for bringing her back."

Luke nodded, evidently unsure how to respond, but his good manners and self-control won out as usual. "Actually, it was Glass who brought me. You have a remarkably brave daughter, Mrs. Sorenson."

Sonja smiled as she released Luke and wrapped her arm around Glass. "I know." She led them inside to the tiny but neat living room. Glass's eyes darted around, but she saw no evidence of packing, or any intention to leave.

"What's been going on over here?" she asked without thinking. "Do they know how much longer the oxygen will last? Are there plans to evacuate?"

Sonja shook her head. "No one knows. The Chancellor hasn't emerged from his coma, so Rhodes is still in charge." Glass felt a pang of sadness for Wells—it had been three weeks; at this point, it seemed like the Chancellor might never recover. Especially not in time to make it off the ship.

"So what are they telling people?" Glass asked, shooting her mother a look. The night before she fled for Walden, she'd seen her mother and Rhodes together—and they had looked cozier than friends had a right to be. But Sonja just shook her head.

"Nothing. There haven't been any updates, any instructions." She sighed and her face fell. "But people are talking, of course. Once they closed the skybridge, it became clear that . . . well . . . that things weren't going to get any better."

"What about the dropships?" Glass asked. "Has anyone said anything?"

"Not officially. The entrance to the launch was still shut, last I heard. But people have already started heading down there, just in case."

She didn't need to say anything else. The ship had been

designed with enough dropships for the population of the *original* Colony. After three centuries in space, that number had more than quadrupled. Not even the harsh population controls enacted a century ago had managed to make much of a dent.

For children on Phoenix, the limited number of dropships had always been something of a joke. When someone gave a stupid answer during tutorial, or messed up during a game on the gravity track, one of their friends would inevitably say something along the lines of "We're giving away your seat on the dropship." It was safe to laugh about, because humans were supposed to stay on the Colony for at least another century. And when they finally did return to Earth, there'd be plenty of time for the dropships to shuttle everyone back and forth. No one had ever imagined what would happen in the event of a large-scale evacuation. The prospect was too grim.

"We should go now, then," Glass said firmly. "There's no point in waiting for an announcement. By then, it'll be too late. All the spots will be taken."

"I'll just get my things," Sonja said, her eyes darting around the room as she took inventory of her scant possessions.

"There's no time," Luke said, taking Glass's mother by the arm and leading her toward the door. "Nothing is worth losing our chance at getting to Earth." Sonja nodded, her eyes flickering with fear, and followed Luke through the door.

The closer they got to the launch deck, the more crowded the halls became—filled with anxious Phoenicians, some laden with bags and children, others carrying nothing but the clothes on their backs.

Luke grabbed Glass with one hand and Sonja with the other, guiding them through the crowd toward the stairwell. Glass tried not to make eye contact with any of the people she passed. She didn't want to remember their faces when she thought about the dead.

CHAPTER *18*

Clarke

"It's not serious," Clarke told Sasha as she finished cleaning the cut on her neck and turned to rummage through their dwindling bandage supply. She reached into the box, then hesitated, unsure whether to use one of the remaining bandages. While Sasha's wound wasn't deep and would certainly heal on its own, it'd feel good to be able to do *something*.

"You're going to be fine," Clarke said, wishing the same were true for the girl lying on the far side of the cabin, her poor, disfigured face covered with a blanket no one would want to remove. Clarke had asked to examine Priya's body one more time before they buried her, to see if there was any important evidence she and Wells had missed in their shock and horror.

Wells nodded at her from where he was standing guard at the doorway, and Clarke followed him outside.

"Bellamy's gone insane," he whispered to Clarke, and explained what Bellamy had done, how he'd tried to force Sasha to give him information she didn't have. "You need to talk to him."

Clarke winced. There was no doubt in her mind that she'd driven him to do it; telling Bellamy about Lilly had pushed him over the edge. But she couldn't imagine filling Wells in on what had happened in the woods. "He's not going to listen to me," she said, glancing around the clearing, somehow both relieved and disappointed not to see Bellamy anywhere.

"I'll go look for him," Wells said wearily. "Will you stay here and keep an eye on Sasha? If Bellamy comes back and finds her gone, he'll murder all of us." He grimaced at his choice of words, then closed his eyes and rubbed his temples.

Clarke's hand extended out of habit, trained to ruffle Wells's hair whenever stress prompted this uncanny imitation of his father. She caught herself just in time, and placed her hand on his shoulder instead. "You know none of this is your fault, right?"

"Yes, I know." It came out sharper than he'd evidently

meant, because he sighed and shook his head. "Sorry. I mean, thank you."

Clarke nodded, then glanced over her shoulder at the infirmary cabin. "Does she really need to stay in there? It seems cruel to make her sit so near—" She cut herself off before she said *the body*. "Priya."

Wells shuddered, then looked over at the other side of the clearing where a mutinous-looking Graham was standing with his friends. They were too far away to hear, but their heads swiveled back and forth between the grave Eric was digging, and the infirmary cabin behind Wells and Clarke. "I think it's best to keep her away from the others for now. We can't risk angering the Earthborns if something happens to her. Look what they've done already, unprovoked."

He was speaking calmly, logically, in the same tone he'd use to talk about water shifts and firewood duty, but there was something in Wells's expression that made Clarke wonder if perhaps he had another reason for wanting to keep Sasha safe.

"Okay," Clarke agreed. After Wells left, she took a deep breath and walked back into the cabin. Sasha sat cross-legged on a cot, running her finger along the bandage on her neck.

"Try not to touch it," Clarke said, sitting down on the edge of her own cot. "The bandage is sterile, but your hands aren't."

Sasha's hand dropped to her lap as she shot a glance at

Priya. "I'm so sorry," she said quietly. "I can't believe they did that to her."

"Thank you," Clarke said stiffly, unsure how to respond. But when she saw that the pain in Sasha's face was real, she softened slightly. "I'm sorry we brought her here with you. It'll just be for a little while."

"It's okay. You should take your time. It's important to spend time with the dead. We always wait until the third sunset to bury anyone."

Clarke stared at her. "You mean, you leave the body out?"

Sasha nodded. "People grieve differently. It's important to give everyone time to say good-bye in their own way." She paused and surveyed Clarke thoughtfully. "I suppose it's different on the Colony. Death is rarer there, isn't it? You have medicine for everything?" Her voice was frayed by a mix of wonder and longing that made Clarke wonder what kind of supplies the Earthborns had, and how many people they'd lost from a lack thereof.

"A lot of things. But not everything. A friend of mine lost his mother a few years ago. It was terrible. She'd been in the hospital for months, but in the end, there was nothing they could do."

Sasha drew her knees up to her chest. She'd removed her black leather boots, revealing thick socks that stretched all the way up her calves. "It was Wells's mother, wasn't it?" she asked.

Clarke blinked at her in surprise. "Did he tell you?" she asked.

Sasha turned away and began fiddling with the edge of her scraggly black sweater. "No, I just can tell he's suffered a lot. You can see it in his eyes."

"Well, he's caused quite a bit of suffering himself," Clarke said, slightly more harshly than she'd meant to.

Sasha raised her head and stared at Clarke with an expression that was more curious than hurt. "Haven't we all? You know, it's funny. When I thought about kids on the Colony, I imagined you all as totally carefree. After all, what could you have to worry about? You had robot servants, medicine that allowed everyone to live to a hundred and fifty, and you spent all day surrounded by stars."

"Robot servants?" Clarke repeated, feeling her brow furrow. "Where'd you hear that?"

"Just from stories people told. We knew most of it probably wasn't true, but it was fun to think about." She paused and looked sheepish, then started to slip her feet back inside her boots. "Come on, I have something to show you."

Clarke stood up slowly. "I told Wells we'd stay here."

"So he's in charge?"

It was an innocent question, but it still rankled Clarke. Yes, Wells had been working hard to keep the camp from dissolving into chaos, but that didn't mean he got to order everyone around. "He's not in charge of me," Clarke said. "So where are we going?"

"It's a surprise." Seeing Clarke's hesitation, Sasha sighed. "Don't you trust me by now?"

Clarke considered the question. "I suppose I trust you as much as I trust anyone here. After all, you aren't on Earth because you committed a crime."

Sasha looked at her in confusion, but before she had time to ask a question, Clarke turned to quickly check on her patients. Molly and Felix were unchanged, but there was something odd about the Walden girl's lip. It seemed to be stained with something—was it blood? Clarke suppressed a gasp as she thought back to Lilly's final days, when her gums bled so badly, it became difficult to talk. But when Clarke grabbed a scrap of cloth to wipe the blood from the girl's mouth, it came away easily, almost as if it were . . .

"Are you ready?" Sasha asked.

Clarke turned with a sigh and nodded. Perhaps Sasha could show her some medicinal plants the Earthborns used. At this point, she was ready to try anything.

She opened the door and they stepped into the clearing. "It's okay," she called to the boy and the girl Wells had assigned to guard the cabin, imbuing as much authority as possible into her voice. "I'm just taking the prisoner for a bathroom break."

The girl stared at them warily, but the boy nodded. "It's fine," Clarke saw him mouth to the girl, who remained unconvinced. Clarke didn't blame her. There was still no evidence to support Sasha's claim about the rogue Earthborns. As they crossed the tree line, the back of Clarke's neck prickled, and she started to wonder if it was really a good idea to go off in the woods with Sasha alone. A chilling thought passed over her. What if *Sasha* had been the one who killed all the Colonists?

They walked along in silence. When Sasha stopped to examine a plant growing along a fallen log, Clarke had trouble thinking about anything other than how far they'd walked, and if anyone would be able to hear her scream. She kept seeing Priya, her blue, puffy face and the terrible words etched into her feet.

She looked up and saw Sasha staring at her. "Sorry, what did you say?" Clarke asked.

"Just that you should probably pull up this wintershade. It's growing awfully close to your camp."

Clarke glanced at the log, briefly registering the bright red berries. "Are those good?" she asked, suddenly unable to remember the last time she'd had anything to eat.

"No! They're *really* poisonous," Sasha said, lurching to

stop Clarke from touching the berries, though she hadn't even started to reach for them.

A thought crashed through Clarke's head, then seemed to settle in her chest. "What are the symptoms?"

Sasha shrugged. "You throw up a lot, I think. You basically can't get out of bed for a week."

Clarke raced through a list of the sick kids' symptoms: nausea, fever, fatigue. "Oh my god," she muttered, thinking about the stain on Molly's mouth.

"That's it," Clarke said, turning to face Sasha. "That's what's making people sick. They must've eaten the berries."

Sasha's eyes widened, and then she gave Clarke a small smile. "They're going to be okay, then. They tell you to stay away from wintershade, but unless you eat a whole bush, they're not fatal."

Clarke exhaled as relief washed over her. "Is there any sort of antidote?"

"Not that I know of," Sasha said, thinking. "But when we were seven a friend of mine ate some on a dare. You should've seen the look on his parents' faces when they found out, oh my god. But after a week or so he was totally back to normal— which for him meant causing all kinds of trouble. So I think you just have to wait it out."

Clarke grinned and, before she thought better of it, pulled Sasha into a hug.

"So where are you taking me?" she asked, suddenly happy to be out in the woods. It felt like a long time since she'd been anywhere but the infirmary cabin.

"Keep walking. We're almost there."

They set off again, and after about ten minutes, Sasha stopped, looked over her shoulder to make sure no one besides Clarke was watching, then pulled aside a pile of brush, revealing the entrance to some sort of tunnel in the hillside. "This way," Sasha said. "Come on. It's perfectly safe."

Again, Clarke felt a prickle of unease as she thought about how far they were from the camp. But as she caught sight of Sasha's smiling, eager face, her suspicion slipped away. *They* were the ones who'd captured Sasha, who'd tied her up, denied her food, kept her away from her family. If she trusted Clarke, then Clarke owed it to her to return the favor.

She watched Sasha duck and disappear into the cave, then took a deep breath and followed her inside.

Clarke's chest tightened as she was surrounded by darkness. She reached her hands to the side, trying to figure out how large the space was. But then her eyes adjusted to the dim light, and she saw that the cave was larger than her bedroom back on the Colony. There was plenty of air, and enough room to stand up straight.

The dirt-packed ground was covered with piles of objects. Some she recognized, like broken seats from the dropship and an outdated tablet, like the ones they gave to little kids to play with at home. But there were lots of things she couldn't identify, scraps of metal that looked similar to the ones Clarke had discovered in the woods, but not entirely the same.

"What is all this stuff?" Clarke asked, kneeling to examine a cracked water container.

"I found it after the first dropship crashed," Sasha said quietly. "The Colonists left most of it behind, but I couldn't just abandon it in the woods. I'd spent my whole life imagining what it was like on the Colony, and now that there was real stuff from space, right here . . . I needed to find out more." She reached down and picked up the tablet with a wry smile. "I guess you don't use these to summon your robot servants."

Clarke was about to make a joke about sending a robot servant to make them something to eat, when a glint of burnished silver caught her eye.

Sasha followed her gaze. "That one's my favorite," she said, scooping it up. "I think it's—"

"A watch," Clarke said, suddenly numb.

Sasha gave her a funny look and handed it to her. "Are you okay?"

Clarke didn't answer, couldn't answer. She ran her finger along the face, then, trembling, over the silver band. "*Clarke*," Sasha called, her voice sounding far away. "What's wrong?"

She turned the watch over slowly, although there was no

doubt in her mind what she would see. There they were. Three letters carved into the metal.

D.B.G.

It was her father's watch, the one that had been handed down through her family since her ancestor David Bailey Griffin carried it onto Phoenix right before the Exodus.

Clarke blinked rapidly. This couldn't be real. She had to be hallucinating. There was no possible way for the watch to have made it to Earth. Her father had been wearing it the last time she saw him, moments before he died. Before he was given a lethal injection and floated into space.

She ran her finger along the band, and shivered as a chill passed through her whole body. Like she'd just held hands with a ghost.

In the end, they let her say good-bye to her father. Since Clarke had been charged but not yet sentenced, the Chancellor permitted the guards to escort her from her cell to the medical center.

Unfortunately, the Chancellor's decision came too late for Clarke to see her mother. She knew that her mom was gone before the guards even told her—she could see it on their faces.

The guards led Clarke to a part of the medical center she'd never been in before. Apprentice medics didn't participate in executions.

Her father was sitting on a chair in what, at first glance,

appeared to be a regular exam room, except that there were no cabinets full of drugs, no bandages, no scanning equipment—nothing that was needed to save a life. Only the tools to end it.

"Clarke," her father said with a smile that didn't reach his wide, haunted eyes. "It's going to be okay." His voice was shaking, but his smile never wavered.

She broke free of the guards and flung herself at him. She'd promised herself she'd try not to cry, but it was useless. The moment she felt his arms around her, a series of sobs tore through her body. Tears streamed down her face and onto her father's shoulder.

"I need you to be brave," he said, his voice finally cracking. "You're going to be fine, you just need to stay strong. Your eighteenth birthday isn't far off; they'll retry you then, and you'll be pardoned. You *have* to." His voice lowered to a whisper. "I know you'll be okay, my brave girl."

"Dad," Clarke sobbed. "I'm so sorry, I'm so sorry, I never meant—"

"Time's up," one of the guards said brusquely.

"*No!*" Clarke dug her nails into her father's shoulder, refusing to let go. "Dad, you can't, don't let them, no!"

He kissed the top of her head. "This isn't good-bye, sweetheart. Mom and I are going to see you in heaven."

Heaven? Clarke thought in confusion. Unbidden, the old song lyric popped into her head. *Heaven is a place on Earth.* How could she be thinking of something so ridiculous at a time like this?

He took her hands and clutched them in his. He was still wearing his watch—they hadn't confiscated it yet. Should she ask for it? It'd be her last chance to have something to remember him by. But the thought of her father unclasping it with his shaking hands, leaving his wrist oddly bare as they strapped him down to the table, was too much for Clarke to endure.

A guard grabbed her arm. "Come on."

Clarke cried out as if she'd been burned. "No," she yelled, trying to wrench herself free. "Get off of me!"

Her father's eyes filled with tears. "I love you, Clarke."

Clarke planted her feet into the floor, but it was no use. They were dragging her backward. "I love you, Dad," she said in between sobs. "I love you."

Clarke was holding the watch so tightly, her palm felt numb. She kept her eyes on the second hand, but of course it didn't move; the watch had stopped working years ago. When Clarke asked her father why he wore it, he'd told her, "Its job isn't to tell time anymore. It's to remind us of our past, of all the things that are important to us. It may no longer tick, but it carries the memory of every life it recorded. It beats with the echo of a million heartbeats." Now it was holding her father's.

"Are you okay?" Sasha asked, placing her hand on Clarke's shoulder.

She flinched and spun around. "Where did you get this?"

she asked. She'd gone so deep inside the memory, she was surprised to hear her own voice echoing in the cave.

"In the woods," Sasha said. "Like the rest of this stuff. One of the Colonists must've lost it in the crash. I would've given it back, but by the time I found it, they were all gone."

Could it be? Could Clarke's father have been *sent to Earth* instead of executed that day? What about her mother? She knew it was crazy, but she couldn't think of any other reason the watch would have ended up here. By rights it should've been given to her after her father's death, but since she was in Confinement herself, it would've been archived with the other historical artifacts, part of the collective heritage of the ship. And yet it wasn't back up on the Colony, locked in a dusty archive box. It was here, on Earth.

She thought of her father's good-bye, how he'd told Clarke that he would see her in heaven. She'd always thought that was a strange thing to say—he'd never been one to really believe in the afterlife. Was it actually a *message*? Maybe he'd wanted her to think of the song lyrics, and make the connection, since surely he couldn't have said such a thing in front of the guards?

It took all of Clarke's control not to spill everything to Sasha. She was desperate to share her theory, to have someone confirm that she wasn't being crazy. For all she knew, Sasha had met her parents.

But as Sasha looked at her with an expression of confusion and pity, Clarke simply stammered, "This watch . . . looks familiar." Hope swelled up within her, filling the cracks in her broken heart, and she knew she couldn't bear to have anything sweep it away. Not yet. Not until she found out definitively what had happened to the Colonists.

The more she thought about it, the more it seemed possible. Maybe her parents were part of that first expedition. They'd been sentenced to die, but Wells's father could have taken pity on them. He couldn't spare their lives publicly, but what if he was able to put them on the secret initial mission to Earth? After all, who better to send than the people who had been researching the planet their whole lives?

"Sasha," Clarke said, using all her strength to keep her voice steady. "I need to see your father. There are things I have to know about the first expedition."

Sasha stared at her, her face suddenly inscrutable. Finally, she nodded. "I suppose it's okay. But I can't take you all the way to the compound. You'll have to wait in the woods while I go find him. They'll never forgive me if I brought you inside."

"That's fine," Clarke said. "I understand."

"So you want to go right now?"

Clarke nodded. Her chest was so tightly wound with anxiety, she wasn't sure she'd be able to breathe for much longer, let alone talk.

"All right, then. Let's do it."

Clarke followed Sasha out of the cave, and once their eyes adjusted to the sunlight, they set out. Sasha began explaining the route, but Clarke barely heard her. She couldn't stop running her fingers over the watch's cold metal as she turned over all that had just happened in her mind.

She was so distracted that when Sasha stopped short, Clarke walked right into her. "What's going on? Are we here already?"

Sasha turned and placed a finger over her lips, urging Clarke to keep quiet. But it was too late. A moment later, five figures came crashing through the trees. Wells, Graham, and three others Clarke had seen with Graham before. They'd been collecting wood to make more spears, and the long, pointed sticks they held seemed more menacing than they had in the clearing.

"What the hell?" Graham bellowed as one of his minions grabbed Sasha's arm. His eyes flashed dangerously at Clarke. "Were you helping her *escape*?"

"Graham," Wells shouted, hurrying toward them. "Knock it off."

Graham ran toward Clarke and twisted her arm roughly behind her. Two of his friends fanned out behind him, surrounding her. "You've really pushed your luck this time, Doctor. You're coming with us," Graham snarled.

Clarke scanned the boys, weighing her options. There was no way she could fight them, and they were blocking her path. "Listen," she began, trying to think of a way to explain why she had taken Sasha so deep in the woods—but before she had finished the sentence Graham doubled over, letting go of her arm.

For an instant, Clarke couldn't figure out what had happened. But then she saw Sasha struggling against the boy who was holding her, and realized she'd kicked Graham to give Clarke the chance to escape. Clarke's eyes locked on Sasha's green ones, and Sasha mouthed, *Go.*

Clarke gave a small, grateful nod before she took off running, leaving the rest of them behind.

CHAPTER *19*

Bellamy

He was packing up again. He'd done it twice before, but each time, something had brought him back. Octavia had disappeared during the fire. Clarke had been bitten by the snake.

But now he was leaving for good. He'd dealt with Wells's mind games and Clarke's treachery for the last time. As he stuffed a few protein packets into his pocket, a new wave of anger rose in his chest at the thought of everything he'd given up to bring Clarke safely back to camp. He'd lost Octavia's trail, and wasted *days* waiting for the Earthborn girl to talk. He should've left Clark in the woods, letting her limbs swell and her airway close up so that she'd never be able to utter another lie again. She'd tortured Lilly and then had been twisted enough to claim that Lilly had *wanted* to die.

There wasn't much to bring. He had a blanket. His bow. A few water-purifying tablets. He and Octavia would figure the rest out on their own. Before Wells had knocked Bellamy to the ground, the Earthborn girl had whispered, "Four miles northwest. Halfway up the mountain."

Bellamy didn't know what he would find there—Sasha might have been telling him that the other Earthborns lived on the mountain, or that the rogue group had been spotted near there. Maybe it was a trap. But right now it was all he had, and he wasn't going to waste any more time.

Bellamy left without saying good-bye to anyone. Let them think he was heading off to hunt. Wells had disappeared and there was no sign of Clarke, thank god. He didn't think he'd be able to look at her again. The idea that he'd almost *slept* with the girl who'd killed Lilly was enough to make him vomit.

The more distance he put between himself and the camp, the easier it became to breathe. The air smelled different here than it did in the woods closer to the clearing. Perhaps it was the species of trees, or the makeup of the soil, but there was something else too. The scent of leaves and dirt and rain had been mingling for centuries, undisturbed by any humans. It felt cleaner here, purer, a place where no one had ever spoken and no one had ever cried.

The sun started to set, and even as Bellamy picked up his pace, he knew he'd never make it to the mountain before dark. It'd be better to find a place to camp and then set out again in the morning. It was foolish—and dangerous—to explore unfamiliar terrain at night, especially once he crossed into Earthborn territory.

In the distance, he heard the faint sound of running water. Bellamy followed it and found himself on the bank of a small stream. It was so narrow, the trees on either side met in some places, creating an arch of green and yellow leaves.

Bellamy removed his water canister, knelt down, and dipped it into the stream. He shivered slightly as the cold water rushed over his hand. If he were uncomfortable now, what would happen when winter came? There hadn't been any cold weather gear among their supplies. Either they had burned in the crash landing of the dropship, or more likely, the Council hadn't expected the hundred to survive long enough to need it.

Bellamy sat back on the bank, wondering whether it was worth it to use one of the purifying tablets, when he was startled by a flash of movement. As he turned, his eyes settled on a small, reddish, long-haired animal perched on the bank, reaching its snout into the water. Sensing Bellamy's presence, it whipped its head around to look at him.

It had white fur around its large dark eyes, and oversize

ears that twitched back and forth as it surveyed Bellamy. Drops of water clung to its long whiskers, and despite the animal's intense expression, it looked more like a little kid with protein paste all over his face than a predator. Bellamy smiled. He'd seen a few different species of animals in the woods, but none that seemed to communicate so plainly. Before he thought better of it, he reached out his hand. "Hey there," he said.

The creature's black nose twitched on the end of its reddish snout, shaking the water droplets from its whiskers. Bellamy expected it to turn and dash away, but to his surprise, it took a few tentative steps forward, its bushy red tail swishing from side to side. "Hey," Bellamy said again. "It's okay, I won't hurt you." He was pretty sure it was a fox.

The fox sniffed the air again, then trotted forward and gave Bellamy's hand a tentative nudge. Bellamy grinned as its damp nose and wet whiskers brushed his skin.

"Bellamy?"

He wheeled around at the sound of his name, sending the fox scampering away. Clarke was standing a few meters away with a pack on her shoulder and an expression of surprise on her face. "Oh," she said as her gaze followed the fleeing fox. "I didn't mean to scare him."

"Are you *following* me?" Bellamy snapped, rising to his feet. He couldn't believe she had found him here, just when he was finally putting some distance between himself and camp. When he was finally getting away. "Never mind." He shook his head. "I don't even want to know."

"I wasn't following you," she said quietly, taking a step forward. "I'm going to find the Earthborns."

Bellamy stared at her, momentarily stunned. "*Why?*" he asked finally.

She paused. There'd been a time when he'd thought he'd been able to read Clarke's thoughts, to see past the defenses she put up. But he realized now it was all in his head. He'd wanted so badly to have someone on Earth he could trust, to have someone, after Lilly, who he could actually love, but he didn't know the least bit about her.

"I . . . I think my parents were in the first group of Colonists. I need to find out what happened to them."

Bellamy stared at her. He certainly hadn't expected her to say that. But he forced himself to stifle his curiosity. There was no way he was letting Clarke drag him into any more of her insanity.

"Sasha told me how to get to where she lives. She said it's less than a day's walk from here."

"Well then, you'd better get moving," Bellamy snapped.

He started collecting wood. Without saying a word to Clarke, he arranged the kindling in a pile, grabbed a match from his pack, and lit a small fire. Let her be the one to leave first.

When he finally looked up, he saw that Clarke was still standing in the same spot. The firelight reflecting in her eyes made her look younger, and more innocent. Underneath his anger, he felt a pang of affection—not for the girl standing in front of him, but for the girl she'd pretended to be. Was that Clarke really in there somewhere? The Clarke who could look so gravely serious one moment and then burst into laughter the next? The girl who found everything on Earth miraculous, and kissed him as if he were the most incredible find of all?

"You look creepy standing there. Either come down or get going," he said gruffly.

Clarke edged toward the fire, dropped her pack, and slowly lowered herself to the ground. A cold wind swept through the trees, and she brought her knees up to her chest and shivered. Just a few days ago, he would've wrapped his arms around her, but now, they hung like twin weights against his sides. He wasn't sure he wanted her to stay. But he didn't tell her to leave either.

They spent the next hour watching the dancing flames in silence, listening to the sound of the cracking twigs and the wind echoing above them.

CHAPTER 20

Glass

It was far worse than any nightmare. Even in Glass's darkest moments, she'd never have imagined trying to shove past her neighbors—the people she had grown up with—in an attempt to secure a spot on the dropship before they did. She passed one of her old tutors, struggling to drag a large bag down the crowded corridor. "Leave it!" Glass had yelled at her as she hurried past. But her words were lost amid the frenzy of shouts, footsteps, and sobs.

Up ahead, Cora's father stood in the middle of the corridor, looking desperately from side to side as he scanned the surging crowd for his wife and daughter. He called their names while blinking rapidly, evidently trying to message them on his cornea slip. But his efforts were in vain. The network had shut down, rendering everyone's devices useless.

By the time they had made it down the stairs and into the corridor that led to the launch deck, it was so crowded that they almost couldn't move. Luke did his best to push his way through the people closest to the wall, pulling Glass and Sonja steadily behind him. Glass winced as she knocked against a man clutching something in his arms. He was holding it so carefully, she assumed it was a child, but as she hurried past she realized it was a violin. She wondered if he was an actual musician or just a music lover who thought to grab the relic from its preservation chamber, the one thing he apparently couldn't leave behind.

Many of the other people in the crowd weren't from Phoenix—not that it mattered anymore. They were no longer Phoenicians, Waldenites, or Arcadians. They were all just desperate, terrified people doing everything in their power to get off the doomed ship.

Until recently, the thought of the Colony failing had concerned Glass about as much as the prospect of the sun exploding—something she knew would eventually happen, but far after her time. She remembered when she was seven, the year her tutorial group had studied the inner workings of the ship. A member of the engineering corps had led them down to the engine room and proudly displayed a complex ventilation system and series of airlocks. All the machines and generators had looked so solid and shiny and invincible, like they would last forever. What had happened between then and now?

A shout echoed from the other end of the corridor, prompting cheers to ripple down the hall. "Someone must've managed to open the door to the launch deck," Luke said softly.

"Do you think it was the Vice Chancellor?" Glass asked. It wasn't clear who was in charge, or who the remaining guards were taking their orders from. The few guards still in uniform had abandoned their posts, joining the sea of bodies to fight their way toward the dropships. The terror in the air was palpable.

The crowd pushed forward suddenly and Sonja stumbled, crying out as her ankle twisted underneath her. "Oh no," she said as she took a lurching step forward, her eyes filling with pain and panic.

"Luke." Glass pulled on his sleeve to get his attention. "I think my mom is hurt!"

"I'm fine," Sonja insisted through clenched teeth. "Just keep moving. I'll catch up."

"*No*," Glass said as a chilling sense of déjà vu washed over her. When Glass had been nine or ten, there'd been an evacuation drill on Phoenix. It'd all been clearly planned out ahead of time. When the alarm sounded, the children would file out of their classrooms and walk two by two down to the launch deck. Most of the kids had been in the type of exuberant good mood that came from missing tutorial, but Glass had found the whole ordeal frightening. Would the Council *really* send children to Earth without their parents? What would it be like to leave without saying good-bye? It'd been enough to reduce her to tears, although luckily, no one but Wells had noticed. He'd taken her hand, ignoring the giggles and taunts, and held it until the drill was over.

Luke pulled them both over to the side of the hall, and then bent down so he was eye level with Glass's mother. "Everything's going to be fine," he reassured her. "Now, show me where it hurts." She pointed to the spot. Luke frowned, then turned around. "I'm going to have to carry you," he said.

"Oh god," Glass muttered, feeling her breath catch in her chest. They were already so far back in the crowd—they couldn't afford to slow down anymore.

"Luke?" another voice echoed hers. Glass spun around and saw Camille staring at them. Her cheeks were flushed, as if she'd been running, and sweat clung to the hair that'd come loose from her ponytail. "You're here! You made it!" Ignoring Glass, Camille pulled Luke into a hug, then reached down to grab his arm. "The dropships are filling up. We need to move quickly! Come with me!"

Some of the concern drained from Luke's face as he smiled in relief at his ex-girlfriend, his childhood friend whom he had known as long as Glass had known Wells. "Camille," he said. "Thank god you're okay. When Glass told me what you did, I . . ." He trailed off. "Forget about it. There's no time. You go on," he said, giving her a nod. "We'll be there in a second."

Camille looked from Luke to Sonja to Glass, and her face darkened. "You need to move," she said, looking only at Luke. "You'll never make it if you have to take care of them."

"I'm not leaving them," Luke said, his voice suddenly hard.

Camille looked from Luke to Glass, but before she could respond, she was knocked to the side by a large man shoving his way down the packed corridor. Luke grabbed Camille's arm to steady her, and as she regained her balance, she placed her hand on top of his.

"Are you serious? Luke, that girl is not worth dying for." Even with the roar of the crowd, Glass could hear the venom in Camille's voice.

Luke shook his head as if to keep the words from getting too close to him, but even as he shot Camille a look of frustration, Glass felt a cold wash of fear. Camille wanted Luke to come with her—and Camille didn't stop until she got what she wanted.

"You don't know her. You don't know what she did," Camille insisted.

Glass caught her eyes in warning. She wouldn't dare tell Glass's secret, would she? Not here and now, not after Glass had helped her get safely to Phoenix. They had a deal. But Camille's eyes revealed nothing. They were hard and dark.

"I don't know what you think you're talking about, but I love her. And I'm not going anywhere without her." Luke took Glass's hand and gave it a firm squeeze before turning back to Camille. "Look, I'm sorry you're upset, but I never meant to hurt you, and I hardly think this is the—"

Camille cut him off with a bitter laugh. "You think this is because you *dumped* me for her?" She paused. In that brief moment Glass felt her heart go still in her chest. "Didn't you ever wonder what really happened to Carter? What Infraction he was suddenly accused of?"

Luke stared at her. "What could you possibly know about that?"

"He was arrested for violating population laws. *Apparently*, some girl on Phoenix named him as the father of her unregistered child."

A woman holding a baby paused to stare at Camille, but then tore her eyes away from the group and kept moving.

"No," Luke whispered. His grip on Glass's arm tightened. Around them, people were shouting and running forward toward the dropships, but Glass couldn't bring a cell in her body to move.

"They didn't even bother to run a DNA test, from what I heard. They just took the little slut's word for it. I guess she was trying to keep the real father safe. But, honestly, what kind of person would do something like that?"

Luke turned to Glass. "It's not true, is it?" It was more of a plea than a question. "Glass. It can't be true."

Glass said nothing. She didn't have to. He could see the truth written on her face. "Oh my god," he whispered, taking a step away from her. He shut his eyes and winced. "You didn't . . . you told them it was *Carter*?"

When he opened his eyes, they blazed with a fury far worse than anything she could've imagined. "Luke. . . I . . ." She tried to speak, but the words died on her lips.

"You had them kill my best friend." His voice was hollow, as if the emotion had been burned out of him. "He died because of you."

"I didn't have a choice. I did it to save *you*!" Before the words left her mouth, she knew it was the wrong thing to say.

"I would've rather died," he said quietly. "I would have rather died than let an innocent person take the fall for me."

"Luke," Glass gasped, reaching for him.

But he had already turned off in the direction of the launch deck, leaving Glass's fingers clutching empty air.

CHAPTER *21*

Wells

"I'm sorry about that," Wells said, releasing Sasha with a sigh.

He hadn't been all that surprised when he and the others stumbled across Sasha and Clarke in the woods, heading in what was surely the direction of the Earthborns' camp. He couldn't even bring himself to be angry with Clarke—she was only doing what he should've done himself. It had taken every ounce of his willpower to turn toward Graham with a condescending stare and order him back to camp. "I'll handle this. You should go get in the water. That looked like it hurt," he'd added with a meaningful glance at Graham's crotch, where Sasha had kicked him. One of the other boys snickered. They had all exchanged uncertain glances, but then started walking toward the stream. Without another word, Wells had taken Sasha back toward camp, staying silent until they'd been walking long enough to lose the others.

"I'm sorry about everything," he continued. It wasn't enough, but he needed to say it, anyway. "We should've let you go a long time ago." Keeping Sasha as their prisoner had made sense at the time, but now Wells couldn't look at the marks on her wrist without feeling a surge of nausea and regret. If the next dropship landed right now, and his father emerged, what would he think? What would he say to Wells when he found out that they'd essentially kidnapped the very first Earthborn they'd encountered? Would he deem his son a hero or a fool? A coward or a criminal?

"It's okay," Sasha said, tilting her head to the side, as if trying to survey Wells from a new angle. "Although, for a second there, I thought you were actually furious." She lowered her voice in a terrible imitation of his. "*I'll handle this.*"

"Why would I be furious?" he asked.

Sasha gave him a searching look. The early evening sky was a deep orange, and the light filtering through the leaves made her green eyes glow. "Because I'm supposed to be your prisoner."

Wells looked away, suddenly embarrassed. "I'm sorry I got carried away. We were all scared after Asher and Octavia, and I didn't know what else to do."

"I understand," she said softly.

They'd both stopped walking, and although the light was fading, Wells was in no hurry to get back to camp. "Want to rest for a little bit?" he asked, pointing to a moss-covered log that lay ahead.

"Sure."

They sat, and for a long moment, neither of them spoke. Wells was staring straight ahead, watching the trees fade into silhouettes until they were almost impossible to distinguish from the shadows. Then he glanced over at Sasha, and saw her looking at him with an expression he hadn't seen in a long time. Not since the days when he and Clarke used to sit on the observation deck, sharing the bits of information they'd saved up all day for each other, knowing that the other was the only person in the universe they wanted to share it with.

"It's not your fault," Sasha said, breaking the silence. "You were doing what you thought was best to keep them safe. It isn't easy, making those kinds of decisions. I know that. And I also know the difference between you when you're trying to be the leader and you when you get to just be a boy."

"It's funny you should say that," he said, surprised.

"Say what?"

"That you see the difference between me as a leader and me as a person."

"I believe I said *boy*," she corrected. He could hear the

smile in her voice. Above them, the blossoms on one of the strange nocturnal trees were glowing pink, as if the petals were clinging to bits of sunset.

"Well, I gave myself a promotion."

"Person is definitely a step up from boy." Sasha nodded in mock gravity. "Although I'm not sure they're quite the same species."

He reached out and tugged lightly on a piece of the silky black hair that swept down her shoulders. "I haven't decided yet if *we're* the same species."

She grinned and bumped his shoulder playfully, then scooted over to close the distance between them. "Why is it funny, though?" she asked.

Wells had almost forgotten his original point, he was so lost in the sight of her, her eyes luminous in the evening light. "Oh, just that I always used to think about my father that way. There was the Chancellor, and then there was my dad. Sometimes, it felt like they were two completely separate people."

"I know exactly what you mean," Sasha said quietly. "Your dad is going to be so proud of you when he comes down."

If *he comes down*, Wells thought. He fell silent as the now-familiar pain crept into his chest.

"Look!" Sasha was pointing up to the sky, where the first intrepid star was emerging from the gathering darkness. "Make a wish."

"A wish?" Wells repeated, wondering if he'd heard her correctly.

Sasha pointed to the sky. "You're supposed to make a wish when the first star appears."

Wells turned to Sasha to see if she was joking, but her face was sincere. It must be some Earthborn custom, he realized. If stars granted wishes to people living in space, his life would be very different. His mother would still be alive. His father wouldn't have been shot.

He had nothing to lose, so he closed his eyes. He started to wish for his father to come to Earth, but then he realized what his father would think of that. *Non nobis solum nati sumus.* Instead, he thought, *I wish that Bellamy would find Octavia, and that we could live peacefully with the Earthborns.*

He looked back at Sasha, who was watching him with a small smile. "Don't you want to know what I wished for?" he teased, but she shook her head emphatically.

"Oh no," she protested. "You can't ever tell anyone your wishes. They have to be secret."

Wells knew plenty about keeping secrets—after all, he'd learned from the best.

Wells hadn't been able to forget about his father's lie. He'd spent the week following his birthday paying extra attention to everything the Chancellor did or said, hoping some small detail would explain why he'd lied about missing dinner for a Council meeting. But there was nothing. Wells's father still left at precisely the same time each morning, before the circadian lights in the hallway began to chase the darkness away, returning just in time to kiss Wells's mother on the cheek before she went to bed—she'd been so tired lately—and interrogate Wells about his schoolwork. His mother liked to joke that "how did you do on your calculus exam?" was Chancellor-speak for "I love you, and I take pride in your accomplishments." Wells knew his father really was at work late, because he'd snuck out multiple times, hurrying to his father's office and pressing his ear against the door. Each time, his pounding heart had been appeased by the sound of the Council arguing in weary tones, or the soft clank of his father's cup on his desk that marked another sip of tea.

So why couldn't he shake the feeling that his father was hiding something—something big?

By the time Unity Day came around, Wells could hardly look at his father without feeling a stab of unease. Wells always hated Unity Day, when he had to spend the whole morning standing between his parents, doing his best not to look bored as visiting children from Walden and Arcadia marched by.

For as long as Wells could remember, he'd spent the ceremony staring up surreptitiously at the boughs of the Eden Tree. If he looked at just the right angle, he could imagine that he was an explorer lost in a forest. Sometimes, he fought a hungry tiger.

Other times, he built a boat to sail down a dangerous river.

But this year, he couldn't take his eyes off his father. The Chancellor, who normally observed the proceedings with a bland smile, was staring intently at one of the orphans from the Walden Care Center. It was so unlike him that Wells found himself startled into speaking.

"What's going on?" he whispered to his father.

"What are you talking about?" The Chancellor gave a brief, sharp look before returning his attention to the kids from the Care Center, who'd begun to recite the poem they had been taught for the occasion.

Anger bubbled up in Wells's chest. "What are you hiding?" he hissed.

This time the Chancellor looked straight at him. "I have no idea what you're talking about," he said, speaking very slowly. "Now be quiet and behave yourself before you embarrass me and your mother."

His tone was normal—clipped, terse—but there was something different about the Chancellor, something in his eyes Wells hadn't seen before.

Fear.

"You *can* tell me if your wish came true, though," Sasha whispered. She was sitting so close to him, Wells could feel her breath on his cheek.

"What?" he asked, startled.

"Your wish. Has it come true?"

"Oh," he said, suddenly confused. "Is it supposed to be immediate? Because mine might take a while."

"I see." There was a faint hint of disappointment in her voice, which confused him.

"What did you wish for?"

Sasha leaned forward and kissed him.

Wells hesitated for a moment, a million thoughts whirring around his brain, but then Sasha slid her arms around his waist, and all those thoughts were silenced. He pulled her closer to him, losing himself in the kiss. Finally, she broke away and put her mouth to his ear.

"That's what *I* wished for," she whispered, her breath tickling him.

He reached out and brushed a strand of hair away from her face. "I'm glad your wish came true." He felt like he could stay in the woods with Sasha forever. There was nothing he wanted more than to spend the night watching the stars appear, using each silvery glimmer as an excuse to bring his lips to hers.

But of course, that wasn't a real option. *We aren't born for ourselves alone.* Wells couldn't abandon the others after the horror of that day. He needed to get back to help bury Priya, to comfort those who wouldn't be able to sleep. To restrain those whose grief and fear might turn into a need for vengeance.

"You need to go," Wells said, unable to keep his voice from cracking.

"Go?"

"Yes," he said, this time more firmly. "Go home, just like you and Clarke were planning to. It's not safe for you here—you saw what Bellamy did, and I know what Graham is capable of." He reached through the darkness to grab her hand. "Will you make it there safely alone?"

"Home," she said, slightly wistfully. Sasha smiled, a slow, sad smile. "I'll be fine. Thank you." She leaned forward and kissed him again, lightly, before vanishing into the darkness.

If it weren't for the tingle on his lips, he might've thought she'd never been there at all.

CHAPTER 22

Bellamy

Even with the crackle of the flames, the silence was unbearable.

He wanted to ask her why she'd done it. Why she'd lied about Lilly. But whenever he tried to shape his thoughts into words, they died on his lips.

Eventually, he'd grabbed his bow and a few arrows and went in search of something for dinner. By the time he returned with a rabbit slung over his shoulder, Clarke had spread out their bedrolls. He noticed with a strange mix of relief and disappointment that she'd placed them far apart.

Twilight had settled over the trees, and the small campfire glowed in welcome. Clarke was sitting on the ground, turning a watch over in her hand. He wondered where she'd gotten it, and if it had to do with what she'd said before, about her parents having been on the first mission to Earth. The light from the flames flickered across her face, momentarily illuminating what might've been a tear running down her cheek. But when she spoke, her voice was steady. "Thanks," she said, nodding at the rabbit, quickly rubbing her eye with the back of her hand.

Bellamy nodded, but didn't speak as he skinned the rabbit and began methodically placing the chunks of meat on a sharp stick.

"Want me to do that?" Clarke asked as she watched him crouch over the fire.

He winced as a small cloud of ash blew into his face. "I've got it under control."

"And all this time, I thought you just stood around looking pretty."

"What?" Bellamy jerked around to face Clarke, ignoring the sizzle of the meat that was now burning.

"Sorry," Clarke said quickly. "It was a joke. Everyone knows that you're the reason we're still alive."

"No, it's not that." Bellamy turned to salvage the rabbit, before it turned into a charred crisp. *I thought you just stood around looking pretty.* "It just ... you made me think of something." He spoke so quietly, she probably hadn't even heard him over the crackle of the fire, but he didn't care. He just wanted to remember in peace.

"Come on," Bellamy panted. He pulled Lilly around a corner, then paused to let them catch their breath. "You . . . okay?"

She nodded, too winded to speak.

"We . . . need . . . to . . . keep . . . moving," Bellamy said between gasps.

He'd been an idiot to sneak Lilly onto Phoenix. But he'd be worse than an idiot if he didn't get her off.

He'd be a killer.

He should've thought it through. He should've been practical. But the wistful look that appeared in her eyes every time she talked about reading had melted any sense of reason away. She'd been dying to return to the Phoenix library ever since she saw it in elementary tutorial years ago.

The thud of approaching footsteps made them both jump. "Let's just leave the book and run for it," Bellamy said, pulling her down the hall. "That's really what they care about. They might not come after us if they get it back."

Lilly hugged the heavy book to her chest. It was bound in green cloth—the color that always looked so striking against Lilly's dark red hair. "No way," she said. "I've been looking for this one for *years*. I need to know whether she ends up with the boy who called her 'Carrots.'"

"If he knows what's good for him, he'll go find a blond. Redheads are nothing but trouble." Bellamy grinned and reached for the book. "Give it to me. That thing is half your weight . . . Carrots."

She shoved it at him with a smile. "It's about time. I didn't bring you so you could stand around looking pretty."

He grinned, but before he could respond, a shout rang out from around the corner. "They went this way!"

Bellamy and Lilly broke into a sprint.

"There they are, up ahead!"

"Oh my god," Lilly panted. "They're going to catch us."

"No, they're not." Bellamy tightened his grip on Lilly's hand and sped up, pulling her along with him.

They careened around another corner, and then darted into an alcove behind the stairwell. Bellamy dropped the book and wrapped his arms around the trembling Lilly, pressing them both against the wall, praying to whoever was listening that the guards wouldn't look their way. Lilly shut her eyes as the footsteps grew louder, and the guards' shouts more urgent.

But then the sounds faded. The guards had run right past them.

Bellamy remained silent for another minute to be safe, then exhaled loudly. "It's okay," he murmured, stroking Lilly's wavy red hair. "We're going to be okay."

"I can't be Confined," she said hollowly, still shaking.

"You won't be." Bellamy tightened his hold. "I won't let them."

"I'd rather die than be a prisoner."

"Don't talk like that," Bellamy chided with a smile. "I'm not going to let anything happen to you. I promise."

She'd turned to him, her eyes full of tears, and nodded. He bent his head down to kiss her flushed forehead and said it again. "I promise."

He turned to face Clarke. She was sitting with her knees drawn up to her chest, fiddling with the watch.

"She made you promise, didn't she?" Bellamy said.

Clarke looked up, startled to hear him speak. But then understanding dawned on her face, and she nodded slowly.

"She made you promise that you'd . . . end her suffering."

"Yes." Clarke took a deep breath, then continued. "She couldn't take it anymore. She hated the pain, but more than that she hated not being in control of her life. She didn't want to be a prisoner in the lab." The note of pain in Clarke's voice was the same that rang in his heart.

Clarke wasn't lying, he realized. The Lilly he knew was strong, but begging Clarke for mercy was, in its own way, an act of strength. The Lilly he knew would have rather died than become a sick, helpless test subject.

And Bellamy had never even stopped to consider how terrible that must have been for Clarke, having a friend ask her for something like that. He would never forgive the Vice Chancellor, or any of the people responsible for the horrific experiments that'd taken Lilly's life, but he knew now that it wasn't Clarke's fault. She'd loved Lilly as much as he had.

She'd loved her enough to do the terrible, painful thing her friend had asked for.

Bellamy walked over and sat down next to Clarke. "I'm sorry I said those things to you," he said, looking into the fire.

Clarke shook her head. "Don't be," she said. "I deserved most of it."

"No. You didn't deserve any of it." He sighed as Clarke reached for his hand, lacing her fingers with his. "And I certainly don't deserve your forgiveness."

"Bellamy," she said, and her tone made him look up. "We've all done things we aren't proud of." Her brow furrowed, and Bellamy wondered if she was thinking of Wells.

"I know, but—"

"I'm going to need you to shut up now," she said, and kissed him.

Bellamy closed his eyes, letting his lips say everything he was too stupid or stubborn to put into words.

He pulled gently on her lower lip. *I'm sorry.*

He moved his mouth to the soft spot under her jaw. *I was an idiot.*

He kissed the hollow of her neck. *I want you.*

Her breathing was growing heavy, and every time his lips brushed against a new patch of skin, she shivered.

He lowered his mouth to her ear. *I love you.*

It wasn't enough. He wanted her to hear him say it. He

wanted to hear himself say it. Bellamy drew back and took Clarke's face in his hands. "I love you," he whispered, staring into eyes that were aglow with firelight, and something else.

"I love you too."

Bellamy kissed her again, a little harder this time, repeating his proclamation every time his lips pressed against a new sliver of skin. With the fire crackling beside them, he placed his hand behind her head, and lowered her to the ground.

CHAPTER 23

Clarke

Clarke shifted her head on Bellamy's chest, wondering how it was possible to feel so comfortable while lying on the ground in the middle of the night. She'd normally be shivering under the thin blanket, but the warmth that spread through her the moment Bellamy had taken her in his arms hadn't dissipated.

Bellamy's eyes were closed, but every few minutes, he would tighten his hold, or kiss her cheek, or run his fingers through her hair. The fire had gone out, and the only light came from the smattering of stars peeking out from the canopy of leaves.

Clarke shifted onto her other side so her back was against Bellamy's chest. He responded by tightening his hold and drawing her closer, but this time, it seemed more like a reflex. From his steady, rhythmic breathing, she could tell he was asleep.

A faint flicker of light winked at her from the darkness. Maybe the fire hadn't gone out? But this light seemed to be coming from a few hundred meters away, near the rock formation that stuck out of the hill.

Her heart pounding, Clarke twisted back to face Bellamy. "Hey," she whispered in his ear, "wake up." When that didn't work, she gently shook his shoulder. "Bellamy." His head fell to the side, and he let out a loud snore. "Bellamy!" She sat up suddenly, freeing herself from his grasp.

Bellamy's eyes flew open. "What?" he asked, blinking sleepily. "What's going on?" When he saw her expression, concern swept away the drowsiness, and he sat up. "Are you okay?"

Clarke pointed toward the light. "What do you think that is?"

In the darkness, she could see Bellamy's eyes narrow. "I have no idea." He reached for his bow, which he'd laid on the ground next to him before they went to sleep, and rose to his feet. "But let's go find out."

Clarke grabbed his hand. "Hold on, we should come up with a plan."

Bellamy grinned at her. "A plan? Our plan is to see what it is. Come on."

They slipped through the trees toward the light, which grew brighter as they approached. It was *electric*, Clarke realized—it cast a perfect circular glow, bathing the nearby trees and rocks in a warm yellow light.

"Clarke," Bellamy said, his voice tight with worry. He pulled her to a stop. "I'm not sure about this. Maybe we should wait until morning."

"No way." Now that they were so close, she couldn't bear not to find out what it was. She tightened her grasp and stepped forward.

The light source was warm and most certainly metallic. Clarke stood on her tiptoes to reach it, and realized that it was a lightbulb encased in some sort of cage—there were bars on the front, as if the light were a creature that might escape.

"What the hell?" she heard Bellamy whisper next to her. "That couldn't have been burning since the Exodus, could it?"

Clarke shook her head. "No way. It would've burned out a long, long time ago." She took a step back and gasped.

"What?" Bellamy said, startled. "What is it?"

The formation wasn't just a pile of rocks. There were steps carved into the ground, leading down the side of the hill. Clarke didn't hesitate. She moved toward them.

In the yellowish light, she could see Bellamy stiffen. "No way, Clarke. You're not going anywhere until we have at least some idea what the hell this is."

She squinted at something on the step that she'd mistaken for a shadow, and bent down for a closer look. It was a metal plaque with writing on it, although it was old and faded. She squinted. "Mount Weather," she read aloud.

"What does that mean?" Bellamy asked.

A memory jolted through her, and she jumped to her feet with a start. "I know where we are!" she exclaimed. "They told me about this!"

"Who?" Bellamy's voice had grown impatient. "*Who* told you about this, Clarke?"

"My parents," she said softly.

Bellamy stared, wide-eyed, as Clarke told him what she remembered about Mount Weather, how it was supposed to be a shelter for the U.S. government in times of crisis. "But my parents said that no one got there in time."

"Well, maybe they did," Bellamy said. "Could they have survived the Cataclysm here? By going underground?"

Clarke nodded. "And I have a feeling they never left. I think this is where the Earthborns live."

Bellamy looked at the stairs, then back to Clarke. "Well, what are you waiting for?" he asked when she didn't move. "Let's go talk to them."

Clarke grabbed his hand, and together, they started down the staircase into the darkness.

CHAPTER 24

Wells

Wells shifted against the tree trunk, wincing as his exhausted muscles cramped in protest. It was dawn, but he hadn't been able to sleep at all. Eventually he'd given up and volunteered for lookout duty, which the bleary-eyed Arcadian on guard had gratefully accepted.

His eyes drifted toward the grave site, where a new mound of dirt rose up from the grass like a scar. Wells had spent much of the night sitting by Priya's grave, which he'd draped with flowers, although he hadn't managed to do it as artfully as she or Molly had. But at least, he thought with relief, Molly's fever had finally broken. Clarke had asked Sasha to convey what they'd discovered about the wintershade before she left, and the only bright spot in Wells's day was telling everyone in the infirmary cabin that they'd make full recoveries as soon as the wintershade left their systems.

He glanced again at the crude tombstone, which was marked with nothing more than PRIYA. He didn't even know her last name, or why she'd been Confined, or whether she'd ever been in love. Would her parents ever find out that she'd died? If the bracelets were still functioning, then there was a chance they'd been told already. If not, then Wells would have to wait until they arrived on Earth. He imagined a woman who looked like Priya stepping off the dropship, looking around with large brown eyes as she searched for the daughter who'd been taken from her, and while the other parents embraced their children, Wells would have to lead Priya's mother to her grave.

A twig snapped, and Wells jumped to attention, searching the woods for signs of movement, but it was just an errant squirrel. Though he'd never admit it, he'd been hoping it was Sasha.

He knew he was being an idiot. She wasn't going to magically reappear just because he couldn't stop thinking about her. And he'd done the right thing, letting her go home. He just wished he'd thought to ask where her people lived, or if she would ever come back. What if he never saw her again?

Another thought nagged at the back of his mind, refusing

to be dismissed. What if Sasha hadn't really meant anything she said? What if their kiss was just part of her escape plan?

Shouts rose up from the clearing, yanking him from his stupor. They weren't the usual early morning "get your hands off my breakfast" shouts, or the "if you try to get out of water duty I'm going to kill you" shouts. Wells rose to his feet and headed over. He had a feeling he knew what this was about.

A group was clustered around the infirmary cabin, and as Wells approached, two dozen faces turned to look at him. Most appeared to be confused, but a few blazed with anger.

"She's *gone*," Graham spat, striding toward Wells.

For a brief moment, Wells considered playing dumb, pretending that Sasha had somehow escaped. But he knew what his father would have said to that. A true leader owns up to his mistakes, rather than blaming others. Not that Wells thought releasing Sasha was a mistake.

"You said you were going to bring her back, and then you let her go." Graham looked around the group to make sure his words had prompted the proper amount of resentment.

"What were you thinking, Wells?" Antonio asked, his eyes widening in disbelief. "She was the only leverage we had over the Earthborns. They already killed Asher and Priya. What's to stop them from wiping out the rest of us?"

"We don't even know where Sasha's people are, let alone if they realized that we had her. Besides, they weren't the ones who killed Asher and Priya," Wells protested. "It was the other faction of Earthborns. The violent ones."

"That's what *she* told you," a girl chimed in. Wells turned and saw Kendall looking at him with a mixture of sorrow and pity. "But we didn't ever have proof, did we?" The expression on her face made it clear she thought Wells had been played.

"Just admit it!" Graham snarled. "You let her go, didn't you?"

"Yes," Wells said, his voice calm. "I did. It was the right thing to do. She didn't know anything about Octavia, and we weren't gaining anything by keeping her here. We can't just lock people up without a reason."

"Are you serious?" Antonio stared at Wells incredulously. His normally cheery face was twisted with rage as he gestured dramatically toward the crowd. "Your *father* locked us all up for hardly any reason at all."

"So what, then?" Wells asked, raising his voice in frustration. "We're going to keep making the same mistakes? We have the chance to do something different. Something *better*."

Graham snorted. "Cut the crap, Wells. We all know the only thing you're 'doing' is some mutant Earthborn slut."

The fury that Wells had been trying to contain ignited in his chest, and he lunged wildly at Graham, throwing his fists up. But before he could wipe the smug smile off that asshole's face, Eric and another Arcadian boy wrenched Wells's arms behind him. "Let it go, Wells!" Eric shouted.

"See?" Graham turned around to face the others, clearly delighted. "You see? I think he's made it pretty damn clear where his loyalty lies."

It wasn't Graham's words that hurt; it was the look on everyone's faces. Most were staring at Wells like they *believed* Graham, and were disgusted with Wells.

Kendall's lip was trembling. Eric's face was red with frustration. Antonio was glaring. Wells glanced around for Clarke, before remembering that she was gone. He'd done the right thing. Why couldn't everyone see that?

But maybe it wasn't the right thing, a small voice in his head countered. After all, Wells knew that even the greatest leaders make mistakes.

As the Colonel moved past Wells's unit, Wells exhaled and undid the top button of his jacket. It hadn't taken him long to realize that the uniforms he'd admired so much as a child were pretty ridiculous in practice. Just because soldiers on Earth had dressed like this shouldn't mean they had to do the same in space.

"Whoa, check it out. Jaha's going rogue," one of his fellow cadets jeered. "Don't you know what happens to officers who violate the dress code?"

Wells ignored him. While the other cadets always seemed

energized by the training exercises on Walden, they left Wells exhausted. Not the physical component—he liked running laps on the gravity track, and sparring during combat drills. It was the rest of it that left him vaguely nauseous: conducting practice raids on residential units, stopping random shoppers at the Exchange for questioning. Why did they have to assume that everyone on this ship was a criminal?

"Attention!" the Colonel bellowed up ahead.

Automatically, Wells threw his shoulders back, lifted his chin, and pivoted into position as the cadets formed a straight line down the corridor.

"At ease, Colonel," the Chancellor's voice called out. "I'm not here to inspect the cadets." Wells's eyes were trained straight ahead, but he could feel the weight of his father's gaze. "Which is a lucky thing, given some of their appearances." Wells bristled, knowing exactly whom his father was referring to.

"Sir." The Colonel lowered his voice. "Who's in your security detail today?"

"I'm here on unofficial business, so I came alone." Wells risked a glance and saw that the Chancellor was indeed alone, a rare sight for a high-ranking official coming across to Walden. The other Council members refused to cross the skybridge without at least two guards at their side.

"Can I send a few of the cadets with you, at least?" he said, lowering his voice. "There was another incident on Arcadia this morning and I think it'd—"

"Thank you, but I'm fine," his father said in a tone that made it clear the discussion was over. "Good afternoon, Colonel."

"Good afternoon, sir."

When the Chancellor's footsteps disappeared around the corner, the Colonel dismissed them and ordered them back to Phoenix, double time. The cadets broke into a brisk jog. Wells hung back, pretending to tie the lace on his boot. When he was sure no one was looking, he peeled off and headed down the corridor after his father.

His father was hiding something, and Wells was going to figure out what it was. Today.

Wells slowed to a walk when he caught sight of the Chancellor turning a corner up ahead—and saw something he hadn't expected.

His father was standing in front of the Remembrance Wall, a stretch of hallway in the oldest part of Walden that, over the centuries, had become a memorial for everyone who'd died on the Colony. The oldest names were in larger handwriting, carved with knives into the wall by the loved ones left behind. But as time went on and space on the wall grew scarcer, names were carved over by newer and newer names, until the wall was so crowded that most names were almost illegible.

Wells couldn't imagine what his father was doing there. The only times Wells could recall him visiting the wall were during official ceremonies, honoring Council members who had died. As far as Wells knew, he'd never come here alone.

Then the Chancellor reached up and traced the outline of one of the names. His shoulders slumped, radiating a sadness Wells had never seen.

Wells's cheeks began to burn. He didn't belong here, intruding on what was clearly a private moment. But as he started to turn around, taking care to move as quietly as possible, his father spoke up. "I know you're there, Wells."

Wells froze, his breath catching in his throat. "I'm sorry," he said. "I never should've followed you."

The Chancellor turned to look at him, but to Wells's surprise, he didn't look angry, or even disappointed. "It's okay," he said with a sigh. "It's time I told you the truth, anyway."

A chill passed over Wells. "The truth about what?"

"This isn't easy for me to say," his father began, a slight tremor in his voice. He cleared his throat. "A long time ago, before you were born, before I'd even met your mother, I fell in love . . . with a woman from Walden."

Wells stared at him, stunned. He wasn't sure he'd ever heard his father even use the word "love." He was so unemotional, so devoted to his job—it didn't make sense. And yet, the pain in his father's eyes was enough to convince Wells that he was serious.

In a halting voice, the Chancellor explained that he'd met her as a young guard, during one of his patrols. They'd started seeing each other and had fallen in love, although he'd kept the whole thing a secret from his friends and family, who would've been horrified to learn about his feelings for a Walden girl. "Eventually, I realized that it was foolish," his father said. "If we married, we would only cause our families pain. And by that point, there was already talk of me joining the Council. I had responsibilities to people besides myself, and so I decided to end things then." He sighed. "She would have hated this life, being married to the Chancellor. It was the right thing to do." Wells said nothing, waiting for his father to continue. "And then, a few months later, I met your mother and realized that she was the partner I needed. Someone who would help me become the leader the Colony needed."

"Did you keep seeing her?" Wells asked, surprised by the harsh note of accusation in his voice. "That . . . that Walden woman?"

"No." His father shook his head vehemently. "Absolutely not. Your mother is everything to me." He cleared his throat. "*You* and your mother are everything to me," he amended.

"What happened to her? The woman from Walden? Did she ever find someone else?"

"She died," the Chancellor said simply. "Occasionally, I come here to pay my respects. And that is all. Now you know everything."

"Why does it need to be a secret?" Wells pressed. "Why did you act like you didn't want anyone to see you?"

His father's face hardened. "There are things about being a leader that you couldn't possibly understand at your age." He turned on his heel, heading back toward Phoenix. "Now, this conversation is over."

Wells watched in silence as his father strode off, knowing full well that when they sat down together at dinner that night, they would both act like nothing had happened.

He turned back to the wall, to look at the name his father had touched so tenderly. Melinda. He tried to make out her last name, but it was too scratched-over for him to read. As close as he could tell, it started with a B.

Melinda B. The dead woman his father had once loved, whose memory brought him back to the wall over and over again. The woman who, if things had been different, could have been Wells's mother.

Wells reached down and rebuttoned his jacket, then turned back toward Phoenix, leaving the ghosts of his father's past behind him.

"Chancellor Junior was completely out of line," Graham was saying. "And who the hell knows what he'll do next?"

"I don't know," Lila was saying, "we can't just—"

"It's fine," Wells said, interrupting them. "I'll make it easy for you. I'll *leave*."

"What?" Kendall said, startled. "No, Wells, that's not what we want."

"Speak for yourself," Graham snapped. "It's exactly what *I* want. I say we're better off without him."

Wells wondered if Graham was right. Had he done the same thing that his father did long ago, and made an error in judgment because of a girl? What would the Chancellor say, if he were here right now?

"I hope you will be," Wells told them, surprised by the amount of sincerity, and lack of resentment, in his voice.

Then without meeting anyone's eye, he spun on his heel and went off to pack his bag for the last time.

CHAPTER *25*

Bellamy

The stairs led down to an enormous metal door embedded in a rock wall. It had a huge, impenetrable-looking circular lock, but the door itself was ajar.

"Sort of defeats the purpose, doesn't it?" Bellamy pointed to the gap between the heavy door and the rock.

"Not really," Clarke said, slipping past him for a better look. "Until recently, they were the only human beings on the entire planet. There was no one to keep out."

"Can you see anything?" he asked, trying his best to keep the concern out of his voice. He'd been hoping to catch the Earthborns who'd taken Octavia out in the open. Desperate as he was to find his sister, even Bellamy knew better than to waltz right into an enemy compound in the middle of the night. But once Clarke got an idea in her head, there was no stopping her, and he had no intention of letting her go at it alone.

"Not yet." She spun around, and her face softened as she saw the worried look in his eyes. "Thank you," she said quietly. "For doing this. For being here with me."

Bellamy just nodded.

"Are you okay?" Clarke asked.

"It's just Jim Dandy."

Clarke reached over and squeezed his hand. "Aren't you excited? You're finally going to meet people who understand your weird, old-man Earth slang."

He managed a smile, but when he spoke, his voice was serious. "So, do you think they're expecting us?"

"No, not expecting us, exactly. But Sasha said they'd be happy to help us."

Bellamy nodded, hiding his fear. He knew that if something bad happened to Clarke and himself tonight, they'd never be seen again.

"Let's do it, then."

Clarke pulled open the door, flinching as the creak of rusty hinges rang out through the silent night air. Then she slipped in between the gap and motioned for Bellamy to follow.

It was dark inside, but not pitch-black. There was a strange ambient light, but Bellamy couldn't tell where it was coming from.

Clarke took Bellamy's hand, and they crept along what seemed to be a tunnel through the rock. After a few steps, the ground began to slope down sharply, and they had to slow their pace to keep from losing their balance and tumbling to the bottom. The air was much cooler here than it'd been outside, and it smelled different as well—damp and mineral, instead of woodsy and crisp.

He forced himself to take a deep breath and keep his steps slow. The weeks he'd spent hunting had changed the way he moved, his feet seeming to float soundlessly above the ground. Clarke seemed to do it naturally.

But then she stumbled, gasping, and he pulled her close to his chest. "Are you okay?" Bellamy's heart was pounding so fast, it seemed like it was trying to betray him to the Earthborns.

"I'm fine," Clarke whispered, but she didn't let go of him yet. "It's just . . . it drops off here." The stone floor had given way to steep metal stairs.

They made their way down slowly, following the stairs as they twisted sharply downward. It was hard to tell in the dim light, but it seemed like they were spiraling into an enormous cavern. The walls were damp and made of stone, and the farther they went, the colder the air became.

As they descended the stairs, Bellamy thought about what Clarke had told him about Mount Weather. He tried to imagine what it would've been like, running blindly for the safety of an underground bunker, saying good-bye to the sun and sky and the world you knew as you hurried into the darkness. What had gone through the minds of the first people who clambered down these steps? Were they overcome with relief at their good fortune, or sorrow for all those they'd left behind?

"Do they have to go up and down these stairs every time they leave?" Clarke whispered.

"There might be another entrance," Bellamy said. "Otherwise, why haven't we seen anyone yet?" As they reached the bottom, Clarke and Bellamy fell silent, the lonely echo of their footsteps far more eloquent than any chatter.

The stairs ended in a vast, empty space that seemed more like a cave than somewhere humans could've lived for centuries. Bellamy froze and grabbed Clarke's arm as an echo bounced through the darkness. "What was that?" he whispered, jerking his head from side to side. "Is someone coming?"

Clarke gently shook his hand off and took a step forward. "No . . ." Her voice contained more wonder than fear. "It's water. Look at the stalactites," she said, pointing at the craggy rocks above them. "The condensation collects on the rock and then drips down into some kind of reservoir. I guess that's where they got their drinking water during the nuclear winter."

"Let's keep moving," Bellamy said, grabbing hold of her hand. He pulled Clarke through an opening in the rock and into a hallway with dull metallic walls, similar to the old corridors on Walden. Long strips of lights ran along the ceiling, wires spilling out from cracks in the plastic cover.

"Bellamy," Clarke said breathlessly. "*Look*."

There was a plastic case on the wall, similar to the locked boxes on the Colony that housed control panels. But instead of a screen or buttons, there was a sign. At the very top was an eagle inside a circle, holding a plant in one claw and a bunch of arrows in the other. The words ORDER OF SUCCESSION ran above it in two columns. The column on the left contained a long list of titles: President of the United States, Vice President of the United States, Speaker of the House, and so on.

Next to each title were the words SECURE, MISSING . . . and DEAD.

Someone had circled the word *dead* in black ink for the first six titles. Secretary of the Interior had been marked as SECURE at first, but then someone had crossed that out and circled DEAD in blue ink.

"You think someone might've taken this down by now," Bellamy said, tracing a finger across the plastic case.

Clarke turned to him. "Would you have taken this down?" she asked quietly.

Bellamy shook his head with a sigh. "No. I wouldn't have."

They continued down the hall in silence until they reached an intersection. There was another large sign, except that this one had no plastic cover.

→ HOSPITAL

← SEWAGE TREATMENT

← COMMUNICATIONS

→ CABINET ROOM

→ GENERATORS

→ CREMATORIUM

"Crematorium?" Bellamy read aloud, suppressing a shudder.

"I guess it makes sense. You can't float people on Earth, and you certainly can't bury them in solid rock."

"But where do they *live*?" Bellamy asked. "How come we haven't seen anyone yet?"

"Maybe they're all sleeping?"

"Where? The crematorium?"

"Let's keep moving," Clarke said, ignoring his quip.

To the right, a red light began flashing. "That's probably not good," Bellamy said, tightening his grip around Clarke's hand, ready to pull her into a run.

"It's fine," Clarke said, though she'd already begun to

move away from the light. "I bet it's on a timer or something."

The sound of echoing footsteps made them both freeze. "I think someone's coming," Clarke said, her eyes darting from Bellamy to the end of the long hall.

He pulled Clarke behind him, slid his bow off his shoulder, and reached for one of his arrows.

"*Stop it*," Clarke hissed, stepping to the side. "We need to make it clear that we've come peacefully."

The footsteps grew louder. "I'm not taking any chances," Bellamy said, stepping in front of her again.

Four figures appeared at the end of the hall. Two men, and two women. They were dressed similarly to Sasha, all in black and gray, except that they weren't wearing fur.

And they were holding guns.

For one excruciatingly long moment, they stared at Clarke and Bellamy, seemingly bewildered.

Then they shouted something and began running toward them.

"Clarke, *go*," Bellamy ordered as he drew back the bow and took aim. "I'll hold them off."

"No!" she gasped. "You can't. Don't shoot at them!"

"Clarke! *Move it!*" Bellamy shouted, trying to give her a shove with his shoulder.

"Bellamy, *drop the bow*." Her voice was frantic now. "Please. You need to trust me."

He hesitated, just long enough for Clarke to slip under his arm and stand in front of him, her hands raised in the air. "We have a message from Sasha," Clarke shouted. Her voice was loud and firm, though her whole body was trembling. "She sent us here."

There wasn't even time to see whether the name registered on the Earthborns' faces. A strange *whooshing* sound filled the air, and Bellamy felt something sting his upper arm.

Then everything went black.

CHAPTER 26

Glass

Hundreds of bodies were packed onto the launch deck, with hundreds more pushing against them from the ramp. In total, there were more than a thousand people shoved into the bottom of the ship, filling the air with a choking mix of sweat, blood, and fear.

Glass and Sonja had made it onto the deck, but just barely. They were standing all the way in the back, pressed up against the ramp. Sonja couldn't put any weight on her ankle, so Glass had her arm around her, although it was hardly necessary. The crowd was so dense, Sonja could lose her balance and she still wouldn't fall.

Every few moments, the sea of bodies would surge in one direction or the other until the anxious Phoenicians,

Arcadians, and Waldenites seemed like nothing more than a tide of flesh.

Rising up onto her toes, Glass could see people trying to force their way into one of the six remaining dropships. They were already crammed far beyond capacity, and bodies kept spilling back out.

Glass tried to blink away the tears obscuring her vision to count again. Six. There were supposed to be seven dropships. The one she'd escaped from, that had supposedly carried Wells and the other prisoners to Earth, was gone, of course. But what had happened to the seventh?

Even if there were a dozen dropships, Glass and her mother wouldn't make it off the Colony unless they kept pushing their way toward the front. But Glass felt weak and immobile. Every time she moved, pain ripped through her as she thought of the look of disgust on Luke's face, and the pieces of her heart she was trying so hard to hold together would slip from her grasp.

But as she turned to look at her mother, Glass knew she had no choice. She couldn't think about what had happened with Luke, not now. Sonja's own heart had cracked long ago, but the difference was that she hadn't bothered to catch the pieces. Glass had done it for her. Without Glass, her mom wouldn't fight for a spot on the dropship, and Glass wasn't going to let that happen.

She tightened her hold around her mother's waist. "Come on. Let's keep moving. One step at a time." There was nowhere to move, yet somehow, Glass and Sonja managed to wedge themselves between shoulder blades and around elbows.

Glass gasped but didn't look down when she stepped on something fleshy. She kept her eyes fixed on the front of the launch deck, and gripped her mother's hand tightly as they carved a path through the wall of bodies.

They slid alongside a woman whose dress was damp with blood. From the way she clutched her arm, Glass guessed she'd been hit by one of the guards' bullets. Her face was pale and she was swaying back and forth, although there was no room for her to fall.

Keep moving.

Glass swallowed a cry as she shoved past the woman and felt her bloody sleeve brush against Glass's bare arm.

Keep moving.

A man was holding a little girl in one arm and a bundle of clothes in the other, rendering him too bulky to navigate through the crowd. *Drop the bag*, Glass wanted to tell him. But she said nothing. Her only job was getting her mother on the dropship. That was all she could afford to care about.

Keep moving.

A young boy, hardly older than a toddler, sat on the ground, too shocked and scared to do more than whimper and wave his chubby arms in the air. Had he been jostled out of his parent's grasp? Or had he been abandoned in a moment of panic?

She felt a tug deep inside her chest, a jolt of pain in the empty space behind her heart that never fully healed. Glass tightened her grip on Sonja, and extended her other arm toward the little boy. But right before her fingertips brushed against his outstretched hand, there was another surge, and Glass found herself being swept in the other direction.

She let out a gasp, and scrambled to find her footing. When she turned back to look for the boy, he'd disappeared behind a wave of bodies.

Keep moving.

By the time they made it to the center of the launch deck, the nearest dropship was overflowing with bodies, far more than it was meant to accommodate. People were standing in every centimeter of available space, packed as tightly together as they could fit around the seats. Glass knew that jamming people in like that was extremely dangerous—anyone who wasn't strapped in would be thrown violently against the walls during the descent. They'd certainly die, and would probably end up killing some of the seated passengers as well. But no one was stopping them, or forcing the extra passengers off the dropship. No one was in charge.

A new sound joined the chorus of wails and shouts.

At first, Glass thought she was imagining it, but when she glanced over her shoulder, she spotted the musician from earlier standing at the top of the ramp. He'd tucked the violin under his chin and was drawing the bow across the strings. With nearly one thousand people between him and the nearest dropship, he must've realized he wasn't going to make it. And instead of succumbing to panic, he'd chosen to end his life doing what he loved best.

The man's eyes were closed, rendering him oblivious to the confused stares and angry jeers of everyone around him. But as the melody dipped and soared, their faces softened. The bittersweet trills swept the pain out of their chests and into the air. The crushing fear became a shared burden, and for a moment, it felt like something they could bear together.

Glass turned from side to side, searching desperately for Luke. Growing up on Walden, he'd never attended a Remembrance Day concert, and she wanted him to hear this music. If he had to die tonight, she needed to know his last moments would be marked by something other than heartache.

A loud beeping suddenly echoed through the room, breaking the spell of the music, as the door on the farthest dropship started to close. The few people who'd been trying to force their way inside began to frantically claw their way forward, desperate to get on the ship before it launched.

"Wait!" a woman screamed, breaking free from the crowd to run toward the door. "My son is in there!"

"Stop her!" another voice bellowed. A few people rushed forward to grab the woman, but it was too late. She slipped into the airlock, but didn't make it into the ship. When she realized what had happened, she spun around and pounded frantically on the sealed airlock door. There was another, louder beep, then silence.

Behind her, the ship detached from the Colony and started toward the blue-gray orb of Earth. Then a wave of horrified gasps rippled over the crowd.

The woman was floating past the window, her face contorted by a scream none of them could hear. Her arms and legs thrashed wildly, as if she thought she could grab the ship and pull herself back inside. Yet within a few seconds, she stopped moving, and her face turned a deep purple. Glass turned away, but not quickly enough. Out of the corner of her eye, she caught a sickening glimpse of an enormous, swollen purple foot before the woman drifted from view.

Another beep sounded as the next dropship began to launch. Now only four remained. The frenzy of the crowd had reached a fever pitch, the launch deck echoing with the sounds of death and grief.

Gritting her teeth, Glass pulled her mother forward just as the sea of bodies swept them even closer to the ramp. The third dropship detached from the ship and launched. A red-head shoved past them, and it was only after she was gone that Glass realized it had been Camille. Did that mean Luke was close by? She started to cry out his name, but the shout died before it even left her throat.

"Glass," her mother's voice came from behind her. It felt like an eternity had passed since the last time Sonja had spoken. "We aren't going to make it. At least, not together. You need to—"

"No!" Glass cried, seeing a break in the crowd and moving toward it. But just as she did, she saw Camille push a skinny boy off the dropship and take his place. His shocked mother's anguished wails echoed through the deck as the doors closed with a final click.

"*Move aside!*" a harsh voice shouted. Glass spun around and saw a line of guards jogging down the ramp, their boots thudding in perfect unison as they escorted a handful of civilians onto the launch deck. One of them was the Vice Chancellor.

No one heeded the guard's orders. The mass of bodies continued to push toward the remaining dropships. But the guards continued to surge forward, pushing people aside with the butts of their guns to clear a path. "Move it!"

They shoved right past Glass and Sonja, pulling their charges alongside them. As he was led past, Vice Chancellor

Rhodes's eyes settled on Sonja, and a look Glass couldn't quite identify came over his face. He stopped, whispered something to a guard, and then motioned toward Glass's mother.

The crowd parted as three guards stormed toward them. Before Glass had time to react, they'd grabbed her and Sonja and were herding them toward the last dropship.

The angry, violent shouts that followed sounded very far away. Glass could barely register anything but the sound of her own frantic heartbeat and the feel of her mother's hand holding tight to hers. Were they really going to make it? Had the Vice Chancellor just saved both of their lives?

The guards pushed Glass and Sonja onto the final dropship with the Vice Chancellor. All one hundred seats were full save for three in the front. Rhodes beckoned them forward. Glass moved like someone in a dream as she seated Sonja next to the Vice Chancellor, then sat down in the last seat herself.

But Glass's relief was tempered with a sharp, aching sadness at the thought that Luke probably wouldn't be on Earth with her. She couldn't be sure he wasn't on one of the earlier dropships, but she didn't think so. Luke would no sooner have knocked someone out of his way for a spot on the dropship than he would let a friend die for his own crime.

As the final countdown began, Sonja clutched Glass's hand. All around them, people were crying, muttering prayers, whispering good-byes and apologies to those they were leaving behind. Rhodes was helping Sonja with her harness, and Glass began to fumble with her own.

But before her trembling hands could lock the buckle into place, a guard appeared in the door. His eyes were wide and darting madly as he held his gun in the air.

"What the hell are you doing?" Rhodes shouted. "Get off! You'll kill us all!"

The guard fired a shot into the air, and everyone fell silent. "Now, listen up," the guard said, looking around. "One of you is getting off this dropship, or everyone dies." His terror-filled eyes settled on Glass, who still hadn't managed to lock her buckle into place. He took a few steps forward and aimed the gun at her head. "You," he spat. "*Get. Off.*" His arm was shaking so violently, the barrel of the gun almost scraped against Glass's cheek.

A disembodied voice filled the pod. "One minute until departure."

Rhodes fumbled with his harness. "Soldier!" he snapped, in his most commanding military voice. "Stand to attention!"

The guard ignored him, grabbing Glass's arm. "Get up or I'll shoot you. I swear to god I will."

"Fifty-eight . . . fifty-seven . . ."

Glass froze. "No, please." She shook her head.

"Fifty-three . . . fifty-two . . ."

The guard pressed the muzzle of the gun to her temple. "Get up or I'll shoot everyone in here."

She couldn't breathe, couldn't see, but somehow, Glass was rising to her feet. "Bye, Mom," she whispered, turning toward the door.

"Forty-nine . . . forty-eight . . ."

"*No!*" her mother screamed. Suddenly, she was at Glass's side. "Take my seat instead."

"No," Glass sobbed, trying to push her mother back into her seat. "Stop, Mom!"

The man waved the gun back and forth between the two of them. "One of you better get the hell out of here, or I'll shoot you both!"

"I will, please, hold your fire," Glass pleaded, shoving her mom down and turning toward the door.

"Stop!" A familiar form came barreling forward, jumping onto the ship at the last minute.

Luke.

"Thirty-five . . . thirty-four . . ."

"Drop your weapon," Luke shouted. "Just let them go."

"Get back," the guard spat, trying to shove Luke away. In a flash, Luke had jumped onto the man from behind, locking his arm around the man's neck and wrestling him to the floor.

A deafening, bone-shuddering *crack* filled the dropship as the gun went off.

Everyone screamed. Everyone except for one person.

"Thirty ... twenty-nine ..."

Her mother was slumped on the floor, a dark red stain blooming on the front of her dress.

CHAPTER *27*

Clarke

For the first few moments, she couldn't remember where she was. Clarke had woken up in so many different places over the past few weeks—her cell during her final days in Confinement, the overcrowded infirmary tent where Thalia had taken her last breaths, curled next to Bellamy under a star-filled sky. She blinked and listened intently, waiting for something to come into focus. The shadowy outlines of the trees. The sound of Bellamy's even breath.

But still there was nothing. Only darkness and silence.

She started to sit up, but winced as the small movement sent shooting pain through her head. Where was she?

Then it came back to her. She and Bellamy had wound

their way deep inside Mount Weather. Those guards had come after them. And then . . .

"Bellamy," she said hoarsely, ignoring the pain as she jerked her head from side to side. As her eyes adjusted to the darkness, her surroundings came into focus. She was in a small, empty room. A cell. *"Bellamy!"* He had aimed an arrow at the guards. Could they have determined he was too much of a threat? Her stomach roiled as she remembered the guns they'd been carrying.

Something groaned a few meters away. Clarke rose onto her hands and knees and crawled toward the sound. A long, lanky figure was stretched out on the stone floor. "Bellamy," she said again, her voice cracking as relief swept through her. She slumped back down on the ground and cradled his head in her lap.

He groaned, and then his eyes fluttered open.

"Are you okay?" she asked, stroking his hair away from his face. "Do you remember what happened?"

He stared at her, seemingly uncomprehending, then jumped to his feet so quickly, he almost knocked Clarke over in the process. "Where are they?" he shouted, looking around wildly.

"What do you mean?" she asked, wondering if he was still waking up from a nightmare.

"Those Earthborn bastards who knocked us out." He

swatted at his neck. "They shot us with tranquilizer darts or something."

Clarke brought her hand up to her own neck. The foolishness she felt for not understanding what had happened turned to dread as she realized what it meant. The supposedly peaceful, civilized Earthborns—Sasha's people—had knocked Clarke and Bellamy unconscious and dragged them into a dark cell.

"Are *you* okay?" In the dim light, she saw Bellamy's face soften as his fury gave way to concern. He pulled her toward him and kissed the top of her head. "Don't worry," he murmured. "We're going to get out of here."

Clarke said nothing. This was all her fault. She'd been the one to insist they come down here, the one who had begged Bellamy to come with her. She couldn't believe she'd been such an idiot.

Sasha had lied about Asher. Lied about Octavia. Worst of all, she may even have known what was going to happen to Priya. There was no other "faction" of Earthborns. She must've invented them to make the hundred trust her, to lure Clarke and the rest of them into a trap. Sasha had been so vague when she spoke about the first Colonists, about the "incident" that had forced the Earthborns to expel them. Clarke should've suspected something was wrong.

She closed her eyes and thought about the graves she'd

found. Was that where she and Bellamy would end up after the Earthborns killed them? Or would their bodies remain in this godforsaken bunker forever?

For a moment, all she could hear was Bellamy's breath and her own frantic heartbeat. But then another sound came, the unmistakable tread of footsteps. "They're coming," Clarke whispered.

She heard the clank of metal, and then bright light streamed inside, blinding her. Clarke brought her hand up to her eyes and saw the shadowy outline of a person in the doorway.

The figure stepped forward, and a face came into focus. It was Sasha.

Clarke's fear drained away, leaving only anger and disgust. "You *liar*," she exclaimed, lunging forward. "I trusted you! What the hell do you want from us?"

"What? Clarke, no." Sasha actually had the audacity to look hurt as she backed away from Clarke. "Wells let me go, and I came as quickly as I could. I wanted to make sure I was here when you arrived."

"Right, so you could arrange for us to be sedated and locked up," Bellamy spat.

Sasha shrugged sheepishly. "Sorry about that. But you probably shouldn't have tried to shoot them with your bow." She stepped forward and tried to put her hand on Clarke's arm, then winced as Clarke pulled away. "The guards were only doing their job. As soon as I heard what had happened, I ran down to get you. Everything's fine now."

"If this is your idea of fine, I'd hate to see what you think is bad," Bellamy said, his voice colder than the damp air.

Sasha sighed and pushed the door open further. "Just come with me. I'm taking you to see my father. Everything will make sense after you talk to him."

Clarke and Bellamy exchanged glances. She knew he didn't believe Sasha any more than she did, but their only shot at escaping was to get out of the cell. "Fine," Clarke said, taking Bellamy's hand. "We'll go, but then you have to show us the way out."

"Absolutely." Sasha nodded. "I promise."

Clarke and Bellamy followed her out of the cell and into a dimly lit hallway. Most of the doors they passed were shut, but when she saw one that was open, Clarke paused a moment to look inside.

It was an infirmary, or something like it. The equipment was similar to what they had on Phoenix; she recognized a heart-rate monitor, respirators, and an X-ray machine. Yet the narrow beds were covered with ragged, mismatched blankets, or in one case, what appeared to be animal fur.

And most striking of all, it was empty—no doctors, nurses, or patients in sight. In fact, as Sasha led them through a series of corridors, Clarke didn't see a single person anywhere. "I thought you said there were hundreds of you. Where is everyone?" she asked, curiosity momentarily overpowering her wariness.

Bellamy was less easily distracted. "Probably out kidnapping more of our people."

Sasha stopped and turned to Clarke. "No one's actually lived down here for fifty years. Now the bunker's mainly used to store all the generators and the medical equipment, things that couldn't be moved to the surface."

"So where *do* you live?" Clarke asked.

"I'm going to show you. Come on." Sasha led them around a corner, past another open room full of empty metal cages that Clarke could only hope had once contained animals, then stopped in front of a ladder that extended up through an opening in the ceiling.

"After you," Sasha said, gesturing toward the rungs.

"Like hell we're going first," Bellamy said, grabbing Clarke's hand.

Sasha glanced between Clarke and Bellamy, then pressed her lips together and stepped lightly onto one of the lower rungs. She scaled the ladder so quickly, she'd nearly disappeared through the opening when she called for them to follow her.

"You first," Bellamy said to Clarke. "I'll be right behind you."

It was harder work than Sasha made it look. Or perhaps that was just because Clarke was shaking so much, she had to use all her strength to keep her hands from slipping.

The ladder disappeared into some sort of airshaft, almost a vertical tunnel. It was so narrow that Clarke could feel the back of her shirt scrape against the rock wall. She closed her eyes and kept climbing, imagining that she was climbing through the Colony, not under thousands of pounds of stone that felt like they were stifling her, crushing down on her until she couldn't breathe. Her hands were sweaty, and she tried to wipe them on her shirt, terrified that at any moment, she'd slip and crash into Bellamy. She forced herself to breathe steadily.

Finally, after what felt like an eternity, she glimpsed daylight above her.

As she grasped the top rung, a hand reached down. Clarke was so exhausted that she grabbed it without hesitation, and allowed Sasha to pull her up onto the grass.

While Clarke gasped for breath and rose shakily to her feet, Sasha reached down for Bellamy.

"Do you climb that thing every day?" Bellamy panted, placing his hands on his knees and taking a deep breath of the cool morning air.

"Oh, there's a much easier way in and out. But I thought you'd appreciate the view from up here," Sasha said, smiling. They were standing at the top of a hill looking out over a valley filled with wooden structures. There were dozens of small houses whose narrow chimneys were sending streams of smoke into the air, a larger building that might've been an assembly hall, and a few fenced-in areas filled with grazing animals.

Clarke couldn't stop staring at the people. They were everywhere: carrying baskets full of vegetables, pushing huge piles of firewood in wheeled carts, running down the streets and greeting one another. Children laughed as they played some kind of game along the dirt path that wove around the houses.

Clarke turned to Bellamy and saw the same look of awe reflected in his eyes. For once, he was at a loss for words.

"Come on," Sasha said as she started to make her way down the hill. "My dad is waiting for us."

This time, neither of them protested. Bellamy took Clarke's hand, and they followed Sasha down the slope.

Before they even reached the bottom, dozens of people had stopped to stare at them. And by the time they set off down one of the dirt roads, it seemed like the entire village had gathered to catch a glimpse of Clarke and Bellamy.

Most of the Earthborns merely looked surprised or curious, though a few were glaring at them with open suspicion, or even anger.

"Don't worry about them," Sasha said cheerfully. "They'll come around."

Up ahead, a tall man was standing with two women, who were talking animatedly, clearly arguing. He listened to them both, nodding gravely and saying little. He had close-shaved hair and a gray beard, with pronounced hollows underneath his sharp cheekbones. Yet despite his somewhat gaunt appearance, he radiated strength. As his eyes fell on Sasha, Clarke, and Bellamy, he excused himself from the women and strode forward with powerful, purposeful steps.

"Dad." Sasha stopped in front of him. "These are the Colonists I told you about."

"I'm Clarke." Clarke stepped forward, extending her hand without thinking about it. She still didn't know whether she could trust these people, but something about the man compelled her to be polite. "And this is Bellamy."

"Max Walgrove," he said, shaking her hand firmly, then reaching over to do the same to Bellamy.

"I'm looking for my sister," Bellamy said without preamble. "Do you know where she is?"

Max nodded, his brow furrowed. "A little over a year ago, a few members of our community broke off, believing that they'd be better off living by their own rules. They were the ones who took your sister—and most unfortunately, killed those two kids."

Next to her, Clarke could sense Bellamy growing frustrated. He clenched and unclenched his fists, and when he spoke again, his face strained with the effort of keeping his voice steady. "Yeah, Sasha keeps mentioning this other 'faction' you have running around. But so far, no one's been able to tell me how the hell I'm supposed to find my sister." He crossed his arms and surveyed the Earthborn leader through narrowed eyes. "And how do I know you're not the one who took her?"

Clarke tensed and tried to give Bellamy a warning look. But Sasha's father seemed more amused than insulted by Bellamy's accusatory tone. He turned to glance over his shoulder at a field enclosed by a wooden fence. On the far side, a group of children seemed to be playing tag. Max raised his hand in the air, and they all began running toward them.

As they came closer, Clarke realized that they weren't all children. An older girl was with them, her long dark hair streaming behind her as she ran, laughing, across the field.

"Octavia!" Bellamy broke into a sprint, and in a flash, he'd swept her into his arms. He was too far away for Clarke to hear, but by the way his shoulders were moving, he was either laughing or sobbing. Possibly both at the same time.

A strange mix of feelings welled up in Clarke's chest as she watched the reunion. She was overjoyed that Octavia was safe, but part of her ached thinking about the reunion that she might never get to have.

Blinking away tears, she turned back to Max and Sasha. "Thank you," she said. "How did you find her?"

Max explained how he'd sent a team to keep watch on the

rebels. When he learned that they had kidnapped a Colonist, they staged an attack to get her back. "We just rescued her last night," he explained. "I was going to escort her to your camp myself today, but then you found us." There was a slight twitch at the corner of his mouth, as though he was trying to keep from smiling.

"I don't know how I can ever thank you enough," Bellamy said, walking over with Octavia. "You *saved* her."

"You can thank me by keeping your group in line this time, and by keeping to yourselves. Sasha's told me that you're good people and that you treated her well, but I can't risk another tragedy."

"What happened last time, exactly?" Clarke asked tentatively. She was desperate to ask about her parents, but she needed to hear the whole story first.

"A little over a year ago, one of your dropships crashed about ten kilometers from here. We'd always known about the Colony, but there'd never been any way to communicate, so coming across strangers from space was a bit . . . startling. But they were in bad shape, so we tried to help the survivors. We gave them food, shelter, access to our hospital—whatever they needed. They'd been sent to this location because they knew about Mount Weather, which they hoped would provide shelter and supplies. Of course, they hadn't expected anyone to be living here."

"Do you know what brought them to Earth?" Clarke asked. "The mission was secret. None of us knew anything about it until Sasha told us."

Max nodded. "They'd been sent to test Earth's radiation levels, to determine if the planet could support human life again. We made that part easy for them, of course."

"Who were they?" Clarke cut in. "Were they volunteers, or scientists, or prisoners like us?"

Max frowned, but to his credit, he answered her question without pressing the point. "Most seemed hesitant to discuss their pasts, but I gathered that they weren't exactly model citizens. Not criminals, exactly, or I suppose they would've been killed. Or *floated*—as I've heard it." He grimaced slightly, then continued. "More like people who could disappear without causing much attention."

Clarke nodded, taking the information in. "And after they arrived here?" she prompted.

"In the crash landing, they lost the ability to send messages back to the Colony. None of them had ever imagined they'd be separated from the ship indefinitely. So I suppose tensions started to run high. We hadn't planned on making them permanent members of our community, and they certainly hadn't counted on staying here forever." He paused for a moment, and then his face hardened. "I still think it was an accident, what happened with the child. But not everyone saw it that way. All they knew was that one of our children—a little boy—had taken a few of the Colonists fishing. He volunteered to show them our best fishing hole, proud to be useful, but when they finally came home at dusk . . ." Max winced at the memory. "They were carrying his small body between them. He'd drowned, the poor boy." He sighed. "I'll never forget the sound of his mother's screams when she saw him."

"It was an accident," Sasha said hollowly. "I know it was. Tommy slipped off that rock, but none of the Colonists knew how to swim. They *tried* to save him. Remember how wet they all were? They said that blond woman practically drowned herself trying to get to him."

"Perhaps," Max continued. "But they seemed more defensive than sorry. And that's when the fighting started. A number of our people—the family of that boy, the same group who came after your group as soon as you landed—refused to give them any more food, said they needed to go fend for themselves. I suppose the Colonists got scared, but they went about it the wrong way. Started stealing, hoarding, even threatening people with violence. At the end, I didn't have a choice. They had to be banished.

"It was a . . . difficult sentence to carry out. I knew most of them were good people. And I knew they didn't stand much of a chance out there on their own. But I never thought that when I delivered the sentence, they would *fight back*. And of course, after that, I had to defend my people. I didn't have a choice."

"So they're all dead?" Clarke asked quietly.

"Except for the couple, the doctors. They left before things got bad, said they disapproved of the way the other Colonists were behaving. They wanted to strike out on their own, see as much of the planet as possible."

"Doctors?" Clarke repeated, forcing the word out as the air drained from her lungs. She reached out for something to grab on to and felt Bellamy at her side, steadying her with his strong arms.

"Clarke, are you okay?" he asked.

"Were they . . . do you remember their names?" She closed her eyes, suddenly afraid to see the look on Sasha's father's face when he heard the question. "Was it Griffin?"

But she had to look. When she opened her eyes, the Earthborn leader was nodding. "Yes. David and Mary Griffin, I remember."

Clarke laughed, then gasped as the weight that had been pressed against her chest for the last six months broke apart. Her face was wet; she reached up a hand and realized that she was crying. She wasn't alone on Earth.

Her parents were alive.

CHAPTER 28

Glass

She couldn't hear the countdown.

She couldn't hear the screams.

All she could hear was the sound of her mother's ragged breath.

Glass was on the floor, cradling her mother's head as blood blossomed on Sonja's chest, turning her shirt a deep red Glass had always tried and failed to achieve with dyes.

The deranged guard was shouting something at Glass, but she couldn't make sense of it. There was a flurry of movement as Luke locked his arms around the man's neck and dragged him off the dropship.

"It's okay," Glass whispered as tears streamed down her

cheek. "You'll be okay, Mom. We're going to make it to Earth and then everything will be fine."

"We're running out of time!" someone shouted. In the back of her mind, Glass registered that the door was about to close, that the countdown was somewhere around thirty seconds, but she couldn't process the implications.

"Glass," her mother said hoarsely. "I'm so proud of you."

She couldn't breathe. Couldn't speak.

"I love you, Mom." Glass forced the words out of her mouth and clasped her mother's hand. "I love you so much."

Sonja squeezed it back, just for a moment, before she sighed and her body went limp.

"Mom," Glass gasped as a sob tore through her. "No, please..."

Luke reappeared at Glass's side. Everything that happened next was a blur.

Her mother's last words rang in her head. Louder than the screams and shouts from outside the dropship. Louder than all the alarms. Louder than the frantic thud of Glass's broken heart.

You're so brave, so strong.

I'm proud of you.

"Want me to walk you back?" Wells asked, shooting a nervous glance at the clock. "I didn't realize how late it was."

Glass looked up. It was close to midnight. Even if she ran, she still wouldn't make it home before curfew. Not that she would run—that was a surefire way to catch a guard's attention. "I'll be fine," Glass said. "None of the guards really care if you're out past curfew, as long as you don't look like you're up to something."

Wells smiled affectionately. "You *are* always up to something."

"Not this time," Glass said, slipping her tablet into her bag as she rose to her feet. "I'm just an overworked, studious girl who lost track of time doing her math homework." In the old days, before her dad left, Glass would never have been caught dead studying. But now, it was one of the only chances she had to see Wells. And, weirdly, it was kind of fun.

"You mean, you lost track of time watching *me* do your math homework."

"See? This is why I need your help. You're all about the logic."

They were sitting in Wells's living room, which was even neater than usual. His mother was in the hospital again, and Glass knew he wanted to make sure the flat was in perfect condition whenever she came home.

He walked Glass to the door, then paused before he swiped it open. "Are you sure I can't walk you back?"

She shook her head. If Glass were caught breaking curfew, she'd be given a meaningless warning. If Wells were caught, it would mean weeks of frosty treatment from his father—hardly what he needed right now.

She said good-bye and slipped into the dark, empty corridor. Glass was glad she'd gotten to spend some time with her best friend, even if they had been studying. She barely saw him anymore. When he wasn't at school, he was with his mother at the hospital, or at officer training. She'd see him even less when they finished school and Wells became a full-time cadet.

Glass moved quickly and quietly down the stairs and onto B deck, which she'd have to cross to get to her own residential unit. She paused for a moment as she passed the entrance to Eden Hall. Remembrance Day was coming up. While she'd spent the past few weeks agonizing over her dress—she had to work so much harder to find something, now that she and her mother were living off their own meager ration points—she'd made very little progress in the date department. Everyone assumed she would go with Wells. If neither of them found a date, they probably would end up going together, but it would just be as friends. She could no more imagine kissing him than she could envision moving to Walden.

Then again, Glass had never spent much time thinking about kissing *anyone*. The real fun was in making the boys want to kiss *her*. Picking out a dress that was sure to send a boy's heart racing was far more fun than letting him drool all over her face, like Graham had that one time he'd cornered her at Huxley's birthday party.

Glass was so absorbed thinking about her outfit for

Remembrance Day that she didn't even see the guards until they were right in front of her. There were two of them, a middle-aged man with a shaved head and a younger man—a boy really, just a few years older than Glass.

"Everything okay, miss?" the older man asked.

"Yes, fine, thank you," Glass responded with a well-practiced mixture of politeness and indifference, as if she had no idea why she'd been stopped and couldn't be bothered to find out.

"It's past curfew," he said, eyeing her up and down. His gaze made her uncomfortable, but she knew better than to let him realize that.

"Is it?" she asked, flashing him her warmest, most brilliant smile. "I'm so sorry. I lost track of time studying at a friend's flat, but I'm on my way home now."

The older guard snorted. "Studying? Yeah, what were you studying? Brushing up on your anatomy with one of your boyfriends?"

"Hall," the younger guard said. "Cut it out."

His partner ignored him. "You're one of those girls who thinks the rules don't apply to you, aren't you? Well, think again. All I have to do is enter a record of this incident, and you're going to find yourself in *very* different circumstances."

"That's not what I think at all," Glass hurried to say. "I'm sorry. I promise that I'll never break curfew again, no matter how hard I'm studying."

"I wish I could believe you, but you strike me as the kind of girl who loses track of time about as often as she takes off her—"

"That's enough," the younger guard said in a commanding tone.

To Glass's surprise, the bald guard fell silent. Then he narrowed his eyes and said, "All due respect, *sir*, but this is why they don't have members of the engineer corps patrol the halls. You might know a lot about spacewalks, but you don't know much about keeping the peace."

"Then you'll have to make sure you don't end up on another one of my patrol shifts." The younger guard's voice was light, but his gaze was intense. "I think we can let her off with a warning this time, don't you?"

The older guard's mouth curled into a sneer. "Whatever you say, *Lieutenant.*" The title spoke louder than his bitter tone. Clearly the younger guard outranked him.

The younger one turned to Glass. "I'll escort you home."

"I'm fine," Glass said, unsure why she was blushing.

"I think it's best if I do. We don't want you to have to go through this same process again five minutes from now."

He nodded at his partner, then set off with Glass. Perhaps it was because he was a guard, but Glass was acutely aware of his movements as they walked down the corridor. How he seemed to shorten his naturally long stride to match her pace. How his sleeve brushed against her arm when they turned the corner.

"Do you really do spacewalks?" Glass asked, eager to fill the silence.

He nodded. "Once in a while. Those kind of repairs don't happen very often, though. They require a lot of preparation."

"What's it like to be out there?" Glass had always loved to stare out the ship's small windows, wondering what it would feel like, to go into the stars.

He stopped and looked at Glass—really looked at her, not the way that most guys did when they gave her a once-over, but as if he could see what she was thinking. "Peaceful and terrifying at the same time," he said finally. "Like you suddenly know the answers to questions you never even thought to ask."

They'd reached Glass's door, but she found that the last thing she wanted to do was go inside. She fumbled with the thumb scanner clumsily.

"What's your name?" she finally asked as the door opened.

He smiled, and Glass realized that it wasn't the fact that he was a guard that was making her chest flutter.

"I'm Luke."

Luke never let go of her hand. Not when the dropship detached from the launch deck with a violent shake that made most people scream. Not when the beeping alarm and rumble of the thrusters gave way to a startling silence. Not when Earth began to approach, closer and closer, until the window filled with gray clouds.

"I'm so sorry," he said, raising their interlocked hands to kiss her fingers. "I know how much you loved her. How much she loved you."

Glass nodded, worried that if she spoke, the tears would come again. The pain was so new, so raw, she hardly knew what shape it would take, what sort of scars it would leave. If her chest was going to burn like this for the rest of her life.

But she *would* have a life—a life filled with trees and flowers and sunsets and rainstorms, and best of all, Luke. She didn't know what would happen to them once they reached Earth, but whatever it was, they could face it, as long as they were together.

The dropship began to rumble, and Luke squeezed Glass's hand a little harder. Then the entire ship began to thrash and careen to one side, unleashing a torrent of screams.

"I love you," Glass said. It didn't matter that Luke couldn't hear her. He knew. No matter what happened, he would always know.

CHAPTER 29

Wells

Once he'd packed, Wells walked quietly toward the little cemetery to pay his respects. Night had fallen, and the flowers draped over the headstones were glowing. Wells was glad Priya had thought to decorate the graves with living plants. Growing up on the ship, none of them had ever known true darkness, and this way, their dead would always have some light shining down on them.

But as he crouched down next to Priya's marker, Wells shivered. Had she sensed that she'd soon join the others?

He stood up and walked over to Asher's grave, running his fingers along the wobbly capital letters carved into the wood. He paused, wondering why they seemed strangely familiar.

The writing on all the markers was different, yet he was sure he'd seen block letters like that before.

"Good-bye," Wells whispered before swinging his pack over his shoulder and stepping into the woods.

He crossed the tree line and took a deep breath of the cool forest air. He was surprisingly calm about setting out on his own, more relaxed in the woods than he'd been all morning at camp. The sound of the wind rustling through the leaves was a welcome change from the malice-tinged whispers.

He'd indulged fleeting fantasies of setting out on his own before, although in those scenarios, Clarke had always been with him. Or, more recently, Sasha. His heart lurched in his chest as he thought about her returning to the camp and finding him gone. What would she think when the others told her that he'd left? Would he ever see her again? And what would happen if his father came down? Would he try to find Wells, or dismiss him as a disgrace?

"*Wells*," a voice called out to him through the darkness. He turned and blinked as Kendall's slim outline appeared in the shadows. "Where are you going?"

"I'm not sure yet. Away."

"Can I come with you?" she asked with a mix of eagerness and wistfulness that made it clear she already sensed what his answer would be.

"I don't think that's a good idea," he said carefully. "You'll be much safer if you stay with the group."

Kendall took a few steps closer. Hardly any moonlight filtered through the thick canopy of leaves, yet her large, luminous eyes were looking at him so intently, he almost shivered. "Are you going to find Sasha?"

"No . . . I have no idea where she went."

In the darkness, Wells could see Kendall nod. "That's good. She's dangerous, you know. Just think what those Earthborns did to Priya."

"That had nothing to do with Sasha," Wells said, unsure why he was defending her.

"What kind of person would do that to someone?" Kendall continued, as if she hadn't heard him. "Hang someone from a tree? Carve a message into her feet? You'd have to really want to make a point." Her voice had taken on a strange, almost singsong quality, and a chill danced down his spine.

"You can't trust the Earthborns, remember that." She took another few steps forward, until she was standing less than a meter away from Wells. "I know she's pretty, that girl. But she's not one of us. She doesn't understand you. She won't do whatever it takes to keep you safe."

Wells's breath grew shallow as an icy realization seeped into his brain. That was why the writing on Asher's grave seemed familiar. The block letters—they looked a lot like the ones carved into Priya's feet.

What if the Earthborns hadn't killed her? What if—

"See you," Kendall said with a smile as she bounded off to camp. Wells froze. Should he go after her? Warn the others? Was the dread in his stomach a real warning, or just paranoia?

A branch snapped up ahead and Wells whipped around, his heart racing. *It's probably just an animal*, he thought, wishing that he'd swallowed his pride and asked Bellamy to teach him how to shoot. He hadn't even brought a spear with him.

But then the shapes ahead resolved into three distinctly human figures. Wells tensed, scanning the ground for something he might be able to use as a weapon. A large stick, or maybe even a rock. He could fight hand to hand if it came down to it—he'd been at the top of his officer training class in combat—but he wasn't sure he'd be able to handle all three if they came at him at once.

He found a sharp-looking rock and ducked behind a tree, holding it at the ready. And then, as the strangers moved closer, *laughter* rang out through the trees.

"Clarke?" he called out in shock, dropping the rock with a thud. The moonlight shimmered on her hair like a halo, illuminating her wide, delighted smile. Bellamy was with her . . . and was that *Octavia*?

When they spotted Wells, all three grinned and hurried

over to him, talking at once. Slowly, he pieced together what had happened: Octavia's capture, Bellamy and Clarke's visit to Mount Weather, and everything Sasha's father had told them.

Wells's heart sputtered at the sound of her name. "So, you saw Sasha? Is she okay?"

He and Clarke locked eyes as understanding dawned on her face. She'd always been good at noticing the small details, seeing things before anyone else—it was what made her such a good doctor, he thought. She flashed him a meaningful smile, and Wells knew that she understood what Sasha meant to him, and that she was okay with it. "Sasha's good," she said. "She's going to come visit soon, after she's had time to convince the rest of the Earthborns that we don't mean them any harm." She paused, as if trying to decide how much information was appropriate for her to share. "I think she wants to see you."

"Are you going somewhere?" Octavia asked, reaching over to tug at Wells's pack.

Bellamy and Clarke exchanged glances as Wells told them what had happened that morning, how everyone was furious that he'd let Sasha go, how he had decided to leave before they could kick him out.

"That's ridiculous," Bellamy said with more indignation than Wells ever thought the Waldenite would muster on his behalf. "You can't just *leave* because Graham and a few of the others threw a hissy fit. They need you. *We* need you."

"Please, Wells," Clarke interjected. "Everything's going to be fine. Especially once we tell them how you were right about Sasha. If you hadn't let her go, we never would've gotten Octavia back." She shot a glance at the younger girl, who was already setting off down the slope, eager for her big entrance.

"I guess . . ." He shifted his pack from one shoulder to the other, then turned to Bellamy. "Congratulations, man. I'm really glad you found her. You never gave up on her, and it paid off." He glanced at Clarke, then back to Bellamy. "I think we all have a lot to learn from you."

Bellamy shrugged. "I don't really know how to live any other way. I've always been taking care of her. It's like . . . we aren't born for ourselves alone. You have to take care of other people."

Wells looked up sharply. "What did you just say?" Bellamy had spoken casually, as if that were a phrase that people used all the time. But Wells had never heard anyone say it on Earth. In fact, it had been years since he heard the saying spoken aloud, but that didn't mean he didn't think about it every day.

There were some things you never forgot.

CHAPTER *30*

Bellamy

Bellamy stared at Wells, wondering if the kid had finally cracked under the pressure. Why was Wells looking at him like that?

Bellamy shrugged. "It's just something my mom used to say about Octavia and me. How we were lucky to have each other, and how it was my responsibility to take care of her." He snorted as the bitter memories stirred inside of him. "*My* responsibility, because she sure as hell wasn't going to do it." He fell silent for a moment. "I think it's something my father used to say, though he used it to explain why he was never able to see us."

Wells seemed to pale at these words. "Hey . . . are you

okay?" Bellamy asked, shooting a glance at Clarke to see if she'd noticed how strange Wells was behaving. But before she had time to react, Wells continued.

"Was . . . was your mom's name Melinda, by any chance?"

The word landed with a thud on Bellamy's chest. He hadn't heard anyone say his mother's name in years. Not since the day the guards came inside their flat and found her lying cold and still on the floor. "How—how did you know that?" Bellamy asked hoarsely, too stunned to inject a note of hostility or suspicion into his voice.

In a strangely calm voice, Wells told Bellamy about his father's secret past, his affair with the Walden woman and his long-standing commitment to her family. "We live not for ourselves . . . it's what my father always said to justify the sacrifices he had to make, like not spending enough time with me and Mom . . . or not marrying the woman he loved. But I never knew they had a child together."

The world around Bellamy seemed to spin, melting into a blur of shadow and starlight as his brain reeled. The only thing that kept him tethered to the ground was the sensation of Clarke's hand on his arm. The Chancellor—the man who'd been shot because of him—was his *father*? He couldn't talk. Couldn't breathe. But then he felt Clarke's arm around him, and he took a deep breath. As he exhaled, his surroundings came back into focus. The dark outlines of the trees, the patches of star-filled sky, Clarke's stunned expression, the nervous face of the kid Bellamy had once thought he hated, but now seemed to be . . . something else entirely. "So that makes you . . ."

"Your half brother." Wells let the final word hang in the air, as if giving both of them time to examine the shape of it before they claimed it for their own. "I guess you and Octavia aren't the only siblings in the Colony anymore."

A laugh escaped from Bellamy's lips before he had time to stop it. "Half brothers," he repeated. "This is insane." He shook his head, and with a grin, extended his arm and reached for Wells's hand. "Brothers."

CHAPTER *31*

Clarke

"Half brothers," Clarke said for what was probably the twenty-ninth time that night. She reached over and ran a finger along Bellamy's cheek, as if she might find some sign she'd overlooked that he and Wells were related.

Bellamy smiled as he gently removed her hand, then brought it to his lips to kiss it. "I know it's hard to believe. I'm just *so* much better looking." But then his grin faded. "Does it weird you out?"

Clarke turned to look at Wells and Sasha, who'd returned to camp even earlier than expected. They were sitting on the other side of the campfire, a little apart from the rest of the group. Through the flickering flames, she could see Wells smiling at the Earthborn girl, who seemed to be blushing. A few people were looking at them warily, but now that Octavia was back, it'd been fairly easy to convince the group that she'd been telling the truth about the rogue Earthborns, and most had been quick to forgive Wells for letting her go.

Clarke sighed and rested her head on Bellamy's shoulder. "The thing is, the fact that you're related to my ex-boyfriend isn't even the weirdest thing about you."

Bellamy wrapped his arm around Clarke's waist and tickled her stomach. She laughed, and reached around to retaliate, but Bellamy sat up sharp as something on the other side of the fire caught his attention.

"It's true!" they heard Octavia cry, flipping her long dark hair over her shoulder. She'd spent the past hour regaling the group with tales of her time at Mount Weather.

"And how do we know you didn't come back to spy on us?" a voice asked. Clarke's muscles tensed as Graham strode over toward Octavia, the fire casting a flickering light on his smirk.

His voice was a mix of playful condescension and hostility, but Octavia didn't let that faze her. She tilted her head to the side and gave Graham a searching look from under her dark lashes.

"You might find this hard to believe, Graham, but there are far more interesting things to see on Earth than your little spear collection. If I had to spy on you, I'd fall asleep."

The people sitting near Octavia laughed, and to Clarke's surprise, Graham actually smiled, though even in the darkness, she could see it didn't extend to his eyes. "Oh, trust me, my *spears* are about as big as anyone can handle," he protested. Octavia giggled.

"Should I go punch that kid in the face now, or later?" Bellamy growled.

"Later," Clarke said. "I'm comfortable sitting here." She'd only joined the group around the fire a few minutes earlier, having spent the past hour in the infirmary cabin, making sure Molly, Felix, and the others were well on their way to recovery as the wintershade left their systems. The look of relief on Eric's face when Clarke helped Felix to stand for the first time since he'd gotten sick was enough to make Clarke forget that she had walked nearly twenty kilometers in one day.

Clarke shifted so she was leaning against Bellamy. He wrapped his arms around her waist and leaned back, so they were both looking up at the sky. The roar of the fire was enough to muffle the voices of everyone around them, and with their eyes tilted upward, it almost felt like they were the only two people on Earth.

She wondered if her mother and father were looking up at the same sky, feeling the same way. Earlier that day, Bellamy had told her that once Octavia had recovered from her ordeal, they'd both go with Clarke to help her look for her parents. The Griffins had nearly a year's head start, but it didn't matter, Bellamy promised. They wouldn't stop until they found them.

The thought was both thrilling and terrifying, almost too much to wrap her head around. So for the moment, she contented herself with leaning against Bellamy, letting the sound of his steady heartbeat temporarily drown out the rest of her thoughts.

"Look at that," Bellamy whispered in her ear.

"What?"

He took her hand, gently extended one of her fingers, and pointed it toward a pinpoint of light moving quickly across the sky. "Did you ever make wishes on meteors on Phoenix? Or was that just a Walden thing?" he asked, his breath warm on her skin. "You probably already had everything you wanted."

"I definitely didn't have everything I wanted," Clarke murmured, snuggling against his chest. "Though I think I might be getting close at the moment."

"So you don't want to make a wish?"

Clarke looked up again. The speck of light was moving awfully fast, even for a meteor. She sat up a little straighter. "I don't think that's a falling star," she said, unable to keep the note of anxiety out of her voice.

"What do you mean? What else could it be?" But then she felt him grow rigid behind her, a sudden realization settling into his bones. "You don't think . . ." He trailed off and tightened his hold around her.

They didn't have to say it. While the rest of the group sat around the fire in blissful ignorance, Bellamy and Clarke knew the truth. The spot of light wasn't a star—it was one of the dropships.

The hundred would soon be the hundred no longer.

The rest of the Colony was coming to Earth.

ACKNOWLEDGMENTS

I am deeply grateful to everyone at Alloy for being a part of this adventure. I'd never hijack a dropship without any of you.

Huge space hugs to my brilliant editors, the staggeringly clever Joelle Hobeika, and the endlessly creative Katie McGee, for their unfailing dedication to this series. It's also a great privilege to work with Josh Bank, Sara Shandler, and Les Morgenstein—people whose vision takes storytelling to new heights.

Many thanks to my editor, Elizabeth Bewley, for her keen guidance, and to the publishing wizards at Little, Brown for their hard work and enthusiasm for *The 100*.

It takes a village to keep an author sane during the writing process, and for that I am eternally indebted to my friends for their unwavering support. Thank you for the coffee, encouraging texts, glamorous viewing parties, and for reminding me to be excited when I could barely remember to do my laundry. And special thanks to my Scholastic colleagues for making the office a constant source of inspiration, wisdom, and bookish mirth.

Above all, I'm grateful to my family. Every word I write is shaped by the stories you gave me, stories tucked into piles of books, shining out from late night movies, and swirled into choruses of raucous laughter. I love you more than all the stars in the galaxy.